Readers love *Dog Days*
by TA MOORE

By TA MOORE

Bone to Pick
Ghostwriter of Christmas Past
Liar, Liar

WOLF WINTER
Dog Days
Stone the Crows

Published by DREAMSPINNER PRESS
www.dreamspinnerpress.com

TA MOORE

STONE THE CROWS

REAMSPINNER
PRESS

Published by
DREAMSPINNER PRESS

5032 Capital Circle SW, Suite 2, PMB# 279,
Tallahassee, FL 32305-7886 USA
www.dreamspinnerpress.com

Stone the Crows
© 2018, 2019 TA Moore.

Cover Art
© 2018, 2019 Bree Archer.
http://www.breearcher.com
Cover content is for illustrative purposes only and any person depicted on the cover is a model.

Mass Market Paperback ISBN: 978-1-64108-076-7
Trade Paperback ISBN: 978-1-64080-543-9
Digital ISBN: 978-1-64080-542-2
Library of Congress Control Number: 2018934250
Mass Market Paperback published March 2019
v. 1.0

Printed in the United States of America
∞
This paper meets the requirements of
ANSI/NISO Z39.48-1992 (Permanence of Paper).

To my mum and the Five. You've always believed in me. And to Lynn, who has always believed in Dog Days.

A WOLF winter isn't white. It's red as blood.

In Durham, mild-mannered academic and occasional dog Danny Fennick had spent years pretending to be human. That all blew away on the storm that heralded the end of the world, the cold, savage Wolf Age before the twilight of the gods. Against his will Danny was drawn back into the bloody pack politics of the Wolves and, somewhat more enthusiastically, into his Wolfish ex-lover's bed.

His ex is Jack, who has vied his whole life with his twin brother, Gregor, to be Crown Prince Pup of the Numitor's Pack. The two are connected and even the end of the world isn't enough to quell fraternal rivalry.

Then the monsters started to crawl out of human skin, infected by the putrid bite of a prophet. Among the Wolves, who resented the gods who made and then abandoned them, they are sentenced to their role, hobbled and shunned, and they see the end of the world as an opportunity to improve their lot.

With a reluctant truce called between the warring brothers, the three of them managed to defeat the prophet and his monsters before he could leave the

Numitor with no heirs to usher in the wolf winter. But that wasn't enough. The prophet hadn't worked alone, and the Numitor had to be warned of the treachery that brewed against him.

The question was—would they make it in time?

Littermates slay each other, kin defiles kin
In the fang age, the cold age, the Wolf Age
The wolf winter shall call the ravens down.
~ the Catechism of the Wolves

Prologue

"WHAT'S IT mean, then?" Terry demanded. He planted himself at the barrier and ignored the grumble of irritation from the line behind him.

There were over a hundred families crowded into the space, shuffled into roughly drawn lines. Children leaned against their parents' legs or were carried in their arms. People wearing Aran sweaters and hospital bracelets slouched in wheelchairs. IV bags were zipped into coats as the users leaned on their companions' arms. Some of them were back for a second day, with the hope that it would be their turn on the military transit for evacuation to Glasgow. Others just needed supplies, dressings, and meds.

They could all wait. He had.

Terry dragged his son's arm up to display the strip of black tape slapped onto his too big borrowed jacket. Jimmy tugged back against him.

"Dad. Dad, please don't," he begged.

Terry ignored him and lifted his arm up higher so the tag couldn't be missed. His fingers wrapped easily around the bony, wasted wrist. "Go on. Fucking say it. You put it on him. Say it."

The woman on the other side of the barrier—girl, he'd have said if it weren't for the clipboard and the white jacket and the power over life and death—couldn't meet his eyes.

"Sir," she said. Her voice cracked. "Please. We have to process everyone in the queue. We're doing everything we can to make this as quick as possible."

Someone shoved him. "You've been seen. Just move."

A mutter of agreement rippled through the hall.

"We all have kids."

"…I need my meds!"

"…daughter went yesterday. She's all alone."

Terry shrugged the hands off and reached down to drag his son up into his arms. He remembered when he'd grumbled that it was getting harder, that piggyback rides wrecked his back and the kid could walk. Now all that chunky muscle and growth-spurt-ready chub had leeched away, the down jacket seemed like the only weight to him.

"What's the black tab for?" His voice cracked as he yelled. He could taste the salt and bile on the back of his tongue. "I know. I already fucking know. Just admit it."

Now she couldn't avoid looking. Her gaze dropped to the careless black slap of tape and then back up to Terry's eyes. Her face was scrubbed and raw-looking from the wind. She still had adolescent spots on her chin, for fuck's sake.

One of the other doctors stepped in. He was lean and dark, with a beak of a nose and nervous hands.

"It's triage." He put a reassuring hand on the woman's shoulder. "Everyone here needs to be evacuated. We have to prioritize those with the most need and the best likely outcomes."

"And where does my son go on that list?" Terry asked.

The woman clutched the clipboard to her chest and grimaced. She tried to say something, but it wouldn't come out.

"I... Doctor Blake?" She glanced desperately around at the other doctor.

"The survival rates for your son's condition, as I'm sure the doctor's explained, are poor," Doctor Blake said. "In addition he isn't undergoing intensive care that needs continuity. He's low on the list."

The first doctor bit her lip. "I'm sorry."

He spat in her face. The gob of phlegm hit her just under the eye and slid down. She flinched back with a shocked gasp and scrubbed at her cheek with her sleeve. Blake looked sour and waved a hand to call someone over.

"You." A big man in a paramedic's uniform—Harris nametag velcro'd on his breast pocket—grabbed Terry. "Out."

There was no point in a fight. They all *knew* what the black tag meant. He just wanted them to say it.

"I'm so sorry."

The woman's apology drifted after him as Harris shoved Terry, with Jimmy still clutched clumsily in his arms, out through the doors and into the narrow entry. The long glass windows were flowered with frost, and the recently shoveled path was already under half a foot of snow.

"You got a place to go?" the paramedic asked. He glanced down at Jimmy—at the peaked bald face under a flap-eared fur hat—and his mouth twitched. "There's shelters. If you and the kid need—"

"No." Terry picked at the edge of the tape with his nails. It was stiff and shiny, hard to get hold of. When he finally managed to rip it off, the tape left a stripe of sticky residue on the red sleeve. It would collect fluff to match the one from yesterday. "All we need from you is a seat on the bus."

"Dad," Jimmy said. He reached up and patted Terry's face with a cold hand. "It's alright. We can come back tomorrow."

The tag would be the same color—just another stripe of fluff on his sleeve.

"I've got money," Terry lied. He ignored Jimmy's exhausted protest and grabbed for Harris's arm. "You can have it. All of it."

Harris pulled away. "Whose kid would I kill?" he asked.

"I don't care."

"I'm sorry."

Of course he was. When your son was dying, everyone was very, very sorry. They were sorry to tell you the diagnosis, sorry when they said the treatment wasn't working, and sorry when they said your kid was too likely to die to deserve a ride to Glasgow.

"Let's go home, Dad," Jimmy said.

Terry carried him. When he bought his boots, they said they were waterproof. Maybe they were. He'd only worn them on the occasional walk with the dog.

But snowproof they weren't. His socks were wet and half-frozen. He couldn't feel his toes anymore, just the occasional jab of pain through the bones.

The wind battered him. It chilled his jaw and froze his joints. He stopped outside the butcher. The window was empty, and a bitterly ironic sign for summer BBQ deals was still pasted to the glass. He slid down until his hips caught on the low windowsill.

"Dad?"

"Just a minute," he said.

There was a gun. It wasn't his. It belonged to the farmer he did work for sometimes. A shotgun they used for gulls. He could... what?

Jimmy tugged at his jacket. "Dad. Dad."

He looked up as a stocky old man limped toward them, his weight divided between two sticks. A white collar showed over his coat. Terry didn't know him, but there were a lot of people in town he didn't know.

"Father."

"Father," the priest parroted back, with a nod of his head to Jimmy. "I heard what happened back there. The boy's sick."

There was no "sorry" in the priest's voice, no pity. It was refreshing and disorienting at the same time.

"He'll be fine. We just need to get to Glasgow." It was a lie. At that point even Terry knew that. But the lie was all he had.

"Those doctors didn't think so."

Terry lifted his chin stubbornly. "What do they know? If they were any good, would they have sent us out here?"

The priest dragged himself closer, his legs awkward as he moved through the snow. He wasn't as old as Terry had thought. The lines of his face were scars and wear, not age. He leaned against the window and smiled with closed lips at Jimmy. Then he turned his attention back to Terry.

"Do you believe in miracles?" he asked.

"I'm not religious."

The priest chuckled. Gapped teeth flashed against the red of his mouth, and his breath was visible as he panted from the effort of getting there.

"You don't have to be." He reached out and laid a scarred hand on Jimmy's. A smell clung to him—something sour and musky. Terry felt embarrassed to notice it. "You just have to be desperate."

Chapter One

"I'M A pathologist," Nick had protested as the hospital administrator shoved a clipboard and hi-vis vest at him. "What good am I going to be to a relief effort?"

No one had listened. It was all hands on deck as the SNP proved they could manage their own disasters without any help from England. Except they couldn't, and it was small comfort that, by all accounts, neither could anywhere else in the UK. The winter had swept across the country with brutal, climatic efficiency, and all their glorious civilization ground to a frozen halt.

Helicopters were grounded, train tracks frozen over, and most importantly, the off-licenses were either sold out or looted.

Nick only had one bottle of whiskey left, and that would not be enough.

Faced with the prospect of an unstocked liquor cabinet—otherwise known as a filing cabinet—Nick added an extra shot to his tepid coffee. He took a drink and grimaced as the bitter burn hit the back of his throat. At this point he could probably just drop the pretense and admit it was just whiskey in a coffee mug.

Nick took another drink, apparently determined to chase that empty bottle, and closed his eyes for a second. Last night's hangover poked at his eyelids with raspy fingers, and the little bit of professional pride that wasn't numb with the cold hissed reproachfully at him.

"Fuck you," he told it. His voice echoed back to him dully as it bounced off the walls. "This is your fault anyhow."

He sighed and opened his eyes. The world had gone to hell, and Nick was apparently going to face it sober, but there was still work to do. He turned and cast a grim eye over his makeshift base of operations.

It was billed as an *Entertainment Center* on the sign outside.

Even at its best, Nick couldn't imagine it had been that entertaining. It was a corrugated iron box with a flat plastic roof in the middle of a run-down trailer park, probably sweaty hot in the summer and definitely Baltic in the winter. There was a heavy cover that turned the small pool into a stage and a poster still taped to the front door. The paper was yellowed and the tape brittle. It advertised a tribute act to the pop band Bucks Fizz (Buck the Frizz) as a headline event in the 1980s. From the layer of dust in the pool, it had been drained since that concert, but the smell of chlorine still lingered in the air.

Not even the real Bucks Fizz could liven up the atmosphere now. Frost crusted the dips in the metal, the paintwork was fractured and peeling where the ice crystals had pushed through, and corpses wrapped in tarps and plastic sheets were laid out along the edge of the pool. It looked like a particularly macabre holiday brochure photo.

Nick was the only doctor in Ayr who still had a full practice list.

He fished his voice recorder out of his pocket and turned it on… probably. The cold had cracked the casing, and the LED had given up the glowing ghost a week earlier. It didn't look like it was working, and there was no way to tell if it was or not until he stumbled over to the Trauma Base to use the only computer hooked up to the generator.

Until then—Nick tapped his thumb on Record—he just had to take it on faith.

"This is Doctor Nicholas Blake," he said. His accent slurred down-market as he talked. Exhaustion and, to be fair, booze had eroded a natural talent for mimicry and one year of elocution lessons. His vowels had gone all Glasgie. He thought about caring and decided he didn't. "I am continuing to process the dead recovered from Ayr."

It was stark, said out loud like that.

Nick tucked the recorder into his breast pocket, where hopefully it would still pick up his voice. He looked at the body laid out on the flimsy Formica table he'd dragged over from the kitchens to serve as a makeshift slab—not ideal under normal circumstances, but these were hardly normal circumstances, even for Scotland.

He remembered scoffing over weak tea with his colleagues in Edinburgh as the snow piled up outside. They'd made fun of the soft Southerners who thought a bit of snow was the end of the world and joked about missing *I'm a Celebrity* this year. The Scots were used to bad weather, cold winters, wet springs, and the legend of summer. When winter came early, it was just something to grumble about and stock up on whiskey.

Even as the helicopter took off from the hospital roof and Nick perched on a box of antibiotics and saline and peered with that familiar queasy fascination at the retreating earth, he'd thought it was all under control. It would be a few hard months, and once it was over, farmers would apply for compensation for their dead sheep, the *Guardian* would write op-eds about global warming, and the odds would be significantly better for a white Christmas next year.

He'd been wrong. They all had. It probably didn't make any difference to the dead, though.

"Deceased is a teenage female," Nick recited for the record. He picked up his digital camera and breathed on the lens to melt the glaze of frost. The first photo was of the girl's pale face, bruises discoloring her temples and the hollows around her eyes. Even in death the cold pinched her lips and left them chapped and dark. The clips still in her hair, rhinestone butterflies against wet-dark curls, were quietly macabre. Nick lifted her arm. The flesh was stiff and chilled under his gloved fingers. "Identifying mark of a rose tattoo on inner forearm. Initials *I-C* are included. No ID was found with the remains."

He snapped a picture of that, the ink dull under dead skin, and set the girl's arm back down on the table. Two more pictures, to chronicle the mole on her hip and the scar on the back of her ankle, and he set the camera aside.

"Cause of death is presumed to be hypothermia."

Nick put the envelope containing the girl's personal effects on her chest and sealed the body bag. He scrawled a number in Sharpie on the plastic, and job done. The girl would join the rest of the logged remains in the deep end of the small pool and then be transferred to the shallow, temporary grave site in the waste ground outside the trailer park.

And that was it. Nick's job was done. On to the next corpse. Sometimes the body would present with injuries inconsistent with the cold as a cause of death, but even then, all he did was chronicle the injuries the same way he did scars and tattoos. It wasn't a job that really required twelve years of medical school and nearly a decade of experience. A janitor with a checklist to work off could have done the same job.

Not that Nick had anything else to do. He was only meant to be there for three days—an in-and-out mercy mission to drop off medical supplies and evacuate the critically ill and vulnerable to a world-class hospital with an emergency generator and prepared staff. That was four weeks ago.

The medical supplies had been used up. Contact with the world-class hospital had begun with platitudes about finding a way to get them out and ended with silence. The critically ill were mostly under Nick's care now.

So Nick logged the dead, tried not to think about how much he missed picking them apart, and waited for his whiskey to run out. Once it did—he picked up the mug and took a gulp that warmed him up just enough to make him realize he was freezing—he'd see what came next.

The cold was brutal, and the equipment they'd been given wasn't sufficient for the conditions. Nick was nearly forty, nearly fit, and he drank too much even before the snowpocalypse. His fingers had lost sensation. He needed booze to control the scratchy cough that woke him up at night, and he'd skipped meals because his stomach ached as though it couldn't digest what he shoved in there. It might have been years since Nick treated a live body, but if he put his mind to it, he could probably diagnose himself.

But once he did, there was only one real resolution on the table and he wasn't ready to lie down in the pool with the rest of the corpses—not yet. There were still a few shots of whiskey left and plenty of remains to chronicle.

Nick shifted the girl's corpse. The next in line was a contorted, naked man with bloody hands and feet.

"Presumed cause of death is hypothermia," Nick said tiredly. "Injuries are consistent with 'terminal burrowing,' and with the state the remains were—"

Someone hammered on the door. It made the whole building rattle as it vibrated out along the metal walls. Up in the corners of the roof, ice cracked and dropped onto the corpses. Nick jumped in reaction and nearly knocked the dead man off the table.

"Fuck," Nick spat out. His heart skipped a beat and then another before it finally, sluggishly started again. It felt as though it were wedged in the base of his throat, like a chicken bone. He swallowed hard and rubbed his knuckles against his chest to shift the ache. "Shit."

He yanked the dead man back onto the center of the table and folded the tarp over him, as though he might still care if someone saw his frostbitten genitals.

Whoever was outside had stopped banging on the door. Apparently it wasn't as urgent as they had thought. Nick grumbled under his breath. Before they decided to give up, they'd woken every dog in the area and set them to howling. Nick stripped the gloves off as he stalked to the door. He yanked it open, and the blast of cold that blew in shocked the irritation out of him. It had gotten dark while he was working under the glare of portable generator-powered lights, and the storm had picked up again. There was no fresh snow to add to the grubby drifts piled up against the nicotine-beige caravans, but a wind armed with ice had blown in off the sea.

The dogs filled the night with frantic, aggressive noise that bounced off the metal sides of the trailers. It made it difficult to place anything.

"Hello?" Nick asked sharply. The cold worked under the heavy cuffs of his jumper and dug down into his bones. It dried out his nose as he inhaled. "Nelson? This isn't funny, you idiot."

He grabbed his coat from beside the door and shrugged it on as he stepped outside. The snow came up to his ankles, a bitter trickle down into his boots, and the wind flapped the long tails of his coat behind him. It splayed his shadow over the snow like grubby wings.

"Nelson?"

He took a step forward and looked around for the idiot paramedic. Back in Edinburgh, Nelson had been a "two sugars in a sugarless tea" joker. The last weeks stuck in a shoddy trailer site on the edge of a shrinking, snowbound town had edged the practical joker into an almost manic need to coax a laugh from someone. It wasn't working.

Nick held his coat closed over his chest with one hand and ventured another precarious step outside. He squinted against the wind and wiped his nose on his sleeve.

"Hello?" he said.

Something familiar and bitter teased at his nose. He had a good sense of smell. He'd always been the "do you smell that?" guy. But he couldn't quite place that smell. The cold dulled everything. He took another step. His feet were already soaked.

"I'm not in the mood." Nick scowled into the dark. "Jim? What is it? Does Jepson want to see me?"

Someone groaned in the dark. The sound was low and wet and suggestive. Nick would have blushed if he weren't so cold. He licked his lips and felt the sting of spit in open cracks.

"Go to hell."

Nick turned and stumbled through the snow, back toward the still-open door. His shoulders were hunched and tense, the muscles knotted into a tight ache. He shouldn't have slept with Nelson. It would have been a bad idea even if they weren't stuck there until the weather eased off.

If. A paranoid voice creaked a correction in the back of his brain. If it eased off. It was his gran's voice, old Scottish pessimism to the point of preaching the apocalypse and a clip around the ear if you left your shoes on the table or your hat on the bed, or the other way around, just to be safe.

She was born around here, he remembered—up north a few miles—a "proper Highlander" as she always said.

Nick reached the threshold and kicked the clumped snow off his boots. "Go ahead and freeze, then," he tossed sourly back over his shoulder.

But something made him hesitate in the doorway—maybe the smell, still naggingly familiar, or the second groan that clawed its way over the wind. That time it sounded... thick instead of wet. Across the trailer park, he saw lights flicker down at Jepson's trailer. The trauma leader was still up and at work. Her silhouette paused in front of the grubby net curtains, and someone joined her there.

Maybe not at work. Nick started to turn away, but then he stopped and looked again. Heavy jackets and layers made everyone the same shape, more or less, but the second figure was shorter than Jepson. So unless the surgeon had decided to kiss a girl and see if she liked it, that meant it was Nelson.

Blood.

The scent finally worked its way far enough up his nose that he could pick the copper and salt stink of it out from the sharp ozone smell of the snow and the distant salty reek of the sea.

Nick lurched back out into the snow. "Copeland! Harris!" he yelled for his neighbors. The wind caught his voice and stretched the words out thin and tinny from his lips. "Someone's hurt out here. Help!"

The door on one of the shabby vans creaked open, and Copeland looked out. Her hair was matted down on one side, and her broken arm was strapped carefully across her chest. She used her teeth to pull her heavy padded jacket over her shoulder as she gingerly came down the metal-grille steps.

"Who is it?" she asked, eyes wide and afraid.

"Don't know," Nick said. "I thought it was Nelson playing silly buggers, but…."

He jerked his head toward Jepson's caravan. Copeland looked in that direction, and, even though there was no one visible at the window anymore, she blushed.

"Maybe they're just… I mean, Doctor Jepson is married."

He snorted.

Copeland pulled a flashlight out of her pocket with her good hand and thumbed it on. The narrow beam of bright light flicked back and forth over the snow for a second and then stopped abruptly on a patch of dark, half-melted snow in front of one of the unused caravans. "Doctor Blake. There. Oh my God, they're bleeding."

Nick shifted direction and lumbered toward the stain. The snow was up to his shins as he veered off the trodden-down path and into the heavy, iced-over drifts. He caught his foot on something—a pot, an old bit of fence—and pitched forward onto his knees.

Other lights were going on across the park. He heard doors open and some voices demanding to know what was going on and others yelling at the dogs to shut up.

The beam of the flashlight flittered away and played randomly over the side of the caravan as Copeland hammered on the side of Harris's van.

"Wake up. Come on, man, we need help," she yelled.

Nick scrambled back to his feet and batted the ice off his knees with both hands. The wind caught his coat and viciously flapped it back and forth. Despite the cold, he had broken out in a slimy sweat under his arms and an itch at the back of his neck. The blood trail went from blotch to drip to smear before it disappeared under the trailer, dragged under the cracked brown latticework that covered the base. Old horror-movie instincts made him hesitate at the hole, where the smell of blood was so strong that it was impossible to mistake for anything else.

"Hey, are you okay?" Nick asked. Stupid question, but he felt like he had to break the silence. "Do you need any help? I'm a doctor. If you're hurt."

A rough rattle of air, almost lost under the wind, was his only answer. Nick took a deep breath, tasted the whiskey still on his tongue, and crawled into the gap. Snow soaked through his jeans, the chill of it jabbed into his knees like needles, and he had to fumble blindly in front of him to avoid the metal bars and pipes.

"...go...."

Nick squinted into the dark. He could just about make out a figure curled up against the trailer's tire, half-naked with a dark blanket hitched up over their hip. Something about the voice was.... Did he know them? It wasn't someone from the Relief Team, though. Maybe it was just the accent. Everyone up here burred their words like his gran had when she got merry.

"It's alright." Nick grimaced as he caught his shoulder against a sharp strut. "We can help. You're going to be okay."

Behind him he heard Copeland and Harris arguing as they got closer, her voice quick and panicky over his sleep-blurred questions. Nick was almost close enough to the man to touch his white sleeve when Harris demanded, "Who the hell is it, then?" and turned his torch under the trailer.

It wasn't a blanket. Blood coated the man's leg and stomach in a thick, almost syrupy film over raw skin. His chest was dappled with it too—arterial dark splatters that dripped onto the frosty ground in slow, persistent splats.

Nick didn't know him. The torch picked out the sharp lines in his lean, angular face and bounced back oddly from green eyes that looked too bright for the amount of blood. He was beautiful. It was an odd thing to notice in all that gore, but Nick couldn't help it.

"I don't need your help," he rasped out, his lips curled back from the words. "I don't need anyone's help."

"Of course you don't," Nick said. "You look like you're thriving under here."

His brain scrambled to pull up the half-forgotten, heavily depleted list of supplies stored in the old toilet block.

"Harris! Get in here and help me. You're the emergency medicine expert."

"I told you. I can die… on my own."

The man lifted his head off his arm, and Nick realized that the awkward lines of his folded body had created a sort of tourniquet that was now released. The steady drip of blood turned into a gush that steamed as the cold air hit it. Some ingrained habit from med school, back before they all agreed he was better with the dead, made Nick lurch forward and clap his hand against the man's throat. With his body pressed against the man's shoulder, he was close enough that it felt like an embrace—but somehow more intimate, with the bubble of the man's life caught in Nick's hand. The wound was wide and ragged, the edges bulging around his fingers as he tried to pinch them together.

"Who is it?" Harris persisted in the background. "What are they doing out here?"

Copeland's voice cracked. "Does it matter? We have to help him."

"What if it's a trick? What if those idiots come back to try and steal drugs we don't have?"

It felt alien. He was used to cold blood, still and settled under the skin. Not this hot gush, eager to escape and soak the ground. The man struggled against Nick's attempts to help him, his bloody hands slick and slippery as he pushed at Nick's arm and face. Blood smeared up over Nick's eye and into his hair. Through the glaze of red, he saw, for a second, a woman hanging off the man's shoulders by one wasted arm. Her fingers, so sharp and hard they looked like shrink-wrapped bone, plucked at the edges of the wound to try and open it.

Nick gasped and tasted rot and wine in the back of his throat. As though she could feel his attention on her, the woman looked up. Dirty, elflocked hair swayed back from her face, and Nick saw the sharp blade of an eroded nose and a glimpse of a dry yellow eye.

His bladder clenched and nearly spilled a night's worth of whiskey down his leg. He didn't want to see any more. Nick squeezed his hand tighter, resisted the pick-pick of dry fingers, and ducked his chin to wipe the blood off his face with his shoulder.

When he looked up, the woman was gone. He shuddered in relief, and the injured man stared at him as though he could tell what Nick had just seen.

"Tell him."

"Who? I don't know who that is. You'll have to tell him yourself," Nick said, the taste of metal and copper slipping onto his tongue. He glanced over his shoulder and yelled at the dithering Harris. "Just get in here and *help* me. He's bleeding."

"Tell the Old Man," the man said. The sharp clarity had faded from his eyes, leaving them dull and angry. He sagged against Nick, a heavy weight of muscle and bone and despair. "Tell him… I died first, if nothin' else."

"You're not dying. I got you," Nick insisted. He could feel the blood push against his fingers and run down his arms. The warmth of it was almost pleasant, even if it was in danger of making him a liar…. "Besides, I don't even know your name."

"Gregor." The man's head fell forward, and his chin braced against Nick's hand. "Tell him his favorite son died, but I went first."

Chapter Two

THERE WAS no hot water. In fact, there was no water at all. Nick stood in the cubicle bathroom of the trailer he'd been assigned and scrubbed his arms roughly with antibacterial gel. Most of the blood was gone. Just rusty remnants dried into his knuckles and cuticles remained, but he still didn't feel *clean*.

It wasn't the blood, really. It was the memory of the hot, slippery *aliveness* of it. Cold blood didn't bother him. It was just platelets, proteins, and plasma. But living blood was… different. Even though it wasn't.

The inability to shake that superstition was one reason why he was a pathologist and not a surgeon. That was the *only* superstition he allowed himself, though, and he knew it was irrational. The world was a rational place. It made sense. Nick took bodies apart, weighed them, and put them back together for burial.

There were no secrets there, no hidden pocket where the soul was wedged.

Blood was just blood, and death was the finish line. His granny had been crazy, God rest her sour old soul, and Nick was not.

That had been Nick's mantra all through university. He hadn't needed it for years, but it still settled his mind. The woman he'd seen, or *thought* he'd seen, was just like the horrors his gran called up for her clients—shadow, a susceptible mind, and something to tip the balance. In Nick's case, the something was whiskey and stress.

He glanced at his reflection in the fly-specked, age-yellowed mirror over the sink. His face was the only thing that looked back. Nick grimaced at the bony, oil-black, stubbled reflection. That was scary enough.

Someone rapped on the door.

"Doctor Blake? You decent?"

"Not usually."

Copeland pushed the door open and stuck her head in anyhow. Her hair was wet and stringy around her face, her teeth chattering with the cold. She wiped the drip of her nose on the back of her good wrist.

"They asked me to check on you," she said. "Mostly to get me out of the way, I think."

"I'm fine."

"Are you sure?"

Nick just shrugged. He lifted the clean sweater from where he'd hooked it over the shower door handles and pulled it on. Well, cleanish. It wasn't covered with blood, but he only had two sweaters, and they'd been there two weeks with no water. The heavy wool smelled of sweat and sheep—a sharp lanolin stink that rose through the aired wool.

"How's our guest?"

Copeland blinked hard and cradled her cracked forearm protectively. She caught her lower lip between her teeth and shook her head. "They're still working on him, as best we can here. He's still alive. I don't know why."

There was a tremble of shock in her voice. She was a junior doctor, newly minted, and none of this had been covered in her training.

"I can't help there," Nick said. "In my line of work, we don't see the people who didn't die."

"Could an animal have done it?" Copeland asked him abruptly. "A fox or a dog or something."

She trailed off as though she knew how stupid that sounded, but she still waited for an answer.

Reduced to a bullet list on an autopsy, the injuries were just dry facts—frostbite, multiple incised wounds to the left thigh, hip, and stomach—cause of significant degloving of areas, sharp-force trauma to the neck, resulting in the severing of the jugular vein. It was more of a catalog than just a trauma.

The vividly sharp memory of how the laid-bare muscle had twitched, the fat, twisted rope of it pulling through wet flesh and over bone, was what cut through that protective disassociation and filled Nick's throat with bile.

"Badgers don't use knives," he said.

"I know," she said. "I just… what the hell, right? What. The. Hell."

Nick handed her a threadbare towel. It was bleached and rough, with muddy spots of hair dye stained into it, but it was dry and didn't smell too bad. She sniffed and took it to scrub her face and then rubbed it halfheartedly over her matted curls.

"You don't need to worry," Nick told her. He carefully patted her good shoulder and then used the grip to nudge her out the door so he could get by. "Jeffers has radioed the cops. So they'll be here in the morning. They'll set up a security detail again, and whoever did this won't be back."

The thermos of coffee had been made that morning. Nick glanced at his watch and recalibrated his internal clock. Make that yesterday morning. He lifted down two mismatched mugs from the shelf—FML and a pug in headphones—and poured them both a drink. It was the ritual of it more than the taste.

Copeland took the mug and drank the bitter black sludge without complaint.

"It's just…." She spat the rest of the words out as though she wanted to get it over with. "Will they take him away? The man."

The immediate answer that popped into Nick's mind was that of course they would. But where would they take him? Even before the cold snap, the general hospital wasn't set up to deal with the sort of injuries Gregor had. Now they only offered bare-bones services—antibiotics, plasters, and somewhere to sit—and had lost over half of their staff.

How would they even get him there? Some efforts were made to keep the big roads open. Crews of men were out in the cold with shovels and salt, but the cities were impassable with snowdrifts and abandoned cars.

"I don't know," Nick admitted.

"He scares me," Heather said quietly. She gave Nick a quick, abashed look from under her lashes. "I know. It's stupid. He can't even walk, but... it feels like he brought something bad with him."

For a second Nick saw the dry-jerky face of the woman under the trailer, the tendon-twisted mouth and dry, puckered eye. His hand itched with the memory of hard, frayed fingertips picking at him. Old habit made him reach to his throat, but his fingers just found skin instead of the cold iron of the old charm his gran had given him.

Nick hadn't worn it in years, because Gran was crazy and he was not.

"It's just habit," he said. Copeland gave him a confused look. Apparently she thought he was still talking to her, and maybe he was. "It's a dark and stormy night, an injured stranger turned up and was taken in, and we're trapped out here until morning— all things that ghost stories and films have trained people to be afraid of."

She wrinkled her nose at him over the top of her coffee cup. "Maybe that's because people who aren't afraid of those things get ax murdered."

"Maybe," Nick admitted. "That doesn't mean that every dark night comes complete with a serial killer. For every family murdered by a masked psychopath in a horror movie, there's a whole street of people whose lives never changed."

"...probably changed when they found out their neighbors were ax murdered," Copeland muttered into her cup. When Nick laughed, she laughed and quickly set the cup down. "Sorry. You're right, I know. It's just... every time I feel I'm finally on top of things, something new goes wrong. We get sent here, we get stuck here, I break my arm… someone *spit* on me."

Her voice broke, and she had to blink hard and sniff again. Nick cringed at the thought that she was going to cry. He didn't feel up to being a good shoulder to cry on, but he supposed his own clinical lead, back when he was a resident, hadn't felt like it either when Nick broke down on him.

Everyone did it eventually, most of them with less excuse than Copeland. Nick recalled that he had come unraveled over a bad day, a one-night stand, and a needle jab.

He took the coffee cup from her. "Stay here," he said. "Tomorrow things will look more normal."

"I couldn't," Copeland protested, although she didn't move her feet. "It's your bed."

"Trust me. My bed has a better mattress," Nick said. "I doubt I'd get any sleep anyhow, so you're welcome. If you want to stay."

She bit her lip and then nodded with a quick jerk of her chin. "Thank you," she said. "I don't want to be alone tonight."

Nick took her shoulders, turned her around, and gave her a gentle push toward the back of the trailer. "Go. Sleep. If an ax murderer breaks in, you can get out the window while he kills me."

She hiccupped out a laugh and nodded.

"Thank you," she said. "You know, everyone at the hospital always said you were this cold fish? You've always been really nice to me, though. I guess they were just jerks."

She shuffled down the hall to the bedroom, and Nick poured the coffee down the sink and listened to the rattle of the door as it was folded back and the creak of the crappy mattress as she flopped onto it.

Once she started to snore—a ridiculous "bee whistle and snort" noise—Nick went back to work. He was tired. His eyes felt gritty, and nervous energy made his fingers jitter. But every time he closed his eyes, he *felt* the caravan shift as *something* creeped up on him.

Just because you could dole out good advice didn't mean you could take it. Besides, Nick's gran had taught him to be afraid better than most.

Sometime before dawn his body decided to bypass the usual procedures and just plugged on. He woke with a full-body jolt as thunder growled overhead. His heart was in his throat, and for a second, he had no clear idea where he was. The blurry scrawl of his own writing slowly resolved itself, and he realized he'd passed out on a pile of paperwork.

Nick groaned and braced his hands against the edge of the table to push himself upright. His neck and the small of his back spasmed as he shifted position. He had to peel a sheet of paper off his face, and he rubbed his cheek absently in case he'd left it smeared with ink.

He checked his watch. It was nearly six o'clock in the morning, but the only light was the dim-bulb glow of the nearly dead camping lantern. He reached over and turned it off, a small nod to conserving power long after it was too late.

The dark chilled him. He could hear the bee drone of Copeland snoring and the angry skirl of the wind. It should have been soothing. Before the disaster he used to sleep to the white noise of thunderstorms on repeat. Instead it twitched at his nerves. He reached for the light with an instinctive jerk of motion, but he stopped himself before he hit the switch.

"There's nothing there."

He clenched his hand into a fist, nails sharp against his palm, and made himself sit and wait. Each breath caught in his throat as though it might be his last, but he held his nerve.

Nick got up and staggered as one leg nearly buckled beneath him with pins and needles. He leaned on the back of the couch and limped to the window to peer out. The sky was so black it was almost green in places, and he could see a wall of white in the distance. Thunder grumbled again, and a single finger of lightning jabbed down out of the sky.

It hit the ground outside and left a smoking divot, and the flash of light as it struck made Nick flinch and twitch his head away from it. Out of the corner of his eye, he saw his shadow against the wall and the glitter of something bright as it turned to look at him. For a sharp, stomach-twisting second he thought it was Gregor. No, he *knew* it was. At the same time, he knew it couldn't be.

Nick closed his eyes and pressed the heels of his hands against his eyelids hard enough that he could feel the fluid shift and blobs of color popped. When he opened them again, he found his reflection peering at him from the window. He'd just forgotten to draw the curtains.

You can catch things in a mirror. It was his gran's voice in the back of his head—sharp and so Scottish she made Glasgow-born Nick sound like someone from the middle of England. She had a sharp, clear voice, the sort that assumed it would be heard—even years after you wanted it to stop. *Things you can't throw back.*

Only thing Nick had ever caught in a mirror was a stray gray hair or a new line around his eyes. But he still reached out with the same twitchy care he'd give a spider, as though his reflection might skitter unpredictably, and tugged the curtains shut.

"Not a ghost," he said aloud—too loud. He paused for a second until he was sure the buzz of Copeland's breathing was uninterrupted, and then he finished the thought in a quieter voice. "Just a guilty conscience."

Although, at this point, Nick supposed it could easily be both. He twisted his hands together and picked at the dry crust of blood still ingrained around his nails. The dead didn't require comfort and were past reassurances, but he should have remembered his training.

Never make promises you can't keep. Especially never make promises that you *won't* keep.

Every junior doctor had that clipped into their ear, usually more than once. It was human nature to want to comfort people, and it was in the nature of junior doctors to think they could save the world.

Last night, with Gregor's life caught in his hands, Nick had forgotten all that.

You aren't dying.

It's going to be ok.

I've got you.

Two of those promises Nick *couldn't* keep. Even if he'd spent the last decade in a Trauma Unit instead of a morgue, there was always a chance something would go wrong. One of them, though, he just *hadn't* kept.

It had made sense in the moment, as he let Jepson—who had spent the last two decades dedicated to trauma surgery—take over. What point was there in getting in their way when Harris was an emergency medicine nurse? It might look dramatic to stand there and let the blood dry on him, but it wouldn't actually accomplish anything.

All of which was true, but it wasn't why he'd ghosted the scene to go and clean himself up. He'd been afraid. Not of the frayed, pickled face of the hag he imagined, but of what it meant—that he wasn't Dr. Nicholas Blake, who people might call a cold fish but never called crazy. Instead he was still lanky, twitchy Nick Blake, who tried to self-medicate the need to salute magpies away—or worse, Nicky Blake still at his gran's knee, convinced the monsters under the bed were real.

He took a breath, glanced at the curtained window, and twisted his mouth in a sour smile. So he might be a little afraid of the thing in the dark. It still wasn't an excuse. Time to keep the one promise he could. Although, considering the severity of Gregor's injuries, he didn't know what that was worth.

Nick dragged his coat back on. The sleeves were damp. He'd scrubbed at the blood on them with a handful of snow the night before, but it would do until he could scavenge another. A glance in at Copeland showed her passed out on the bed under two duvets. She hadn't even taken off her boots before she crashed. Nick closed the door on her and let himself out.

The north wind promptly tried to shove him back in. He grunted in surprise—usually the wind came from the sea, and the angled rows of caravans deflected it—and got a mouthful of snowflakes, cold and vaguely salty as they melted on his tongue. The door was wrenched out of his hand and blown back hard enough to smack against the side of the trailer. It made the tin box shake.

Nick fumbled his spare gloves out of his pocket and pulled them on. He'd only been outside for a second, and already his fingers felt raw, the skin tender against rough wool. Once the gloves were on, he grabbed the door and wrestled it shut.

He staggered gracelessly down the slippery metal steps and into the snow. The growl of thunder overhead made him curse it for a bad idea and hunch down into his collar. He pulled everything tightly around him in an attempt to hold the warmth in, and he hunched over against the wind.

The shortest way to Jepson was to cut through the trailers, where the snow wasn't as deep and the occasional lighted window could keep you right. It also meant you had to climb over towbars and trip over erratically placed, ankle-height picket fences.

That was how Copeland had broken her arm. She'd stubbed her toe on a raised deck hidden under the snow, and the guy with her tried to catch her as she went down.

"Let people fall," Jepson had told them when they got there, as part of a brisk health-and-safety lecture. "You're less likely to get hurt that way." Nobody listened. It was just instinct to grab for someone you saw going down.

Nick took the longer route and followed the main road that looped through the vans to the central parking lot. The snow was grubby gray there, with shovel scars and pocks from liberally deployed ice. It was slippery, with a half-frozen crust that gave under your heels unexpectedly. But it was easier to walk on.

The lightning strike had left a scar in the snow—a raised welt of ice around a cratered wound, the blackened base just visible as it filled back up. Nick gave it a wide berth, tucked his chin down into his collar, and tried not to think about the lightning-scarred bodies in his morgue.

He was halfway across the park when the rattle of thunder made him stop. The crack of lightning jabbed down to his left. It smashed against the roof of a van and blasted the snow off it. A child wailed—a miserable drone that didn't expect anything to get better—and someone inside flicked a flashlight on and then nervously off again.

They were all right, then. Nick didn't bother to check on them.

Jepson's trailer was a huge bullet of glass and metal, with a full-length bay window at one end and a wraparound deck that was currently home to two long, low white tents with the familiar red cross emblazoned on the side. Jerry-rigged tunnels of nylon fly sheets and aluminum poles created corridors into the trailer.

The light was on inside the van, and the sound of raised, aggravated voices was just about audible over the sound of the storm. Nick skipped going inside and circled around the van to the deck instead. The first tent was empty except for an old woman who sat up in her narrow bed and smiled happily at everyone who came in. Someone had left her at the gates of the trailer park one night, in a nightie and a waxed jacket.

There was nothing physically wrong with her, other than being ninety, but she couldn't go into one of the trailers. She forgot it was cold.

In the second tent, Harris paced nervously back and forth over the ground sheet, a radio gripped tightly in one hand. He stopped when Nick stepped through the entrance, and a look of mingled resentment and relief crawled over his face.

"Are you here to take over?" He tugged nervously at his beard and muttered, "About time. You found the guy. You should be the one to stand watch."

"How is he?" Nick asked.

"Not dead yet," Harris said flatly. He stalked over and shoved the radio into Nick's hand. The heavy, molded plastic was clammy and sweaty from Harris's grip. "More's the pity."

The minute that left his mouth, Harris had the grace to look ashamed. He worried at his beard with his fingers. "Sorry. I don't mean that. I just... this whole thing has me on edge. Isn't everything bad enough without some serial stabber out in the storm? And him...." He gave a leery look over his shoulder. "There's something *off* about him, Blake."

"Is he even conscious?" Nick asked skeptically as he tilted his head to peer at the sheet-draped body in the bed. There was a visible bloom of blood on the cheap Primark cotton.

Harris dragged his attention back to Nick.

"Sometimes," he said. "Doesn't matter. You can tell. Well, *I* can."

He shuddered, glared at Nick like it was his fault, and stalked away. Nick supposed he was glad he wasn't the only one who felt... off-balance after last night. He turned the radio over in his hands—he wasn't entirely sure what to do with it, presumably press one of the buttons—and shoved it in his pocket.

Without the crackle of Harris's almost audible nerves, Nick could hear the slow, labored rasp of Gregor's breathing. He didn't sound like a man in a state to put anyone on edge.

Nick reluctantly stood for a second and then reluctantly walked over to the bed. His lips felt so dry they were stuck together, and he didn't realize he was holding his breath until his chest hurt. Habit made him reach for the patient's notes at the end of the bed, only to remember no one had a reason to write them. It took a second, but he finally made himself look.

The man in the bed was… just a man in a bed. He still had the sort of profile you usually saw stamped on a Roman coin—all sharp bones and clean lines—but nothing unnatural clung to him. The white pad of gauze taped over his neck was stark against freckled skin, but no frayed fingers picked at the edges of the tape. Nick searched the shadows around the bed, but there was nothing.

Of course there wasn't. There never had been.

"You, my friend?" Nick muttered as he put one hand on Gregor's shoulder. "You scared the crap out of me. Keep that to yourself."

The still lines of Gregor's face didn't show any reaction to the sudden sound of Nick's voice. His eyes were sunken, with bruises of pooled blood in the orbits, and his shoulder was dry and fever hot against Nick's palm. Slightly rusty instincts assured Nick that he wouldn't have to worry about Gregor keeping secrets for long.

"Poor bastard. Got all the way here for help, and all we can do is stick a plaster on it and hope for the best."

Nick carefully lifted the sheet draped over Gregor's still body and hissed through his teeth at his first clear sight of the damage done. The blood had been washed off and the edges of the wounds tidied, but that just made it easier to see the butcher's work. It was bad, but it wasn't as bad as Nick had thought in the dark.

A staggered row of clumsy stitches—Harris's work, Nick had seen it before in the morgue—held together a five-inch-long gash that slashed down Gregor's stomach and pulled inked-black lines out of true. The skin on his thigh, from hipbone down, had been raggedly degloved. What tissue was left was stretched back over the raw muscle and held in place with taped-down strips of plastic wrap. It clung to the still exposed patches of muscle, and the iodine stain somehow made the mess look worse.

Nick was about to lower the sheet back over Gregor, but he paused as he noticed that... *mess* was unfair. The edges of the wounds were clean and straight, almost surgically tidy. There were no hesitation marks. It looked as though Gregor's thigh had been opened up with a single confident pass of the blade.

It again reminded Nick of his gran, not of her stories about monsters, but of the easy way she held her old knife, the one with the bone handle and the blade sharpened into a shallow sickle. She'd kept it for butchery—clipped Nick around the ear when she caught him digging for a peach pit with it—and she hardly even bothered to look at her hands as she used it to debone a chicken.

That was what the pattern of injuries reminded Nick of. Whoever had the knife hadn't degloved Gregor's leg, they'd butterflied it.

An odd, dispassionate switch in Nick's brain had flipped. Without thinking, he reached down to examine the inner edge of the wound. His fingers grazed along Gregor's thigh, and then a long-fingered hand with swollen knuckles—probably broken, but with the extent of his other injuries, Nick imagined that Jepson had decided to focus on fixing something else—closed around Nick's wrist.

He hadn't even seen Gregor move. He hadn't thought Gregor could move.

Nick tried to pull his hand back, but the fingers just tightened around his wrist. He looked up, mouth open on a comforting platitude, only to be pinned in place by a glare from bottle-green eyes.

"If I wanted you to touch me, I'd have told you," Gregor said, the words sticky in his throat.

For a second, Nick couldn't catch his breath. He wasn't sure why. It wasn't fear, but it was familiar. It was the same feeling he'd had the first time he sliced a body open in the morgue, or the time he kissed a boy and realized that was why other people liked kissing—a sort of giddy wonder at seeing something strange and rare.

Except this wasn't a revelation about how your life was going to go, about the things you were going to love. It was just a bloody man on a bloody bed.

Nick forced air down his throat and twisted his hand again. "Sorry," he said. "You... I forgot you weren't dead."

Chapter Three

GREGOR LAUGHED—a low rasp of noise that hurt his body on the way out. He supposed he couldn't blame the man. He had forgotten he wasn't dead for a while himself. The back of his throat tasted like old blood, his bones were cold and weary, and he could smell the sourness of the corpse goddess Hela's embrace on his skin.

He let go of the man's arm and tried to push himself up off the mattress. The pain twisted through him like barbed wire anchored in his bones as it shredded his muscles. He could bear that. It was the alien wash of weakness that disoriented him, the clammy sweat that greased his body, the woozy pulse of his heartbeat in his ears.

"Wait." Despite the stink of fear that hung around the man, Nick grabbed Gregor's shoulders and tried to push him back. "You're going to hurt yourself. You need to lie down."

Weak. Not human. Gregor braced himself against the pressure. He looked up into the man's narrow face. It was all bones, hard angles, and beaky nose. His eyes were so dark the pupils blurred into the iris and gave him an odd, piercing gaze. It was the sort of face that didn't meet any of the usual markers for handsome but somehow snuck in anyhow.

And somehow familiar.

"Who are you?"

"Doctor Blake."

Gregor snorted. "I asked who you are, not what you do."

Something rueful flashed over Nick's mobile face. "Isn't it the same thing?" He gave up on trying to get Gregor to lie back down and helped him sit up instead. That he had to accept the help curdled in Gregor's gut. "I'm Nicholas Blake. Nick. We met last night. Do you remember?"

The flash of steel. Pain. Blood in the snow. Shame. The stutter of memory made Gregor touch his stomach. He remembered unmarked skin and hard flesh, an open wound, and his brother screaming. His fingers found a rough zipper of stitches and sore muscles.

"I met a lot people last night," he said. "Some had knives."

The smell of fear thickened. It was sharp and acidic, layered over the musty sweetness that was the doctor's own scent. An odd smell. Despite that, Nick didn't move. He just took a slow breath and held it for a second.

"Nobody here would hurt you," he said carefully.

The kindness in his voice, the low, even seduction of it, made Gregor's hackles rise. He wasn't a horse or a hound to be gentled. It also sent another fragment of memory through his brain—a dark den to die in and a man who smelled like corpses. The weakness of the memory revolted Gregor.

"We're doctors, nurses," the man continued. "Whoever hurt you, they won't get you here."

Gregor's stomach ached too bitterly to risk another laugh. He settled for a sneer.

"If I need protection from you," he growled bitterly, "let them kill me." He tossed the sheet back. The stained cloth fluttered off the bed and landed on the canvas floor in a knot. Cold air hit naked skin and raw flesh. It felt like needles sharp enough to sting. Gregor ignored it. The cold was like pain, something to acknowledge, but not pay attention to. He needed to find his brother. They needed to kill the toothless mongrels who thought they could lay knives on the Numitor's pups. Then Gregor could deal with the unsavory fact that he owed this human a blood debt.

"Don't do that," Nick protested. "For fuck's sake, you shouldn't even be conscious."

Gregor swung his legs over the side of the bed, braced himself, and stood up. The pain made his head swim, and his leg felt stiff and leaden under his weight. He clenched his jaw so tightly it ached, and he reached for the wolf.

For a second he felt nothing, just skin outside and in. Then he found the scraped-clean places where the wolf should be, and wasn't. Gregor snarled and reached again. Again. His mental fingers clawed at the space where the wolf had been until they scored the wound deeper. It didn't bring the wolf back. Gregor's chest tightened, his lungs cramped under his ribs, and his legs buckled under him.

Nick caught him. He locked his wiry arms around Gregor's waist and braced a shoulder under his arm. He was stronger than he looked. Gregor's weight made him stagger, but he stayed on his feet.

"I told you," he said. "You're injured. Come on, get back in bed."

There wasn't enough left in Gregor to fight it as Nick walked him back to the mattress. He sat down on the edge and slumped over.

Nick pressed the back of his hand against Gregor's forehead. "You have a fever."

"Then let me die," Gregor snarled as he smacked the hand away. He took a ragged breath and corrected himself. "No. I'm already dead... as good as dead. Just let me rot."

"I'm not going to do that." Nick grabbed blankets and sheets from one of the empty beds and wrapped them around Gregor's shoulders. "I'm going to go and get Jepson. Stay here. Don't move. Okay? If you rip your leg open again, you could do yourself permanent damage."

Gregor gave him a sour look through sandy lashes. "Too late."

With one last concerned look, Nick left. His coat flapped behind him as he hurried out of the tent, his long legs stretched in a half run. That left Gregor alone. The thought made him shudder. He had always been a lone wolf by choice, up on the old stones and high places, but never alone.

There had always been his brother—his shadow, his fetch, his other half—and there'd always been the wolf.

Now he had neither.

Gregor's toes were warm. He looked down and saw his foot in a stocking of bright red blood. A puddle spread out around it and widened with every breath he took. Good.

The last thing Gregor remembered from before he passed out was the flash of bone-handled knives in the dark and how they'd cut deeper than seemed possible—than *was* possible.

WOLVES DIDN'T dream. They remembered. In sleep they walked the inner Wild of their pasts, whether they liked it or not. Few minded a return to the warm, milk-sweet hours of their first experiences, but you didn't get to choose the memory. There were dark crannies where the psyche kept the worst things, the words and deeds that the waking mind would have to forget all over again.

Gregor hadn't forgotten that, but he had no desire to relive it. The Wild did not care. In yesterday's skin he shadowed his brother and his brother's Dog as they walked along the road. His bare feet sank into fresh-fall snow, and he ducked his head to avoid a low hanging branch heavy with snow.

No. It hadn't been like this. He had been in his wolfskin, four-legged and furred. His memory had never been... altered before. But even in sleep, even in a memory, he couldn't reach his wolf. It hurt to try.

Jack hunched his pack up over his shoulder and nudged the Dog's shoulder as he said, "Your mam will be glad to see you."

The dry look the Dog gave him through snow-misted glasses was the same one Gregor felt crease his face. It didn't sit well with Gregor to find himself in sympathy with a Dog, but better that than in agreement with his brother.

"No. She won't," the Dog said. At some point, once they got back to the Pack, Gregor would have to call the Dog by name. There were other Dogs under the Old Man's protection, useful for when he wanted a newspaper from town or had to send someone out to talk to the cops and teachers, but until they got there, "Dog" was as good as "Danny." All three of them knew what Gregor meant when he barked it. "I'm not going back to petition the Old Man to rejoin the Pack, even if he'd have me. This is about the prophets, their rebellion, and their monsters."

Plenty to be getting on with.

Gregor, with the benefit of hindsight, huffed at the thought as it slid through his head.

Jack snorted. "Plenty to get on with, I guess."

Even as an observer of his own moment, Gregor couldn't tell which of them had the thought first, his brother or himself. That had always been their problem, hadn't it? Which brother had been first? Twelve minutes separated them—twelve minutes and a lifetime of enmity—but had Gregor been twelve minutes early? Or twelve minutes late?

The midwives who dragged them into the world shrugged their shoulders and turned their heads. They weren't their da's only sons, not then, but the Wolf

who bled her life out had been his only mate. So they'd
left the bloody pups on a bed of heather and Scottish
stone to tend to her, and by the time they turned back,
neither could remember which pup they'd laid where.

Gregor knew it was him. He could *remember* the
cold stone on his back, and that second of being bliss-
fully *alone* before the other followed him, squalling,
into the world—his mirror, his shadow, the squatter in
their ma's womb, his twin. Jack.

But just because you knew something, that didn't
mean you believed it. The chance that he was wrong
had been the burr in his tail ever since, until it worked
deep enough to become a lesion. Only one of them
could take their da's place and be the next Numitor
who ruled all the Wolves of Britain, who'd fulfill the
prophets' promise to hand a frozen world to Fenris
before Ragnorak. It should be Gregor—he knew that
in his bones—but twelve minutes could make it Jack.
His lost wolf would make it Jack.

There was a shadow on the road, between the rows
of cars. Gregor noticed it the first time—he wouldn't
remember it if he hadn't—but he didn't identify it. It
stretched as he watched out of the corner of his eye…
and was that another?

It wouldn't do any good. It was done and dusted,
but his throat ached to howl a warning.

It was too late in the real world, hours and blood
between here and then, and too late in the memory as
well. A clot of half-wrecked cars had been abandoned
at the scene of an accident. Their dented bumpers and
crumpled hoods lay under a blanket of grease-stained
snow. The monsters crawled out from under them.

Muscles bulged in thick, stringy ropes under their arms and across their backs. Unlike Job's beasts back in Durham, clumsily put together on the run and no one abomination the same as the other, these all had a settled pattern they shared.

They ran on bone-spike fingers and broken feet. Instead of a wolf's thick hide and heavy fur, they had a ruff of loose skin dappled with cracked, red blooms of calluses. They had tusks instead of fangs, snaggled things made of broken jaw bones. Their skin was smeared with shit and clotted blood to cover the stink of "kill it" that sweated off them, and they were faster than they looked.

It hadn't occurred to Gregor at the time—his mind on the fight, the blood, and the pain—but he wondered how many of Job's failures it had taken until a prophet could make these monsters. How many prophets would it take to do it? No one liked the prophets—to become a mouthpiece of the hated gods was a punishment handed out only to the worst among their packs—but it had never occurred to Gregor that they'd betray the Wolves. Until now.

Gregor cursed—*snarled, he'd snarled*—and threw himself into the fight. The snow was hard under his feet, beaten down and frozen over, and the car doors crumpled when he hit them.

One monster went down, hamstrung and throat-ripped, and then another. It galled a bit that it was so easy to play Jack's ally, but they'd always fought well together, as though they were one Wolf in two skins. Sometimes Gregor wondered if they were, if that was the thing so wrong with them that they couldn't bear their own company.

Seven monsters to two wolves and an uppity dog, and the odds still managed to be in their favor.

The thing in the tattered party dress, velour shredded and wrapped around it like grubby ribbons, had been inked once. Its blotchy hide was covered in smears and lines of color that had probably once been a pattern but now was routed around sagging skin and bone spurs. It lunged at Jack from the roof of a car and bowled him over. The smell of Jack's blood, familial *and* familiar, filled the air as he scraped the skin off his back on ice and tarmac.

Gregor tried to *see* what happened next, but he hadn't been looking. His teeth had been in the throat of a monster, and its claws had taken his ear off.

"You should fix your dogs." A woman's voice. Three prophets had Jack's Dog pinned up against the side of a bus, and a fourth held a knife to his balls. The point of the blade had sliced through worn denim but hadn't drawn blood... yet. A rotting pelt hung over the woman's narrow shoulders, its back paws frayed and dirty where they'd dragged in the mud. The slack face of the dead wolf hid her, and all Gregor could see was a crooked jaw and bloody mouth. Good for the Dog. "You want him intact? Let go of my girl."

Jack shouldn't have.

Jack did. Of course. Gregor had identified the Dog—Danny the Dog—as Jack's weakness way back when they were still kids. Someone else had to have as well.

One Wolf. The odds were against him.

Gregor didn't have a weakness they could put on him like a collar. He hated his brother. The Dog wasn't his mate. So they gave him one. They took the wolf.

MAYBE THE Wild had some small kindness left in it for him, because Gregor woke before he relived the prophets' work with their blades. He opened his eyes and stared up at the stained white canvas pulled taut overhead. The fabric belled and flapped as the wind hit it, and the whole structure flexed with each gust, the howl of the wind shockingly loud.

The storm still raged, then. Gregor closed his eyes for a second and supposed bitterly that he should be glad. Even a wolf would hesitate to venture out while the Wild was that riled up, and the prophets' monsters had been cowed like dogs by the thunder. It was the only reason that Gregor, hobbled and... *ruined*—he might not have his wolf anymore, but he wasn't so weak he had to lie to himself—was able to get away.

"Here."

Cold water touched Gregor's lips. He felt a sharp pinch of resentment at being dropper fed like a sickly pup, but it drowned under the sudden overpowering thirst that hit him. Sleep was hard work, apparently.

He lifted his head enough that he didn't choke and sucked down the cold water to the last drop. It hurt to swallow. His throat throbbed with each gulp, but he couldn't stop. When Nick took the glass away to refill it, Gregor propped himself up on his elbow. He reached up to his throat and touched the thick wad of gauze under his jaw.

The prophet's teeth in his throat, a dominance display for the Wild, and fuck that. He'd ripped his own throat out for her from spite, his blood and her spit sour in the back of his throat.

"Jepson says it looks like you were attacked by a dog on top of everything else," Nick said. He offered the glass to Gregor. "There are a lot of new feral dogs around. People can't feed them, so they turn them out. Now they're starving and not afraid of people. With all the blood, they must have thought you were easy prey."

The details might be off, but the general idea was right.

"They were wrong." Gregor took the glass and drank. It took more effort than he expected. "How long was I out?"

Nick started to say something, stopped, shook his head, and finally spoke. "Not long enough," he said. "You need to rest. With the storm, with the weather, we can't get you the treatment you need. That leg needs microsurgery to get back full function. You've lost a lot of blood that we can't effectively replace."

"What do you care?"

Nick blinked. "I'm a doctor."

Gregor braced his hand flat against the bed and pushed himself up into a sitting position. "I'm your only patient?"

A wry smile tilted the corner of Nick's mouth and creased the corners of his eyes. He was older than Gregor had originally thought. The sharp bones and spare flesh were deceptive.

"You're the first patient I've kept alive in decades," he said. "Maybe I've gotten attached."

"Maybe you shouldn't be so proud of being a doctor, if you're that bad at it." Gregor bunched his fist in the sheet and dragged it back from his leg. There were more black stitches scrawled over his thigh, and the skin they held together was a bit more ragged.

The snort of laughter made him glance at Nick. He looked wicked when he laughed—a full-throated chortle took over his whole face. Gregor felt a sharp cramp of interest that caught him by surprise, not just because his balls were bruised and bloody from the prophets' treatment, but because he didn't fuck humans. Some wolves did. It was forbidden, but they did it anyhow, and a blind eye was turned until it got out of hand. Gregor had never done it. He'd never even thought about it. There'd always been enough wolves eager to share his bed.

But he did share a type with his brother, and Nick fit the dark, lanky, smart-mouthed part of it.

"I'm a pathologist," Nick said dryly as he missed Gregor's brief distraction. "I haven't treated a live patient since… well, like I said, years. I'm just… I'm the one who found you. So, I guess I feel responsible, even if I'm not the one who had to patch you back together."

Gregor curled his lip. It had been a long time since he'd needed a nursemaid, and he never wanted one.

"How long until I can get out of here?"

The silence wasn't empty. Gregor could feel the unsaid words jammed into the space. Jack was the one who was good at words, but Gregor knew what silences meant. His watchdog didn't think he'd get out of there anytime soon, maybe ever. It was the wolf winter, the first cold turn of the world's end, and the weak died of a lot of things.

Gregor leaned back against the pillows and closed his eyes. The wolf was gone, and the place where it had been was still raw and going sour like day-old meat.

He flinched away rather than touch it again, but he swallowed the bitter pill of it.

So he wasn't a Wolf anymore, but that didn't make him human. The Wild still took him when he slept, and he could feel the muscle and flesh stitching back together in the meat of his leg. Slowly, but there, down near the bone, persistently, until he wanted to dig his finger in and scratch.

He would get out of there, but for the moment, he wasn't going anywhere. Not on his own.

"Where are you in such a rush to get to, anyhow?" Nick asked. "Do you have family nearby?"

"I don't know," Gregor said. "I don't know where they took my brother when they were done with me."

He heard the soft grunt of a sucked in breath. Maybe he wasn't as bad at words as he thought.

Chapter Four

IT WAS finally quiet.

Nick lifted his head off his arm and waited. Sometimes the wind only paused to catch its breath, but not this time. After nearly two days, the storm had finally blown itself out—until the next one. He dragged the blanket down from his shoulders, and the nip of cold at his collarbones and behind his ears was painful as he gingerly unfolded himself from the molded plastic chair where he'd spent the night.

As a med student, he used to grab some shut-eye on those things all the time. It never left you particularly rested, but it let you keep your eyes open for the rest of the shift. His back wanted to remind him that his days as a junior doctor were long behind him. It ached from the spasmed muscle in the small of his back to the kink in his neck that didn't want to straighten out.

"Crap," he muttered as he craned his head painfully to the side. His spine grated and then popped loudly enough that he half expected it to wake Gregor.

That, of course, assumed Gregor really was asleep. He'd accepted Nick's presence in the room, but every time anyone else ducked in through the flap, he opened his eyes, lifted his head, and watched them until they left. But Nick's spine realigning didn't seem to have disturbed him. He looked comfortable, sprawled out on the bed, with one arm cocked up behind his head.

Despite himself, Nick looked. Gregor was a handsome man. If he smiled, it might upgrade him to beautiful. Under the bruises and battering, he had long, elegant bones draped with heavy slabs of muscle. Even injured, he moved with confidence... despite his body's inability to follow through.

Half-dead too, Nick reminded himself sharply, and off-limits. Even if he weren't sort of a patient, Gregor was clearly no one's good idea, and Nick had been done with self-destructive behavior for a very long time. He spread his blanket over Gregor. There was no point in wasting his stored body heat, after all, and it hid the shoulders and inked arms.

Nick felt a brief, sharp temptation to just crawl back under the blanket where it was, although that had less to do with his libido and more to do with a desire to just... hide. Since he couldn't, he gave Gregor one last look and left.

When he felt a prickle at the nape of his neck, he stopped at the tent flap and looked back. Gregor hadn't been sleeping after all.

"What if I die when you're not here to keep an eye on me?" he mocked in a low, rough voice as he levered himself up into a partial sitting position. The blanket slid back to his lap and revealed a flash of bruised stitches and broad shoulders that should have been clinical. It wasn't.

Nick decided he didn't want to deal with that twitch of strange lust right then—or, with luck, ever.

"I'm going to see if anyone managed to get through to the police in Ayr," he said. "I'll be back as soon as I can."

Gregor curled his lip in a sneer. "I don't care."

He probably didn't. Any other day Nick would probably have taken him at his word. It was his favorite lifehack—not looking under the surface of anything or anyone. But he'd spent too much time thinking about the past in the last twenty-four hours, and his screwed-up younger self was fresh in his mind.

So scared that you couldn't let anyone get close, in case they realized how scared you were, all sarcastic jabs and adolescent sneers. Although God knows why he tried so hard. He hadn't been an appealing child, and adolescence hadn't done anything to help. No one *wanted* to get close to him back then.

"I know," he said. "I'll still be back."

Gregor rolled his eyes and turned onto his side. He didn't bother pretending to go back to sleep.

ONCE UPON a time, Nick would have found the pristine white duvet of snow—too fluffy and thick for a blanket—to be beautiful. Even now it did make him stop for a second to admire the greeting-card impossible perfection of it through Jepson's picture windows.

The gray sludge of muddy, trodden-on snow was disguised, the shabby beige-and-cream caravans topped with mounds of white like cupcake frosting, and the sky was a brittle, distant blue.

It was also bitterly, flintily cold. It poked like needles under his fingernails and into his ears, eager to suck up any little bit of heat he had hidden.

The storm might be done for now, but another was on the way.

"Drink it."

Jepson shoved the mug at him. She might have retired from the army, but she didn't see that as any reason that people should stop obeying her orders. Of course, she was a surgeon. The army had nothing to do with it.

Nick took the soup and realized he was starving.

"Thanks."

He took a cautious sip. It was hot enough to scald his tongue, and it tasted like…. He stopped and grimaced. It tasted like a mixture of whatever old tins of soup they'd found around stored in cupboards.

"Makes you long for the canteen, eh?" Jepson asked. She pulled her bobble hat off and scratched her short, dense curls. "How's our mystery man?"

"Alive," Nick said. "Conscious."

Jepson *huh*'d and leaned back against the kitchen counter. She had to be about fifty, with a stint in the army and a consultancy in the US behind her, but she looked younger. Nick, with that peculiarly morbid bent that always plagued him, thought she showed more wear under the skin. Her ankles bothered her in the cold, and there were a few scars around her eye where someone had done a very good reconstructive job on her eye socket.

It was a drawback of the job. Whenever he looked at people, he saw the things that could have killed them, or might kill them eventually.

"I am surprised he's either," Jepson said over her own soup. "Between that amount of trauma and the facilities we have here? He's a tough bastard… a lucky, tough bastard."

"I don't know if he'd agree."

That made Jepson give a short chuckle. "Relatively, then," she said. "The cold slowed down the bleeding and made infection less likely. If he hadn't stumbled across us, he would've walked for miles and found nothing but abandoned farms and sand."

"Or his brother."

Jepson sighed with the cup raised to her lips. The steam eddied away from her parted lips. "Doctor Blake, that's not our job. Even if it were, we just can't."

If they'd been friends, maybe Nick would have tried to talk her into it. But he'd never been particularly good at making friends. Until they were loaded onto that helicopter, he'd met her maybe a handful of times in the canteen, in the elevator, and on the stairs. She'd paid a single visit down to the morgue after a particularly bad trauma call.

"I know," he had to admit instead. What were they going to do? Arm Copeland with a flashlight and send her looking for a murderous gang in the empty farms? They'd searched as far as they could manage yesterday, around the fenced-in outskirts of the park, along the narrow ruts the local kids dug, and down to the dunes. The storm blew them back in, but no one had seen anything. "What about Harris? Did he manage to get in touch with the police in Ayr?"

Jepson swallowed and wiped her mouth on the back of her hand. A worried frown settled between her eyebrows.

"No," she said. "He *thinks* he managed to inform them about, ah—"

"Gregor."

Jepson gave him a small nod of thanks and kept going. "But the connection was spotty. He got no reply, and that was the last contact he managed to make."

She sighed again and sat down at the narrow table. Her mouth was tight with worry as she absently tapped her fingernail against the side of the scuffed ceramic mug.

"He's going to take the ATV out later, see if he can run across one of the patrols."

"But?"

"Go with him."

"Why?"

Jepson frowned at the photo frame someone had left in the trailer at the end of their summer holiday. It held a glossy picture of a young child and an old dog.

"He's… a bit off," she said. "We all are, of course, but that house last week, those wee dead lassies. He has daughters, you know, back in Glasgow."

Nick hadn't known. He wished he didn't know now.

Still with a frown on her face, Jepson took a drink of her soup and grimaced. It had cooled enough that she could taste it. She carefully set it down on the table and centered it on a coaster.

"He's wound too tight," she said. "And something about your patient is putting him over the edge, I don't know why. So I want someone with him, and, no offense Doctor Blake, your patients are very... patient."

Nick scratched the back of his head and tried to think of an excuse.

"I told Gregor I would be back," he said.

Jepson tipped her head to the side and gave Nick a thoughtful look, as though she needed to take his measure. It was probably the same look she gave Harris before she decided he was wound too tight.

"I know he's not my patient," Nick said to forestall her. "But it's not like he's got anyone else, and I do feel...."

"Responsible," Jepson finished for him. "That's understandable. Your commitment is even admirable, but it's not helpful. Gregor is in good hands, and he doesn't need you sitting vigil. I need you to keep an eye on Harris."

The only thing Nick could do was nod his agreement. If he argued, it would only convince Jepson that he was too invested in Gregor. It didn't help that there was a guilty voice at the back of his head to remind him that he hadn't sat with Gregor out of commitment. It hadn't even been for Gregor, not really.

It had been because, on some illogical level, he felt like Gregor could protect him from whichever of his gran's monsters came calling. He could justify it to himself, wrap it up in the psychology of Gregor's battered body being evidence that he was just an injured man, and not some hag-ridden carrier of the dead. That didn't change the fact that the minute he left Gregor behind, he started to feel watched again, and the hair at the nape of his neck constantly prickled as though someone—something—were about to touch it.

Not exactly a confession that would reassure Jepson about his state of mind.

"It'll do you good to get out," she told him bracingly. "Stop you finishing that bottle of whiskey in the morgue."

Of course she knew about that. Nick waited for shame, but it didn't arrive. Too much else in his head, and besides, he could make the same jibe to Jepson about finishing Nelson while they were gone. At least Nick didn't have a bottle of Scotch back home waiting for him.

He'd mostly finished that before he left.

"I suppose you're right," he said. "It'll do me good to get out. We probably need to start thinking about cabin fever."

Jepson smiled tiredly and without anything like humor. Her eyes flicked to the satellite phone that was meant to keep them in contact with the disaster-response team in Edinburgh.

"I already am." There was a moment's pause, and Nick thought about asking her what the last news from them had been. Before he could decide if he wanted to know, Jepson shook off her brief mood. Her spine straightened, and she jerked her chin toward the door in a clear gesture of dismissal. "You should go. It doesn't take Harris long to get the ATV ready."

"THE FUCK?" Harris yelled. His voice shattered the silence and startled a flutter of black wings from a nearby tree. Harris stooped, grabbed a stone or chunk of frozen ice from the road, and threw it at them. He missed, and the stone clattered against a low wall that had probably been a high wall before the snow piled up around it. Spite vented, Harris jabbed a finger at the source of his rage. "What the *actual* fuck happened here?"

The tractor lay on its side in the middle of the road, bright green paintwork and yellow tires gaudy against the snow.

Nick got off the back of the ATV. After thirty minutes spent hunched against Harris's back in the bitter cold while the rumble of the engine vibrated up his spine, it took him a second to get his balance. He flexed life back into his fingers as he walked over to Harris.

"Accident?" he said.

There had been plenty of accidents when the first snowstorms hit. Trucks had driven blindly into smaller cars stuck in the snow, and black ice had taken out nearly twenty cars on the motorway, all of them spun into each other like a child's Matchbox car. The motorway was still closed when Nick left Glasgow. The emergency services had managed to get the injured and most of the dead out, but they were too overwhelmed to deal with clearing the road.

Harris glared at Nick like any of that was his fault.

"It's a tractor," he said, each word enunciated slowly and carefully. "They don't just fall over in the middle of the road for no goddamn reason. People don't just leave them there if they do."

He kicked the tractor's cracked windscreen. The crack of impact and the splinter of glass made Nick jump.

"What the hell is wrong with you?" he asked, his voice sharp with irritation.

Harris glared at him, his face bleak with abrupt, unreasonable anger, and he clenched his fists so tightly they looked almost deformed. He hunched his shoulders and took a step toward Nick.

"Shut your hole," he spat. The words fogged thickly off his lips, as though rage really did have heat. Nick took an alarmed step back and then another. "Or I'll shut it for you. Or would you fuckin' like that, you—"

Harris stopped himself, barely, and choked the slur back down. He wiped his heavily mittened hand over his mouth and gave Nick a resentful look. "Sorry," he ground out between his teeth. "I don't know where that came from."

Nick didn't care where it had come from. He was more worried about where it had been going. He'd spent his childhood in one of Glasgow's roughest estates, with a crazy gran and a collection of neurotic twitches. He knew when someone was about to hit him. That sort of black temper didn't stop with one blow.

Anger didn't go away that quickly either.

"Maybe we should go back," Nick said.

Harris's mouth spasmed around what he wanted to say. He smiled tight-lipped as he got control of himself.

"I'd just have to go back out later," he said. "End up spending the night in some dead old farmer's barn. No, we get this done today. The cops can come and get that bloody asshole too. Put him in a jail cell to sleep it off, instead of our hospital."

He stalked along the tractor as he spoke. His feet sank into the snow with every step and made him stagger, but he didn't slow down. It was so wedged into the space that Harris had to climb onto the wall to get to the other side.

"Some bastard wedged it in here," he said. There was a clang as he presumably kicked the underside of it. "They had to have pushed it all the way down here with another tractor. What the—"

He kicked it again. Nick looked back at the ATV, and for a second, he actually considered taking it and leaving Harris there. It was stupid. You couldn't abandon someone in the snow because of one frustrated outburst.

It just hadn't felt like frustration. After a second, Nick shrugged and looked around, one hand lifted to shield his eyes against the sunlight that bounced off the snow. At the top of the field, near a worn old marker that jutted up out of the hedge like an admonishing finger, a group of men in heavy waxed jackets and wellies dug in the snow. The black holes looked like pockmarks against the white.

"What are those idiots doing up there?" Harris growled. He stood on the wall and glared over the top in the same direction as Nick.

"Dead sheep?" Nick suggested. He was a city boy. As far as he could remember, he hadn't been out of Glasgow until he was twelve and his foster family had taken him down to the Lake District. Dead sheep were what most of the farmers mourned at the medical center. But they seemed to have dug down too deep for that, through the crust of snow and into the frozen-hard earth beneath. A row of tires burned sluggishly around the hedgerows like makeshift ovens, the heat positioned to defrost the stony ground.

He waved his arms over his head and tried to attract their attention.

"Hey," he yelled. "Hello up there. Could you give us a hand?"

A few of the workers glanced down toward them. None of them set their labor aside to come and see what they wanted. The most attention they got was from a dog that barked and barked until one of the men cuffed it to silence.

"Fuckers," Harris grouched. He scowled and clenched his fists as he watched the men work. "I should go up there. Make them pay attention."

"What good would it do?" Nick deflected. "They couldn't shift it either, could they?"

Harris grunted and jumped down the other side.

Nick crouched down next to the broken windshield. He pulled the sleeve of his coat down over his hand and pushed the remaining glass out of the way so he could peer inside. The keys were still in the ignition. Nick reached in gingerly and pulled them out. The keyring, a carabiner strung with other keys and a sparkly pink fob that said "Dad's Keys," rattled as he lifted them out.

The smack of flesh on glass nearly made him drop them back into the cab. He caught them by the carabiner, the metal cold enough to sting his fingers, and looked up to see Harris glaring in through the frosted glass.

"What the hell are you doing?"

Nick leaned back out of the cab and shoved himself to his feet. He held up the keys. A plastic tag dangled along with everything else.

"Robbie Dewey." He read it off and glanced at Harris. "You know him?"

Harris wrinkled his eyebrows together. "I think so. He's got a farm up the hill." He dropped back out of sight on the other side of the tractor, and his voice trailed up and over it as he scrunched his way back to the wall. "Nice enough old boy. Helped out with evacuating some of the crofts and housebound up this way. Always had a flask of home brew with him."

By the time Harris, sweating and red-faced, climbed back down off the wall, the stink of anger had left him. He pulled his hat off and wiped his face on the wool. Dense brown-blond curls stuck up around his forehead and curled down around his ears, where they blended into his beard.

"Sorry," he repeated. That time it sounded like he meant it. "I just want to go home, Blake."

Nick shoved the keys into his pocket in a burst of misplaced social conscience. Even if some thief made it all the way out there, if they righted the tractor and backed it down the narrow road they deserved it. Still, he couldn't bring himself to drop the keys back in the cab. It felt careless.

"Last I heard, this is the last evac," he said. "That's our job done."

"Four days ago." Harris pinched his lips together in a thin line. "They were meant to run the evac four days ago."

Everyone knew that. No one had said it aloud until then.

"You know what happened in Aberdeen," Nick said. "They're going to be careful."

It had crackled across the emergency frequencies. Three overloaded medevac choppers packed with the critically ill had been caught in a snap electrical storm on the way down to Glasgow. They had time to radio for help, off-course and over the sea, and then they were gone.

Three pilots, four critical-care paramedics, one teenager, five children, and two preemies lost.

Nick had seen some bad traumas come through his morgue. He was glad he didn't have to do that one.

"I know what Nelson told me," Harris said. "That they're one more storm short of saying there's no way to get us out of here until the weather settles."

The thought made Nick shiver. He wanted to go home, to sleep in a bed that didn't have a £90 Ikea mattress on it, wear clean clothes, and have something to eat other than a communal pot of mixed soup. But there was no one waiting for him—no parents or siblings, no husband or kids. Not even any friends close enough to lose sleep over.

"You'll get home, Harris," he said. "Your kids will be okay."

Harris looked down and kicked the ground to chip a hole in the hard-crusted snow. "Will I? Why are we even out here, Blake? Why are we freezing our asses off for these people?" He jerked his gloved thumb at the men still busily putting potholes in an empty field. "Maybe the preachers were right. Maybe this is God's judgment and everyone here got what was coming to them."

The anger bubbled back up as he spat the last words out. Nick felt that itch of wariness under his skin again, the urge to not make eye contact and get out of the way. Jepson was right. Harris was more than off.

Nothing he could do about it, though. There was no Human Resources to report to out here. Jepson was the closest, and she'd already decided Harris was worth the risk.

"Talking about it isn't going to get it done any quicker." Nick chose to distract instead of debate. "What do we do? Go cross country?"

Harris grunted. "You want to lift the ATV over the wall, stringbean?" he asked. He jerked his thumb over his shoulder at the tractor. "It's in front of the gate. We'd have to haul it over, drive three fields down to the next gate, and just hope we don't hit a gully or a rock or something."

"I thought it was all-terrain," Nick said.

"Not all-weather." Harris walked back to the ATV. "We hit one of your dead sheep under all that snow, we'll flip, and who heals the healers, Blake? I'm not dying out here for some inbred Highland hick."

With a groan, he climbed into the black pleather seat and pulled one glove off with his teeth. His fingers looked a bit too red and swollen around the joints. It was either the cold, or he'd punched the tractor instead of kicking it. Harris didn't seem to notice as he reached into his jacket and pulled out a silver hip flask. He took a swig and then proffered it in Nick's direction.

"Want a hit?" he asked. When Nick didn't reach for it, he snorted. "Who's going to know? You think we're going to get stopped and breathalyzed?"

Nick shrugged to himself and reached for it. He was cold and edgy, and what the bottle of whiskey didn't know wouldn't hurt it. The flask was halfway to his lips when the smell hit him, and he gagged. His eyes watered from the sting of ethanol.

"Bloody hell," he said. "This smells worse than Buckfast."

"Just take a drink," Harris said. He wrestled his glove back on over his swollen fingers. "Dewey isn't the only one who makes home brew around here. Keeps the blood pumping."

Not for long. Nick had opened up corpses whose guts smelled like that gin. He faked a swig with pursed lips and a quick tip of his hand.

"It clears the sinuses, anyhow."

Nick passed the flask back and scrambled onto the back of the ATV. The engine vibrated up through his tailbone as Harris kickstarted it and turned it around. At least, Nick supposed, he had something to worry about other than his old superstitious paranoia.

He freed one hand from his death grip on Harris's coat and rubbed it over his lips.

"Is there even anyone left in Girvan?" he asked. "I thought they'd have gone down to Ayr by now."

Harris looked back over his shoulder, just a glimpse of bloodshot brown eye and breath like a still.

"Oh, no. Lots of people stayed. They say it's not that bad when you get used to it."

The people in the field finally stopped work and turned to watch them go. Nick felt the chilly itch of their regard on the back of his neck as they drove away.

Chapter Five

PEOPLE MIGHT have stayed, but more had left. Houses along the road through town had plywood boards fitted to the windows to protect them from thieves or frost or both. Metal shutters were drawn down over most of the shops, and the few that didn't have them had smashed windows and looted counters.

A charred car sat in the ambulance bay of the Community Hospital parking lot. It had been burned down to the struts and listed sadly in a hard puddle of melted rubber and pocked tarmac. Three black birds perched on what was left of the roof and squabbled over a bloody, dead something.

As the ATV growled in off the turn, the birds took off. One pinched a corner of its dead thing in its beak and tried to make off with it. The other two refused to give up their claim. The bloody thing stretched out long and flat between them as they flapped and fussed.

Long lines of ink showed through, stark against pale skin.

Nick choked back a belch of bile and dug his fingers into Harris's shoulder. "Is that…?" The question dried up on his tongue. How did you ask someone if a bird's dinner was actually part of someone's leg. "Do you see that?" he asked instead.

"What?" Harris glanced over uninterestedly. "The car? There was a lightning storm yesterday. They're lucky if that's the only thing that burned."

"No." Nick pulled at Harris's shoulder again. "The birds. Do you see what they've got?"

"Just some dead thing." Harris pulled into a spot. Like Nick, like Jepson and her coaster, there were some courtesies that hung on even when it made no sense. "What? I wouldn't have thought you were squeamish."

"That's skin," Nick said. "I think—"

One of the birds won the squabble and took off, the ragged strip of skin tangled around its legs.

"What?" Harris demanded irritably.

Nick bit the inside of his cheek hard enough to taste blood. It wasn't the best coping mechanism, but it usually worked. There was a possibility that was the skin someone had flayed off Gregor's leg. Nick had surreptitiously studied the inked lines for long enough while Gregor pretended to sleep. But how likely was that morbid coincidence?

Even if it had been, despite the misfires his brain was making the last few days, there was no proof. The bird was gone. The skin was gone.

"Nothing," he said. "Just… I thought it was something else."

Harris wasn't interested enough to ask what. He fumbled for his flask as he stared bleakly at the glass doors where the instructions for the evac triage and *Automatic Doors Broken—Just Push* were still taped up.

"I hate this place," he said grimly. "All those kids we sent home. All those grannies. We didn't know if they were good or bad. How the hell did we have the right to decide?"

Nick made himself stop looking for birds. "Three's always unlucky," his gran's low, strong voice stated confidently in his memory "Nowt good comes in threes. Remember that." He got out of the saddle. His ears were numb, and his fingers were so cold that the seams of the gloves felt like wire.

"It was bad enough deciding who got to live," he said. "Don't ask me to decide who *deserves* to live."

"They should have sent priests," Harris said. "At least they'd have believed the people that died went somewhere better."

He held the flask out to Nick. This time Nick just shook his head and pushed it back. His lips still itched from the last pretend swig—a stinging prickle, as though the main ingredient was cinnamon. Harris had a stronger constitution than he did.

A short woman in an oversized fisherman's sweater and boots pushed the doors open and leaned out.

"What do you want?" she demanded. "Hospital's closed. If you're sick, keep driving."

She glared at them for a second and then ducked back inside to slam the doors. Through the iced-over glass, Nick could see what looked like a chain threading across the door.

"And I thought the locals couldn't get any friendlier," he muttered.

He walked over and shoved at the doors before the woman could get the padlock on. The doors scraped open enough for him to see a slice of the lobby. It was full of cots and bodies. The stink of BO and grease escaped through the gap and made Nick wrinkle his nose.

"I told you," the woman snarled at him. "We can't help you. Fuck off."

The woman caught her balance and threw her weight back against the door. For all the size of her, she was stronger than Nick. He barely managed to get his foot in the gap to wedge the doors open.

"We don't want anything," Nick snapped out. He hurried the words out before she could interrupt. "We're not sick. We're just looking for the police. Someone was attacked."

"Is he dead?" the woman asked. She pressed her face against the gap. Her breath smelled like Harris's flask. A heavyset man stood up, blankets wrapped around him tightly, and walked between the cots to back her up.

"No."

"Well, don't bring him here. We don't want him."

She slammed the doors against his foot. Even through the heavy leather of his boot, it hurt. Nick cursed, resisted the urge to yank his aching foot back, and glanced over his shoulder at Harris.

"Give me a hand," he said.

Harris grunted and came over to add his weight to the door. Between the two of them, they managed to wrestle the door back open. The woman stumbled backward and tripped over her oversized boots. She landed on the ground with the distinct crack of bone on tile and writhed in pain.

Harris cursed and started toward her. He got a single foot into the lobby when the woman's companion shrugged a fold of blanket away and raised a shotgun. It was an old farmer's gun with rust on the barrel and cracks in the stock, but it was still a gun. Nick went as still as he could, one hand carefully extended to Harris.

"Get that out of my face," Harris snapped. "I just want to help. We're doctors."

"We don't want to take anything," Nick said. "All we came for was to talk to one of the police officers stationed here."

A man in a priest's collar, the white insert frayed and stained, limped in from another room. He wove through the cots—the huddled bodies under the blankets didn't shift—and went down clumsily on one knee next to her. He patted her shoulder and helped her sit up.

"What happened here?" he asked.

"They tried to shove their way in," the man said. His shotgun didn't waver, but his voice sounded a bit unsure. "They want to get help for some friend who got hurt."

Nick cleared his throat. "Actually, we just want to tell someone what happened," he said. "Our friend—"

Harris snorted.

"—doesn't need medical help. Father...?"

"Oh, ah, no need for that," the man said. He tugged at his collar with grubby fingers, adding a fresh stain. "Lewis will do, and I'm sorry, but you have to leave.

It's not charitable, but we've had some problems with people coming through—going up and coming down. Desperate people."

"Fine. After we talk to—"

Nick kicked Harris when he started to argue. He nodded to Lewis. "Okay, we'll leave now," he said. "We didn't mean to cause any problems. We just need to talk to an officer."

Lewis stared at them for a second. Somewhere in the hospital, a child started to cry. Then he nodded. "Wait outside," he said. "I'll get someone to come out to you. I'm sorry. Just, people are scared and anxious."

Nick glanced at the shotgun still pointed at him. "So are we," he said.

"Angry," the man with the gun said. He freed one hand and used it to pull his blankets tighter around him. "People are angry."

"So are we," Harris repeated in an aggrieved growl.

Nick nudged him again, and they backed away from the doors. Once they swung shut, the man dropped the gun and stepped forward to padlock them shut. Then he turned and helped Lewis get their friend back on her feet.

"What the hell," Nick muttered. He bent over and braced his hands on his knees. For once the cold felt good. It cooled the fear sweat on his skin, and the ache of it in his lungs made it easier to slow down his breathing. After a second he glanced up at the glass doors and the shadows of people moving around inside. "What the hell's going on?"

"They're taking care of their own," Harris said. "Maybe we'd have been better off if we'd done the same."

Nick shook his head and straightened up. He shoved his hands into the pockets of his coat and bounced on the balls of his feet. Clouds were thickening overhead like white cataracts over the blue sky.

Footsteps crunched on snow, loud in the awkward silence, and a second later a stocky kid in an oversized jacket ran around the corner of the building. He bolted over to them and stopped in a clumsy stagger of limbs a few feet from the ATV. Under the orange soft-shell jacket, his chest rose and fell as he panted.

"I don't... are you doctors?" he asked. A badly scarred cleft palate repair made him struggle to keep his words sharp. He lifted one hand self-consciously to cover his mouth. "I don't wanna take my medicine anymore. I don't like it. I feel... I don't feel right."

Nick glanced at Harris hopefully. After all, Harris was a dad with two small children, whereas Nick had been unable to master children even when he was one. Harris shook his head quickly, a sick weariness in his booze-glazed eyes, and turned his back to fiddle with the ATV.

"Sometimes you have to take medicine that makes you feel bad before it can make you feel better," Nick said. "What medicine is it?"

The kid screwed up his face unhappily, his lip wrinkled to show the gaps in his teeth. "It's a drink. I gotta drink it."

Nick frowned. "Do you know what the medicine is for?"

"To make me better."

Before Nick could press further, a man in a slick black winter jacket stamped around the side of the building. Bands on the man's sleeves announced he was police.

"Jimmy." He slapped the loop of a leash against his leg with a single curt sound. "Get back inside now."

The boy took a deep breath and held it. His hands were clenched at his sides, and Nick could see the defiance in him.

"Are you okay?" Nick asked quietly. "Do you need help?"

The scarred lip twitched, and the boy deflated as he sighed his lungful of air out. His gaze dropped to his scarred hiking boots and stayed there.

"My dad loves me," he said. It sounded resigned. "That's why I gotta get better."

He dragged his mittened hand over his eyes and turned to go. His dad was close enough now to grab his wrist and yank Jimmy roughly away from Nick and Harris. He dragged him across the parking lot to the locked doors.

The people inside had already unlocked the door by the time he got there, and Lewis pulled the lad inside. He locked the door behind him.

Nick frowned and shifted his weight.

"Leave it," Harris snapped. Apparently he was paying more attention than he let on. "He's the kid's da, man. He knows what's best for him."

It didn't feel like he did, but the moment to protest had passed. Jimmy was gone, and his da had started the short stomp back to them across the trampled snow. His trousers and sleeves were crusted with icy slush, and frost glued his scarf to the stubble on his face. A pair of polarized sunglasses hid his eyes.

"Doctor Harris," the cop said. He wiped his nose on the back of his gloved hand and pulled the scarf down to expose his mouth. "And Doctor Blake. Come to collect the dead?"

There was something familiar about the cop's face, the distinct saddle fracture of his nose and the scar that made a neat, horizontal dash on his lower lip. The name hadn't stuck with Nick, if he'd even been told it, but he was the one who spat on Copeland. Nick only remembered because the child with him—a little boy with a gap-toothed grimace and a diagnosis of childhood leukemia—would be dead soon.

He was always good with the dead. It was the living who slipped his mind.

That boy had been younger than the kid who'd spoken to them, shorter and wasted with treatment and illness—two sick children and trapped out here. Nick felt a flash of pity and supposed his curtness with his son was understandable.

"This is PCSO Terry Muir," Harris said. He reached out and grabbed the snow-scabbed mitten. "Most of the other officers we were working with have gone back to Ayr, but Terry here is a local."

There was a nasty edge to Terry's smile. "I would have left as well, but I didn't make the cut." Nick supposed he couldn't blame him. "So Dan—our pharmacist—said you needed something? Someone had gotten hurt. Although that seems more up your street than mine."

Harris passed the buck with a brusque nod at Nick.

"Doctor Blake," Terry said. "Everything all right?"

For a second Nick thought about being honest. He could just blurt out the confused, delirium-tinged events—a strange naked man injured in the snow, the things in the dark he saw out of the corner of his eye, the birds, the fear. Then he could tap out as obviously crazy and let everyone else deal with it.

But he knew better. Once someone thought you'd missed one signpost to reality, they didn't credit anything else you had to say. Besides, his gran was crazy. Nick wasn't. If he gave that up, he wouldn't have anything to hang on to.

"Not exactly," he said. "We're fine, but two nights ago, an injured man staggered into the trailer park—"

"Looking for help in the wrong place." Terry nodded. "I can see how you'd hate that."

Nick took a second to let that wash over him. He still couldn't blame Terry for being bitter, but he was a bit closer to it.

"Someone had attacked him," he said. The clipped edge to his voice made Terry smirk sourly over the folds of his scarf. "He'd suffered multiple sharp-force traumas to the stomach and leg, in addition to—"

"Are you a police officer now?" Terry asked.

"I've worked with the police in Glasgow," Nick said. He might understand Terry's bitterness—God knows he'd have shared it if it were him—but they didn't have time for it. It was too cold to air grievances for long, and the clouds overhead had gotten thicker. More snow wouldn't be far behind. "I'm a pathologist. I can identify injuries."

Terry shrugged. "Nobody is missing from Girvan. Maybe it was a stranger, fell into barbed wire after a sheep for dinner and ripped himself to hell. It happens."

An incredulous *when* pressed against Nick's teeth. He managed to hold it back.

"He was naked."

Terry snorted out a laugh. "After a sheep for sommat else."

"He said he was attacked by—"

"So would you if you got ripped up chasing a sheep wi' your willy out."

Nick's anger felt like pressure behind his face, and he could hear the metallic scrape in his ears that always came with his temper. His gran had always said he had a wolf's ears for a fight, but he diagnosed himself with a touch of synesthesia.

"Whatever your problem with me," he spat out through tight lips. "A man has been mutilated by someone in this area. His brother is missing. Do you really think that's funny?"

Terry stepped forward and got into Nick's face. "I think a lot of things are funny now," Terry said. He didn't sound like he did. The grim edge to his voice made him into a liar. "You'd be surprised."

His breath stank like fish and ammonia. Nick diagnosed kidney failure even as he drew back from the smell. Harris picked his moment to finally intervene.

"Someone made a real mess of this bloke, Terry," he said. "Tried to take him apart. It's not just us out there. We've got the last batch of evacuees. Old people. Sick people. Children."

He was trying to help, but it sounded like an invitation for a serial killer. Come and get us. Easy prey! Nick took a deep breath of sour air.

"I'm sorry we couldn't evacuate your son—"

"Don't be," Terry interrupted him. "Best thing for him. Like you said, there was nothing your doctors can do for him. Look. I'll get a search party together and radio it in to Ayr so they can send some people out. Don't know what good it'll do. There's lots of places to get lost round here, even more to hide a body."

He stepped back. Nick let out a breath he hadn't consciously been holding as his personal space was released. Terry clapped his mittened hands together to shed the snow and waited. For them to leave.

Nick glanced at Harris, who shrugged uncomfortably. Whatever sense of camaraderie he'd had with Terry seemed to have withered under the weight of the weirdness of the day.

"That man in there nearly shot us," Nick said.

Terry gave him that close-lipped smile again. "Good. If one of these mystery men with knives make it into town, we'll be safe." He glanced up at the sky. "You should go. There's a storm coming, and you city folk aren't as hardy as us locals."

He waited to make sure they did go.

Harris grumbled under his breath all the way back to the road at being called soft—a sour, slightly bigoted mutter of consciousness. Every now and again it poked into Nick's attention, but mostly he ignored it.

He glanced back as they stopped—muscle memory too ingrained to care it was pointless—at the edge of the parking lot. He saw Jimmy in one of the windows, the orange of his jacket starkly bright, just as the kid raised his arm.

There were three grubby stripes against his jacket. Nick had seen it as Terry dragged his son back into the hospital. Like someone had ripped a black tag of tape off the sleeve and left the adhesive to collect dust. The sort of tag he'd seen Copeland slap on when she denied Terry Muir's son a space on the evacuation.

His younger son. Jimmy was a foot taller than the wasted little boy Nick had seen shoved out of the hall with his dad, and he had a thick head of hair under his cap. The first boy had the same missing teeth but no cleft palate. Maybe it was a borrowed jacket, Nick told himself, or shared.

Sheet lightning flickered across the sky. The strobe of light caught in the glass, and Nick took the excuse to look away. He hung on to the ATV and rhymed his mantra off silently to himself. For once it didn't help. It wasn't the familiar paranoia of his childhood, that hollow fear of navigating a world he *believed* was real but could never really see.

It was the jacket of a boy who should have been dying and a patch of pale skin caught on a hedgerow as they passed. Nick didn't ask Harris to stop.

He didn't know what he was more afraid of, that his old affirmation of sanity was wrong and he was just as mad as his gran, or that it wasn't.

Chapter Six

THE WEAKNESS that dogged Gregor was offensive. It dug into the muscles of his thigh and hung there like a tick, fat and heavy with blood. Something as simple as sitting up made his stomach ache and spasm as though it were his first hunt.

He perched on the side of the narrow cot, the metal edge sharp against his ass, and waited for it to pass. It didn't. Fine. He had hurt before. Every line of ink on his body had been earned in a fight. In Durham, the prophets' made-monster had nearly killed him. He'd hung like Odin between life and death, although his only revelation had been the unwelcome realization that he owed his survival to his brother.

Pain was like the cold—something to accept and ignore, even if it did last longer than it used to.

Gregor gritted his teeth and pushed himself up off the bed. His thigh pulsed with hot pressure, as though it was going to explode, and the leg gave loosely under him if he put his weight on it for too long. He ground a curse out between his teeth, dragged himself a pathetic two steps forward, and grabbed the back of Nick's chair for support.

It had been hours since Nick left with a promise to come back. If the wet nurse from his infancy had abandoned him for that long, Gregor thought dourly, his da would have had her sent over Hadrian's Wall in pieces.

Since he had no such authority over Nick's comings and goings, Gregor had to settle for an ill-tempered snarl. It wasn't that he needed Nick, but there was an... easiness... to him that made him pleasant to be around. More so than any of the other humans, who moved too fast and tried to accomplish too much in every single movement.

Not real companionship, not pack, but better than anything else available—not to mention in possession of two intact legs that could have fetched Gregor what he needed.

The bad mood peaked and then collapsed under its own weight. Gregor was left snorting at himself in its wake. Was he such a Pup Prince now that he couldn't wipe his own ass? Did he need some lad to hold his cock while he pissed?

Gregor lurched another few steps forward. It was the baseboard of a bed he grabbed that time, his weight braced against the rod of metal to supplement his damaged muscle. It took two sweaty, resentful breaks for him to reach the flimsy cubicle that carved out a small storage space at the back of the room. The door was locked, although he couldn't see the point of it. The latch was a simple tab of plastic. A human child could have snapped it off.

He limped into the narrow space, grabbed a basin and a scalpel, and then lowered himself onto the low stool positioned in front of the desk. The basin went on the floor, behind his foot, and then he peeled the tape and plastic off his thigh.

It looked worse than it had earlier, with thick scabs scaled over the muscle and white fish-skin-thin tissue peeling back from the stretched flap of wound. An illusion, his slowed healing was now a flipbook of the process. Each stage lingered on, scarred into his skin as though he were a Dog.

Gregor ran his finger along the edge of the wound to feel the puckering tissue. No one would mistake him for his brother again. There was a time when he would have appreciated that, but now Jack would be the Numitor, and Gregor his scarred, "not quite any true thing" brother. It wasn't the distinction from his twin that he'd wanted.

"A new Job," he muttered as he flashed to the resentful, bitter prophet who'd come down over the Wall and made monsters to try and kill both the Numitor's sons. Their maybe uncle, or so the stories said. Although there was one difference—the old rumors said Job had once loved his brother, their father, back when the Old Man was young, before he became the head of all the British wolves.

Gregor took a deep breath that he felt in his severed gut muscles and decided that would not be his fate. He *would* get his wolf back. The prophets had stolen it. They had to know a way to return it to him.

It was possible. A dour, joyless part of his brain reminded him that Job had found a wolf again under the winter moon, a stolen skin rotting into him as he stole its shape.

Enough. Gregor dug the scalpel into his leg. The sharp pain was an almost-welcome distraction as he slid the tip of it under the black line of a stitch. The material edge frayed and then snapped. Gregor caught the knot of it between his fingernails and pulled it out of his leg.

He'd heal faster with nothing human-made in him, and until he got the wolf back, he didn't relish the thought of slicing his leg open later to try and find them.

Blood dripped down his leg and into the basin as he worked. By the time he finished, the plastic bowl was half-full of blood and the wounds he'd started with had already clotted over with thin, white skin.

Gregor wiped the knife clean on his forearm and set it aside. His throat was still stitched. He could swear he felt the itch of the thread when he swallowed, but he couldn't see it to work. If he pulled the stitches out, he might take his throat with it. The Wild could let him die from the irony of it. Sweat ran down his chest and stung in the tender scar on his stomach. He leaned to the side, elbow braced on the desk, and stared at the injury.

If he healed at this rate, if it sped up as he hoped it would when his body was clean of anything but the Wild, questions would be asked. They always had questions, humans. That's how they got the world that they had built over until the Wild came back. They'd asked questions, and the gods had been stupid enough to answer.

Not that Gregor knew that personally. The last few days in Nick's enforced company had probably doubled his lifetime interaction with humans. But that was what Da had always said, and he had dealt with them for long enough.

Gregor pushed himself to his feet. His leg still hurt, but it seemed to hold steadier under him. He half hopped and half limped back to the rows of shelves and hunted impatiently through the boxes of pills and syringes until he found a roll of gauze and some tape.

He tore the paper off the gauze with his teeth, shook the length of it out, and started to wind it around his leg. The white fabric stained as blood wicked through the thin tissues, so he kept going until a thick pad of it covered his wounds.

The final result was a lumpy, twisted loop of fabric that threatened to slip down his leg with every step, but it would do. Gregor shoved the bloody plastic and bits of paper out of sight and started the miserable lurch back to his bed.

He was at his second handhold when he heard the scuff of steps on heavy tarp. What pride he had left made him shove himself up straight. The growl in his throat twisted at his mouth as he lifted his chin.

Nick ducked through the hanging doors, one arm lifted to keep the canvas away from the tray of food he carried. He stumbled slightly when he saw Gregor, surprise and dismay on his narrow face. For a second he fumbled visibly between the need to help Gregor and the decision of what to do with the tray.

"What the hell are you doing?" Nick ducked down and balanced the tray across the seat of one of the ever-present plastic chairs. "Do you not like having a leg?"

Gregor let his spine relax and grabbed the IV stand he'd been using for balance. It wobbled under his weight, but it was better than nothing.

"So is your bed manners the reason you mostly work with the dead?" Gregor asked.

"Bedside manner," Nick corrected him. He jogged over and ducked under Gregor's arm, the sharp blade of his shoulder an uncomfortable crutch. "Bed manners makes it sound like I wipe my dick on the pillow after sex."

It was not that Gregor was fond of being corrected, but he couldn't stop the snort of laughter at the flustered doctor's profane mutter. The wash of lust that filled the air. Hormones sharp and spicy in Gregor's nose, helped too. Nick tightened his arm around Gregor's waist and hooked his fingers over Gregor's hipbone.

"Couldn't someone find you a pair of boxers?" Nick grumbled under his breath. "Or a shirt."

Gregor curled his lip. "I don't need charity from strangers."

"You need clothes."

"I said you couldn't touch without permission," Gregor said. "You can look freely."

He saw the twitch of Nick's head out of the corner of his eye as he took an instinctive glance down. At least the prophets hadn't had a chance to take that from Gregor. Although if he'd been offered the choice, Gregor might have traded his manhood for his wolf.

"I've seen plenty of naked men," Nick said. He ignored Gregor's curious "how many" and went on. "I'm not going to pine away if you cover yourself up."

Gregor grunted his doubt about that but didn't have the energy to argue. He pushed himself off Nick's shoulder as they reached the bed. He could accept a hand across the floor, but not being tucked into bed.

"I thought you'd changed your mind about coming back," he said as he half climbed and half fell onto the mattress. The fresh blood was salt and copper to his nose and wet against his swaddled leg, but Nick didn't seem to notice for all he hovered. "Or does *not long* mean something different when you're a doctor?"

"I thought you didn't care," Nick said dryly. He tugged a sheet from under Gregor's hip and pulled it over him.

"I don't." Gregor leaned back on the thin pillows. "I just don't like liars. Where were you?"

Nick leaned over him, one arm braced against the bed, and narrowed his eyes. "I don't owe you any explanations. I don't owe you anything."

The bubble of anger that burst under Gregor's tongue caught him by surprise. What did he care what the human thought he was owed? If someone who wasn't pack stiffed you on a debt, you just took your pound of flesh. But it galled.

"You saved my life," Gregor said. "It's your fault I'm here, alive. I won't forgive that debt easily. Where were you?"

Nick went to say something and then thought better of it. He pressed his lips together and Gregor frowned as he watched the motion. Nick's mouth tended to look severe, until he cracked that ridiculous, full-face grin, but right then his lips were red and tender-looking—chapped, or chewed.

"Did you fuck someone?" Gregor asked. He let the tinge of anger roll into the question before he justified why. His brother was lost, and for another day at least, he was vulnerable. So it was reasonable to be annoyed that his only ally, his beaky watchdog, had wandered off to fuck some small-pricked human who probably smelled of old sweat and shame. "Who?"

It was hard to read those black eyes. But Gregor caught the flash of temper as Nick drew back from him.

"That's definitely not part of a doctor-patient conversation," he said stiffly.

Gregor snapped his hand up and twisted it into Nick's hair. It was wiry against his fingers. He pulled Nick back down, almost close enough to touch. That ache of inappropriate want clenched in his balls, and the twitch of muscle was raw under the haphazard bandaging job on his thigh.

"We both know I could have you if I wanted," he said.

It was Nick who closed the handspan of distance between them, until his beaky nose touched Gregor's. "Have me?" His breath was sharp against Gregor's mouth, a hint of something sour on his tongue. "You can't even stand up, Gregor, never mind stand to attention. Now let go."

Gregor didn't want to. He had stretched for a reason and realized it was the defiance. If Nick was to play thrall until Gregor was hale again, he needed to do as he was told and speak when spoken to.

"Answer my question," he said. "You kissed someone. Who was it? Unless you *want* me to try and prove you wrong about what I'm capable of?"

The swabs of color on Nick's sharp-carved cheek-bones betrayed a certain interest in that promise. He closed his eyes and visibly squashed the temptation. The muscle along his jaw looked tight under his skin.

"No one. But if Harris offers you a drink, say you're teetotal." He licked his lower lip. Or licked Gregor's lip. They were close enough it was the same thing. "I think they make it with drain cleaner. Now. Let go."

Gregor still didn't want to. That was the only reason he did it.

Nick didn't move for a second. The lean sprawl of his body was close enough that Gregor could feel the outside chill that hadn't seeped out of Nick's skin yet, and then he pulled back. He straightened up and shoved a hand through his hair in a haphazard attempt to flatten it down. It didn't work.

"That was a bad idea." He pinched the bridge of his nose between his fingers and muttered. "Bad enough I'm going mad. Now I'm going stupid."

He stalked off to fetch the tray of food. It was hardly a feast—bread-and-butter sandwiches, a bowl of grease-thinned soup, and a mug of tepid tea—but Gregor couldn't afford to turn his nose up at it. He wouldn't be catching rabbits for a while.

Or ever again if the prophets' work couldn't be undone. That bitter reminder felt like a punch to his already battered spirit, but Gregor chose not to accept it yet. He ate efficiently but with no real enjoyment. Most of his attention was on Nick, who had chosen to pace along the narrow corridor between beds instead of sitting back down on the chair.

"The local police are going to organize a search for your brother," Nick said. He paused by a bed to pick up the clipboard that hung over the end of it and flipped through the sheets. Nick *tch*ed his tongue at something he read and pulled a pen out of his pocket to cross out and correct it. He paused his scribble and looked over his shoulder. "Or... and I'm sorry, but... it might be a search for his body."

Gregor washed down a mouthful of butter with a gulp of cold soup and wiped his mouth on his arm.

No. The prophets wanted them alive. The admission soured what little appetite Gregor had for his meal, but if they just wanted to kill him, he'd be a corpse. No one hobbled a beast for the slaughter. It was a waste of the edge on the knife.

Even though he didn't want Nick to waste his sympathy on Jack, Gregor didn't see how to explain that in a way that wouldn't convince his hosts he needed more guards. So he settled for a different truth.

"He's my brother. My twin. I'd know if Jack were dead."

He imagined that it would feel like being whole, after years of his spirit being tapped by a tick that looked just like him.

Nick didn't look convinced, but he didn't choose to argue either. He went back to his restless patrol of the rows. Gregor finished the tea and sopped up the last of the soup with the crusts of stale bread from his sandwich.

His da would have clipped him round the ear for that. The table had been the one place he and Jack weren't allowed to fight. Manners were important, the Old Man had always said. Turn into a wolf in the middle of a restaurant, and as long as you eat the server wi' the right fork, no one will question it.

Gregor had never cared to fit in with the human world, but he supposed—as he caught Nick glance at him—that he must look like some starveling urchin shoveling grease-wet bread into his mouth. He grimaced as he wiped his hands on the sheets instead of licking them clean.

"I was hungry," he said. It wasn't an apology. It was more explanation than he'd have given anyone else. No wonder humans cared so much for courtesy. To the weak, what people thought of them must matter. "I'm tired. Stay."

Nick glanced at his watch and frowned. "I have work to do," he said. "You aren't even my patient."

"Stay," Gregor repeated. "Stay or I'll die for spite."

The laugh caught Nick by surprise. He caught it after a second, bitten back behind his teeth. Nice enough teeth for someone not a wolf. Not sharp but white and clean. Gregor imagined the dull pressure of them against his forearm—white teeth, pain, and a damp tongue against his skin while he fucked Nick.

If he'd been hoping his cock would shy away from the thought of taking his odd interest that far, he was disappointed. It did prove Nick wrong, though. At least some parts of him could stand. Gregor shifted and reached to press his hand against his cock, but the scrape of rough cotton against skin made him ache harder.

Nick glanced down, stared for a second, and then blushed like a virgin as he jerked his gaze back up to Gregor's face.

"How about I check in on you later," he said as he sidled over and reached for the empty tray. There were just crumbs and cutlery left on it. "We can call it a compromise."

Gregor could have grabbed his narrow wrist and yanked him down on the bed. He didn't think it would take long to fuck the reluctance out of him. It would be easier to do it that way than try and seduce him with words. Somewhere between Gregor's brain and his tongue, words always turned rough and hard.

He just smiled instead. His teeth were white too, and sharp, and he could tell Nick's mind had gone to the same place Gregor's had. He could smell Nick's lust in the air, like heated spice. It would be better if he begged.

"I'll be thinking of you," he said.

Nick lifted the tray and snorted at him. "Yeah, well, if a skinny ass and a lot of woolly sweaters is what gets you going, who am I to stand in your way."

He turned to leave. The back of his neck, between the rough collar and his unruly hair, was as red as his face. Gregor lazily rubbed his cock through the sheet.

"Why did you think you were going mad?" he asked. He knew better than Nick why it was a bad idea.

The question stopped Nick on the spot. His spine looked very straight, and he didn't look around.

"Because I've been there before," he said. "I know the way."

The words seemed to release him. His shoulders sagged down on a sigh, and he stumbled into motion again. Gregor watched him go and then slid his hand down under the sheet. He wrapped his fingers around his cock and traced the familiar path from the head to the root. Pleasure jolted through him along with the dull ache of his still-healing body.

He tried to imagine Nick naked and willing under him. None of the bodies his mind conjured for him felt right, felt real. They were just composites of other men he'd fucked—the wiry body hair of that skinny wolf who'd come up from Leeds to beg for a place or the constellation of moles that spread over Davy Maguire's left shoulder. He was Jack's friend until Gregor fucked him and ruined that.

When none of them worked, he let the Nick in his fantasy keep his clothes on, wool scratchy and ripe as it pressed against Gregor's stomach. Long fingers wrapped around Gregor's cock, cold and chapped rough, and Nick's mouth pressed up against Gregor's throat as he mouthed worries about hurting him.

No one in his life had ever worried for Gregor instead of about him. He didn't need it, but he wanted it. Sprawled out on the thin mattress that smelled of other people's blood and other people's death, he let the shadow-play image of his watchdog take care of him.

It was all quick hands and impatience. He was sure of that. He'd watched Nick fidget for long enough by his bedside. The chill of the winter was replaced by heat and hunger. Gregor closed his eyes, closed out the white canvas and the shrill wind, and chased the hot spasm of pleasure before the pain could catch up with him.

Maybe if he spent himself, the Wild would take him to a sweeter memory than his recent horrors when he finally got to sleep.

Chapter Seven

COLD SHOWERS had less impact when they were the only thing available. Not to mention that, with no way to fix the frost-shattered plumbing, it was more of a cold whore's bath with a washcloth.

Nick stood in the kitchen and wiped come off his thighs as the possibility for a repeat performance faded and the cold water made his balls try to retreat into his body. He felt oddly ashamed, as though he'd caught himself doing something wrong.

Everything that had happened, and he couldn't keep his mind out of his pants for long enough to keep his hands off himself. Or keep his mind off Gregor's *lack* of pants, more accurately, off that heavy sprawl of bone and tight muscle.

He couldn't remember the last time he'd jerked off. It hadn't been worth making a note of it, before all this started, and afterward? Well, the few times he'd had the urge, it hadn't seemed worth it to dig down through the layers and expose his cock to the cold.

Maybe now, though, he'd be able to keep his mind off lean, freckled jaws and heavy cocks. It had all started with Gregor. If Nick kept his distance, maybe it would stop too.

Goose bumps prickled his thighs under the dusting of sparse dark hair. Nick dragged his jeans back up over his damp skin and buttoned up. He wiped his hands on his sweater, tossed the water down the dry sink, and then just stood for a second.

He wanted to crawl back into bed. It was rumpled, and the oversoft mattress smelled of unwashed junior doctor, but he could still curl up and pull the duvet over his head. Nothing could get you if you kept your hands and feet out of the world, not green eyes and rough confidence, not peat-hags, nor birds that taunted you with skin.

His gran had always told him that wasn't true, though. They could get you anywhere. Nowhere was safe.

"Gran was crazy," Nick muttered. "I hope."

It didn't help, and he gave in. Of course he did. Of course he'd always been going to.

Nick ducked into the bedroom, ignored the bed, and grabbed his lumpily packed rucksack from the floor. He pulled out his spare jeans, the Aran sweater he'd never get the stains out of, and more socks than were entirely reasonable, and dumped them all on the creased, summer-floral duvet.

It had worked its way down to the bottom, halfway through a rip in the lining of the bag. Nick's fingertips brushed the cold, rough links of the chain, and he dragged it out with a sigh of relief. It didn't look like much. Nick supposed it never had—just an iron nail twisted into a knot and strung on a cheap chain gran had salvaged from some Primark sparkly she'd gotten tired of.

He could still feel the pinch of her fingers on his neck as she checked he had it on. "Keep it safe. Keep it close," she'd warned him every time. "It will buy you time, but not much."

Even after he'd stopped believing in her dark stories—of clever beasts and wicked gods, of ogres that built walls overnight and men who bound wolves with fingerbones and blood—or convinced himself he had, he'd done as he was told. He just pretended that a talisman wasn't a talisman as long as he didn't wear it.

Well, he needed a new lie, didn't he? Nick dropped the chain over his head and tucked the pendant down under his sweater. It was cold enough to make him cringe, and the point of it jabbed against his chest, but the weight still felt familiar around his neck.

But the other weight, the oppressive sense of eyes on him, faded. It wasn't gone, but he didn't feel sour breath on the back of his neck anymore.

About the best he could expect he supposed.

His search through the bag had unearthed the hat he thought he'd lost. Nick dragged it down over his ears, tucked the chain under his collar at the back of his neck, and couldn't think of another reason to delay going back out.

It was snowing again, but it was the winter equivalent of a drizzle. Huge white flakes spun down out of the sky, each distinct enough to follow with your eyes instead of being lost in the flurry. Nick still stuck his hands in his pockets as he cut between the trailers.

No more vigil at Gregor's bedside, Nick told himself. He'd done what he could—what he was willing to do—for the man. Whatever promises he'd made were as good as kept. So he'd do his job and stick with the dead from then on.

The snow they'd cleared away the night Nick found Gregor had filled in again. Blood was just visible under the new crust of snow like a stain of pink.

He detoured around it and started up the steps to the morgue. The door was pulled open just as he got to the top, and Copeland rushed out. Nick lurched backward and nearly lost his footing on the steps. He grabbed the railing to steady himself, his heart in his throat, and glared at her.

"What the hell?" he said.

"Sorry," Copeland said. She glanced over her shoulder and pulled a face. "I just… it's so creepy in there. I don't know how you do it."

It wasn't hard. The dead never bothered Nick. There was never anything unnatural or supernatural about corpses. They were just dead, usually for very obvious reasons once you peeled back the surface layer of skin.

"No more than a butcher's," he said.

Copeland shuddered and hugged herself, her jacket noisy as the sleeves folded and the rough fabric rubbed on itself. "Now *you're* creepy." Her hair stuck out in wild curls from under her furry hat. The dangling ear-flaps were bigger than her face, and her lips were flushed and swollen.

He supposed whoever she'd been kissing had snuck out one of the windows in the old locker room. Some self-righteous part of him wanted to lecture her about how that would end badly. It would, of course, but Copeland wasn't his responsibility, and if it all went tits up, Nick wouldn't have to fill out the Human Resources forms.

"Not the first person to say that," he said dryly as he stepped to the side to let her pass.

She started to leave and then stopped, her hands twitchy as she waved them in the air.

"No. Jepson sent me to find you," she said. A big, earnest smile spread over her face. "The search party just checked in. They say they've found the missing man."

Nick stared at her. "They can't have," he protested. "We only told them a few hours ago. How could they have—"

Copeland shrugged and pushed him down the stairs, both hands braced on his shoulders.

"I don't know. They just have," she said jauntily. Nick supposed his face must still have looked skeptical, because she sighed. "Just… it's good. Someone's alive. We saved someone. Two someones. It's a win, Doctor Blake."

It certainly sounded like one, but Nick didn't trust anything that came that easily—not before, and certainly not then.

"Harris and I only got back a couple of hours ago," Nick protested. He tried to check that on his watch, but the glass face was misted over. "And the officer in charge didn't exactly give the impression the search was going to be a priority."

Copeland shrugged helplessly. "I don't know how they did it," she said. "I just know they did. Maybe you should do like Jepson said and come along to talk to them. Then you can ask them any questions."

She put her hands on her hips and cocked her head to the side expectantly. The good humor almost fizzed under her skin as the dour little doctor that Nick had gotten used to was unseated by enthusiasm for the win. It felt like kicking a dog to protest further.

"I guess that makes sense," he said. "I was just... expecting a different outcome."

Copeland's smile faded slightly, and she nodded. "Me too," she said. "I guess that this guy is just as tough as your friend."

Nick grunted and, after a brief glance at the swung-shut door to the morgue, turned to retrace his steps. "He's not my friend."

"Whatever." She had to take two steps to each of Nick's as she half hopped through the snow. Her breath was ragged and white as it hit the cold air. "You're the only one he's nice to."

"I wouldn't call it nice."

"Nelson tried to check in on his leg," Copeland said. "He just... stared at him. Now that was creepy. Come on." She drew ahead of Nick in a stumbling run and kicked up snow with her heels.

Three ATVs were parked in front of the old park office, between the huge concrete planters that held dead rosebushes. PCSO Terry Muir held court from the back of one of them—bluff, hearty, and cold— while his two... deputies, Nick supposed, leaned against the wall. Half the trailer park was gathered in front of him, aid workers and evacuees both. Harris was front and center, the earlier tension forgotten as he nodded and grinned.

Jepson stood at the back, her arms crossed and mouth set in the line Nick remembered from her one visit to the morgue. She caught Nick's eye and lifted a finger to tell him to… he didn't know what.

A pale woman with limp, patchy hair hugged her daughter to her hip and leaned forward to say something. Terry shrugged and waved his hand at the trailers and then slapped his own chest.

"…not where I'd want my boy, and you know how ill he was," he said. "He's a different lad now he's home—Dr. Blake."

Lad, not lads. Nick reached up and rubbed his neck where the cheap metal had irritated it. Maybe he'd misremembered. Hundreds of people had lurched hopelessly through the evacuation center, and dozens had yelled and threatened them. No one could blame them.

"Officer Muir," Nick said. "Copeland tells me that you found Gregor's brother? Already?"

Terry still had his shades on. The slight twitch of his chin betrayed the shift in his attention as he looked at Copeland. If he remembered that he'd spat on her, he didn't show it.

"That's right," he said.

"How did you have time to put together a search party?" Nick asked. "We're not long back ourselves."

Terry pulled a flask out of his jacket and unscrewed the lid. "We knew where to look," he said. "All the crannies and crofts where the flotsam ends up. We found the lad up in the hills in the old Kendall place. It's been empty for years. Have to say, looks like this Gregor told you a pack of lies."

He mugged regret, but there was something tight in his voice just under the smug. After a single pull on the flask, he passed it off to Harris, who took a quick slug and glanced around guiltily at Jepson before he passed it on.

"What lies?" Nick asked.

Terry finally stood up off the ATV. He tugged his jacket down straight. "Well, according to his brother, it was Gregor started the fight. Kicked the shit out of the boy, probably not for the first time, and then ran when the tide turned. I'm afraid I'm going to have to take him into custody."

Nick narrowed his eyes, but it was Jepson's cold voice that clipped through the anxious mutter that eddied through the group.

"He's still our patient," she said. "Until I'm content his condition has stabilized, he's not going anywhere."

Terry turned to look at her. "I'm sorry, ma'am, but I don't think that's up to you. This isn't a hospital, and a lot of these people are my responsibility. Locals. Friends." He paused for a second, and Nick wondered how much of that he believed. "If this Gregor is a threat, I can't in good conscience leave him here."

"He can't even walk, Mr. Muir."

"Officer."

"Apologies, PCSO Muir," Jepson said smoothly. Her face was smooth and blank, professionally unreadable under a bobble hat. "The man might never walk again. So I think we're safe."

Terry paused for a second, and his attention flickered over the people huddled up around him. It was the same look that Nick had seen his gran give clients at her séances, an assessment of just how far the hook was down their throat.

"Maybe we should let them take the creepy bastard," Harris said suddenly. His voice was louder than it should have been. He hammered his finger against his temple. "I said from the get there was something wrong with him, something off."

A man with his arm around a bald woman raised his voice in agreement. The few parents—children had been evacuated first—looked at each other, hugged their children closer, and nodded their muted support for the idea.

Nelson turned up at Jepson's elbow. For the first time, there wasn't a cocky grin on the square-built paramedic's face. Nick was bleakly relieved that he wasn't the only one who could feel the tension. Right then he didn't trust his own judgment.

"We don't even know this man is Gregor's brother," Nick said. "It could be one of the men who attacked him. Maybe we should ask some more questions before jumping to conclusions."

One of the two men with Terry shifted off the wall. He had heavy snow goggles worn low over his eyebrows and a scarf glued to his stubble with frost.

"You callin' us liars?" he mush-mouthed through the wool.

"Len, leave it." Terry didn't look around, but the big man still subsided. He was sweating. Nick noticed it in the second before he had to look back at Terry, and the skin around the man's nose was raw and inflamed. "Tell you what, Doctor Blake, why don't we both stick to what we're good at? My job is to make sure my people make it through this winter alive, one way or another. Yours is to… can't say I'm really sure… count the dead? Stack 'em up?"

He laughed as though it were a joke. Copeland joined in at Nick's side with a giggle and an elbow to his ribs to get him to join in.

"Actually, PCSO Muir, Doctor Blake is right," Jepson said. "We don't want to rush to judgment, and we don't need to. Like you said, this man is injured. He'll need medical treatment, and we can provide it. Where is he now?"

Terry scratched his jaw and glanced around the group again and then back to Jepson. Finally he nodded.

"Fair enough, Doctor," he said.

"Major," Jepson corrected him. It was the first time Nick had ever heard her use her rank.

"Okay. I'll call the lads and get them to detour over this way." Terry unclipped a heavy black radio from his ATV. He glanced around and cracked a grin. "Maybe we can do some catch ups while we wait."

He turned and walked away from them. Then he lifted the radio to his mouth. The crackle of static cut through the still air, but Terry's voice was a deliberately low mutter. While he talked, the two men with him stepped away from the wall. The one without the scarf—thin and wiry, with a ginger beard that attempted to hide the lack of a chin—clapped his hands together.

"How about we get some heat going?" he said.

Chapter Eight

A BONFIRE of driftwood, old tires, and cracked plywood doors flared and spat in the middle of the parking lot. The tarmac scorched and bubbled under the heat, and the snow receded in an uneven melt line as the heat built.

It was too hot in the huddle of people around the flames, but after weeks of bone-deep chill, the sting of scalded cheeks and heat-rashed legs was welcome. Flasks passed from hand to hand. Even the occasional teenager or child was given a nip against the cold, and the odd, nervous blurt of laughter was replaced by a low murmur of light conversation. A gray-haired man with radiation scars all down his throat cracked out a verse of an old reel, forgot the words halfway through, and dissolved into laughter.

"Don't engage with him," Jepson told Nick firmly. They stood just outside the circle of melted snow, in the lee of an abandoned pickup truck with a bed full of old rocks. "Don't get into an argument or give him any excuse to... escalate the situation." She grimaced around the words, as though she didn't like being the one to say them.

"We can't let him take Gregor. Something is... wrong," Nick said. It felt too commonplace a word to describe the current situation, but Nick couldn't think of one better. All the words that fit the weird, tense situation they were in—half ghost story and half slasher film—just stalled in his throat because they made him sound delusional. "The officer, Terry Muir, he's the one that spat on Copeland a few weeks ago. His son didn't make the cut for the evacuation."

Jepson rubbed her gloved hand briskly over her face. "I know that," she said shortly. "It's my job to know that. However, right now we need to disarm... whatever this is."

The note of bafflement in her voice was shaded with more anger than Nick's, but it was there. She didn't understand it any more than he did. Nick wasn't sure if it was a relief or not. He fiddled absently with the charm under his sweater and turned it until the rusty point stuck through the wool. Enough to poke into the old clot of scar tissue on his thumb. It was his version of a dreamer's pinch, a reminder of what was real.

"It feels like in school," Nick said. "When the prettiest girl in class pretended to like you and all you could do was wait for the other shoe to fall."

That won a very small, short-lived smile from Jepson. "I never imagined pretty girls being one of your weaknesses, Doctor Blake."

"I hadn't realized there were options," Nick cracked.

The smile faded from Jepson's face, and she frowned over Nick's shoulder at the bonfire. "It reminds me of Afghanistan," she said. "When you had contractors who smiled and screwed you over. I didn't like it there either, but you don't deal with it by challenging them directly."

Nick rocked back on his heels. "You're going to let them take Gregor," he said. "You know they're lying."

"No, I don't. Neither do you," Jepson said. "We don't know this man, and we don't know what he's capable of. Trust me, Doctor Blake, I've known a lot of violent men, and he is one of them. Besides, even if we give him over to Muir's care, and it is an if, I'll make sure he gets all the medical supervision he needs."

"You can't do that," Nick said.

"I don't want to do that," Jepson said. "But I can. What I can't do is put our people at risk, or our other patients. Look, we aren't getting evacuated. The roads are impassable, the storms are so violent that they won't risk flying us out, and apparently they can't find anyone to float us out either. So we *need* to keep the locals on our side. Do you understand?"

"I do. I just…." The words caught in his throat like a stone. If he said them out loud, it would just sound unhinged. Even trapped in his head, they sounded like someone not in touch with reality, but with peat-bog ghosts, ill-omened birds, and an iron necklace to keep the magic away.

"They're scared people," Jepson said. She put a gloved hand on his arm, her fingers striped in green-and-gold wool. "Not bad people. It's Ayr, not Afghanistan. Just... let me deal with it. Okay?" She squeezed his arm and left.

Nick pressed his thumb down harder on the point of the nail. He could do that with a clear conscience, couldn't he? Without Gregor there, without whatever there was about the man that brought up all Nick's obsessive, childhood fears, maybe things would go back to normal.

Except what if—and even the thought made Nick feel sick as he let it into his head—what if he wasn't hallucinating? If the things he saw in the shadows were real... or real enough.

Every therapist he'd ever had—and there had been a lot of them—told him that was the point of no return. As long as he knew that the dead things in the lake were just tricks his mind had been trained to play on him, it was a psychotic experience instead of a psychotic break.

Except Nick's nightmares had always been restricted to... side-of-the-eye phantoms, obsessively adhered-to superstitions that kept his world safe. He'd been afraid of the world his gran convinced him was there, and the defining characteristic of that world was that he could never see it.

He'd never layered his delusions over something solid, never seen a nightmare in a person's face or made up venom in their voice.

On its own, that wouldn't have been enough. Nick had spent most of his adult life with a polite wall between everyone he knew and his issues, his childhood. It had been over a decade since he'd even talked to a therapist about it.

But whether the monsters were real or not, everyone there was about to let something monstrous happen. Maybe not even actively monstrous—maybe they'd just put Gregor in a cell and, come spring, it would turn out he'd died of the cold or infection. Nobody would ever talk about it, and his would just be another name to add to the list in Nick's office.

Nick couldn't just turn a blind eye to that. He'd promised Gregor that they were there to help, and he'd meant it… and Gregor trusted that.

"Still doesn't mean I should care?" Nick muttered to himself as he checked that Jepson wasn't looking his way. She had her head together with Nelson, and his hand was on her wrist. Before she could turn around, Nick slunk farther back from the bonfire and ducked around the pickup. As the cold hit him again, he shivered down into his coat. "He's not even that nice."

The ground along the back fence was uneven with potholes and lumps of grass hidden under the deceptively smooth surface of the snow. Nick followed it down to the narrow, rough chop-out of the hill steps down.

"Doctor Blake?" Copeland's voice stopped him. He turned around and frowned as he saw her trip toward him. She'd lost her hat somewhere, and her hair was tangled around her fire-flushed face. Her feet caught under her, and she nearly toppled into him. He caught her by the elbows, muttered something as she grabbed his jacket. "Where are you going?"

He folded his lips into something tight and smile-like as he tried to set her back on her feet.

"Not really in the party mood, Copeland."

"You can call me Fiona," she said and stretched up on her tiptoes to kiss him.

Her lips were still red and tender-looking, almost raw.

Who did you fuck? Gregor's voice growled through Nick's head as he recoiled from Copeland's advance. He tripped down a step backward and jarred his hip all the way up into his spine.

"What did you drink?" He grabbed Copeland's chin in his hand and leaned down to sniff her breath. It reeked like gasoline and ethanol. She tried to kiss his nose, giggling through puckered lips, and he dodged it awkwardly. "Did you try the home brew that Harris handed out?"

She covered her mouth with her hands and giggled through her fingers. "Maybe. Do you wan' some?"

"I've opened up chronic alcoholics whose liver smelled better than that," he said.

"No," Copeland slurred. She leaned back from him. "It smells good. Like... like... like...."

She stuck on the comparison. Nick hesitated and then cursed to himself. She wasn't his responsibility, but he couldn't just leave her there. Whatever grudge Terry Muir had with them, it had started with Copeland's black tag. He hooked his arm around her waist and half carried, half dragged her down the steps.

"Apples," she announced at the bottom. "It smells like apples."

"It smells like a brewery shit in your mouth," Nick snapped at her. "You can't be this drunk already."

Copeland covered her mouth with her hand and sniffed at the breath that bounced off her palm. "I'm not drunk. I only had a bit. The redhead, he said I had to, that it was hair of the dog that's going to bite me. It was only polite."

"Stupid," Nick muttered the correction. He yanked her hand down, turned her in the direction of their trailers, and gave her a shove. "Go home. Lock the door. Stay there. Don't drink anything else."

The push he gave her moved her forward a few steps and momentum kept her going a few more. She finally stopped and turned around. A deep breath made her cough and then grimace. She lifted her fingers to her sweaty forehead.

"I'm sorry," she said. "I don't... I didn't mean that."

"Go. Lock the door. Sleep." Nick repeated. He glanced back over his shoulder, but the steps down through the ice-covered briars were still empty. "You're drunk, that's all."

She rubbed between her eyebrows, fingers flattened against the bone as though she were trying to squash something.

"I don't get drunk," she said primly. "I have... I have time for fun later. That's why everyone leaves me, because I am no fun, and I don't get drunk."

It wasn't hard to recast that sentence in Nick's own voice. Except, back then, he'd been relieved no one tried to get close to him. It would have been too hard to explain any of the odd little rituals he hadn't managed to shake. He rubbed his sore thumb against his jeans—like that one.

"You're a good doctor," Nick said.

She gave him a sad, surprisingly sweet smile for that and then stumbled around awkwardly to do as she was told. Nick watched her crunch away until she was just a dark, wobbly silhouette. He hesitated, torn enough to take a step after her, but she wasn't the one in trouble. Once she was back in her trailer, she'd be fine. The woman slept like the dead, and whatever toilet bleach was in that home brew, it hadn't killed Harris yet.

Nick turned his back on her and headed for the hospital tent. He tucked his chin down into his collar, his breath warm as it caught in the wool, and squinted at his feet as he walked. The flicker of shadows on the snow made him look up. A black bird stooped across the path between trailers, the shadow of its wings sharp edged and exaggerated on the white ground.

It landed on the roof of a trailer with a thud and a spray of snow. For a second, Nick's brain tried to convince him it was a small trailer, even though it was the same as the ones around it, until it accepted the sheer size of the bird. It was the size of a corgi. It could carry off a corgi.

The bird turned its head to look at him, its black eye shiny over the matching feathers. It shuffled its feet on the roof and opened its beak. No sound came out, but after a second, it clipped its beak shut and fluffed its wings like it had its say.

It was eerie. Nick stared at the bird for a second and couldn't help but wonder if it was the same one he'd seen earlier—the one with the rag of skin.

Before he could decide, the bird crouched and took off from the roof in a flurry of wings. A black feather jostled loose from its wing and spun down. It landed black and ink-line straight in a bush.

Nick reached for it. His fingers brushed the hollow nib, fresh from its skin, and then he thought better of it. Curses or mites, he didn't need either.

He pulled his hand back and someone grabbed the nape of his neck. Hot, sweat-wet fingers slimed his skin and yanked him back and up onto his toes. A fetid, fruit-rot smell, like unchecked ketosis, washed over Nick. It was so thick that Nick could almost taste it, coated on his tongue and down the back of his throat.

"Doctor Blake, is that you?" Terry asked mildly, his voice conversational while Nick dangled like the catch of the day. "We thought it was an intruder. Someone creeping around. Peeping in windows."

Nick twisted his head to the side and saw Terry with arms crossed, his shoulder braced against the side of a trailer. In the periphery of his vision, he could see the blurred edges of the man who had him by the throat, sweat-greasy skin and heavy scarf—Len.

"Well, I'm not. So get your hands off me."

Terry pursed his lips as he thought about it. "How can I be sure, though?" He tilted his head in the direction that Copeland had disappeared in. The fake humor, mocking as it was, slid from his voice and just left the bitter behind. "Maybe you're going to peep in that bitch's window. You seemed sweet enough on her when she told me my kid was going to die."

The snow had thickened. The fat, lazy flakes you could catch on your hand were now small and vicious, hard enough that Nick could feel it ping off his skin.

"We had criteria. If we sent your son, we couldn't send another child—"

"Fuck someone else's kid," Terry snapped. His voice cracked in his throat with the need to be heard. It was raw and angry. He stalked forward and grabbed Nick's jaw. It was the same grip Nick had used on

Copeland, but he hadn't squeezed until the bones hurt. "My son. You told my son he was going to die."

Len choked out a laugh from behind Nick. All the stolen heat from the bonfire had leeched out of Nick's bones, but Len still radiated sickly heat. If it was a fever, it should have half cooked his brain in his skull by then.

"He's alright now, though," he mushed out. "Like my wife. The priest fixed him right up. Didn't he, Terr? Gonna be fine."

Something terrible slid behind Terry's eyes as he looked over Nick's shoulder. Regret, maybe, or contempt. He hid it behind his glasses before Nick could be sure.

"That's right. But see, Doctor Blake, we aren't selfish like you were. We aren't going to save some and leave the rest. We have enough for everyone."

Terry held out his hand and crooked his fingers. Without loosening his grip on Nick's neck, Len handed over the brown bottle he'd swilled from all night. Terry gave it a shake and smirked when it sloshed.

A low, strangled whimper escaped Nick.

"Enough for you," Len said and shoved the bottle into Nick's mouth.

There was no pinched-lip fakery to be done. If Nick wanted to keep his teeth he had to open his mouth. The home brew stung as it hit the inside of his mouth, his tongue numb and itchy at the same time, and the inside of his sinuses burned up to the back of his eyes.

He choked and did his best to block his throat with his suddenly clumsy tongue.

"Drink up, Doctor Blake," Terry said. That awful thing in his eyes was in his voice now, and Nick finally put his finger on what it was. Pity. "It will all seem better once you've got a bellyful of this."

Nick had grown up poor, scrawny, and weird on a sinking estate, where kids were only too glad to get a turn punching down. He wasn't much of a fighter. He was good at getting away.

He pulled his knees up to his chest and kicked Terry in the stomach with both feet. The air grunted out of Terry and he staggered backward, his face blanched gray as he tried to convince his lungs to inhale.

While he wheezed, Nick dragged the iron pendant out from under his sweater, the chain twisted around his fingers, and stabbed the end of it back into Len's cheek, through the mass of wool and into flesh. Len howled as though it were a knife instead of an old nail and let go of Nick. Without the bruising grip on the nape of his neck to keep him upright Nick's knees gave. He went down on all fours in the snow, the landing hard enough to crack the joints, and retched up as much of the home brew as he could force out of himself.

It splashed over the snow, shit brown and stinking, and then Nick saw it move. Tiny, smoky snakes, thin as pins, coiled and squirmed over each other as they tried to get away from the cold. He could see the ice crystals as they formed like scales on the wriggling bodies. The little things struck at each other viciously as they writhed around, and whatever venom they injected melted their bodies down into the puke.

Nick recoiled and scrambled away, his ass in the snow as he kicked at the ground with his boots. One hand reached for the nail—old habits were quick to come back—and he realized it wasn't there. The chain had snapped and the pendant was still in his hand, caught in the foul-looking length of wool Nick had wrenched off Len.

His stomach tried to force more bile up his throat, frantic to get rid of whatever dregs of the things dying in the snow that might still be in him. Nick forced it back down and scrambled to his feet. He staggered and blinked, his head full of fog and panic.

"You should have drunk it. It would have been easier," Terry said, the words squeezed through gritted teeth. He couldn't stand up yet, hunched over as he hugged his stomach, but a grim smile twisted over his mouth when he looked over Nick's shoulder. "Don't kill him."

Nick looked. He wished he hadn't. Under the scarf the flesh from just under Len's cheekbone to his jawline was gone on one side, bone and broken teeth exposed and smeared yellow with pus and serum. His upper lip was split open and peeled back over his gums, and the intact side of his face was broken and twisted out of true. It was all dry and old. The only fresh wound was the puckered tear Nick had jabbed under one eye.

It wasn't the worst injury Nick had ever seen. The face always seemed to be what violent people aimed their frustrations at, and a car wreck could leave a closed casket the only option. It shouldn't have been on someone alive though, not for long, and it shouldn't have smiled.

"My wife," Len said, the tendons visible in the meat of his face. He reached up and touched his ragged lip. "She's a passionate one now."

Nick spun on his heel and ran. He could taste the snow on his tongue when he gasped it in, cold and clean as it melted, but the fog between his ears obscured everything else. Twice he ran into the side of a trailer because he didn't see it until his body slammed into the metal. Once... once he looked back, and the space he'd just staggered through was occupied by an oversized brand-new trailer.

He knew all the landmarks to his madness—the finger twitch salute to magpies, the compulsion to leave by the same door he came in—and this wasn't it. This was new.

"You can't hide," Len yelled behind him. His voice was somewhere between a gargle and a growl. Nick heard metal clatter as Len kicked his way through the swing set. "I can smell ya, scared little man."

Nick forced his tired legs back into a run. He didn't get far before his foot caught in something—a rock, a root, anything—under the snow, and he went facedown. Cold powder wedged its way up his nose and into his eyes. He huffed out a shocked breath and tried to push himself up.

A heavy boot between his shoulders slammed him back down and pinned him there.

"It woulda been easy if you'd drank," Len said. His voice was weirdly calm since he'd caught up. Even. "After you drink, you're alright. You don'... you don' mind so much."

Nick didn't think he believed that. He didn't think there was anything that could make that face in the mirror okay.

He closed his eyes and pressed his face down in the snow, as though he could sink into it and hide himself. Instead a hand grabbed a handful of his hair... and then let go with a low grunt.

Something warm splattered on Nick's neck and ran down into his ears. It smelled like copper and a hint of rot. Nick spat out a panicked curse and scrambled away, one hand twisted around to scrub at the back of his neck.

He rolled over onto his back and stared, his drink-fogged brain incapable of keeping up. Len had a fresh mouth across his throat, just as bloody as the ruined one on his face. His eyes were wide with dull surprise as he pressed his hand to the wound to try to stem it.

"Doc?" he asked. Maybe he thought Nick would help. Even if he wanted to, Nick didn't think he could.

Len sighed wetly and dropped to his knees. Gregor stood behind him in stolen clothes, snow matted into his hair, with a bloody scalpel in one hand. He grabbed Len's head, his fingers dug into the flesh on his forehead, and drove the knife into the base of his skull with a sharp, underhand strike.

The inside of Nick's mouth tasted like fear and nail polish remover. His heart was stutter-fast in his throat, and a dry voice in his head noted that Len's spinal cord was severed between the C1 and C2 vertebrae. It wouldn't kill him instantly—although that was a common misconception—but he'd lose control of his body.

Sure enough, Len's eyes rolled back independently of each other, and his big sweaty body went limp. Gregor let him fall, and hot blood spread out under him, a dark stain that diluted as it spread, until it turned slushy pink.

The last time Nick had seen blood on the snow it had been Gregor's.

"Some things you're meant to mind," Gregor said harshly. His lip was curled in an unsympathetic sneer, and there was something so cold about him that it chilled Nick, down where even the bitter winter chill hadn't reached before.

He stepped over Len's body and grimaced as he put his weight on his injured leg, the denim of his borrowed jeans pulled tourniquet tight around his thigh. The flash of obvious pain softened him, but it also reminded Nick that Gregor should barely be able to hobble. Of course, a small voice stabbed coldly through Nick's thoughts, Gregor shouldn't have survived that first night either.

"What the fuck was he?" Nick asked breathlessly.

Gregor gave the corpse an uninterested look. In his heavy winter coat and layers of Aran sweaters and thermal underwear, Nick was still cold enough to shiver. In jeans and a soft-shell jacket thrown on over a T-shirt, Gregor seemed comfortable.

"He was a monster," he said calmly. "Or would have been, soon enough."

That wasn't as reassuring as Nick had hoped. "What are *you*?"

For some reason that was the question that stumped Gregor. He paused for a second, mouth held tight, and then came to some sort of decision.

"I'm a Wolf," he said.

The shaky, disconnected feeling was shock. Nick could diagnose that with confidence. It didn't help him rein back the words that slipped off his tongue.

"Is this the wolf winter, then?" he asked. It had been on his mind for days, ever since thoughts of his gran and her old stories escaped the hole he kept them in. Of course the wolf winter was the one that came up most often. It was the frostiest, the bitterest of his gran's cold, auld stories, when the gods ended the world in ice and fire. Nick hiccupped out a nervy laugh at the confused look on Gregor's face. "Are the wolves going over the Wall?"

Chapter Nine

GREGOR GRABBED Nick's collar and dragged him roughly to his feet. What little color Nick had drained from his face at the abrupt move, and he gagged.

"Puke on me, and I leave you here," Gregor said harshly. The snow—halfway to hail—pelted his face and slid down the back of his jumper sweater. "Where'd you hear that?"

Nick closed his eyes and swallowed hard. His face was sallow-looking, nearly gray at the temples and the hollows of his cheeks. "Hear what?"

"The wolf winter? The Wall?" The answer didn't spill out of Nick quickly enough, and Gregor gave him a shake in frustration. "Answer me. Or I leave you here."

Doubt scratched at the inside of his brain with sharp, smug little claws made of "I told you so." He should have retreated when the sick-thing stench of the prophets' monsters infiltrated the camp, found another den to lie up in while he waited for his injuries to finish healing. Another day, another night, and he would be whole enough to go and find his brother. To make them give him his wolf back.

Instead he'd come to find Nick. Give him time and he could justify it as being a practicality, that even if he was nearly healed, until he got his wolf back, even human help might be useful. But he hadn't thought about it. He just knew he couldn't leave without Nick, that he wasn't going to let the prophets take anything else from him.

The bleak thought seeped from the wound where his wolf had been. If Nick had played him for a fool, he'd kill him. He twisted his fistful of fabric and hauled Nick up onto his toes.

"I… it's just an old story," Nick blurted out. "My gran used to tell it at night. The wolf winter, when the world would freeze, and the wolves would come down over the Wall from Scotland to eat all the little boys in their beds. Like popsicles."

It didn't smell like a lie, although the stench of the monster laid its taint over every scent, just like fear. Gregor resented that, even though the idea of Nick's death at his fangs was still fresh in his head. He didn't want Nick to be afraid of him, not that sort of fear, anyhow.

"Stop trembling," Gregor ordered. He let go of Nick's collar and pretended not to notice that Nick staggered backward and away from him. "I just wanted to know."

Nick hacked out a skeptical laugh. "I'm not mad, I don't think," he said. "So that means that this is all real, and you just murdered a—"

He was clear enough on what was happening that he couldn't get the *man* out. Instead he just jabbed a finger at the hulk of a thing sprawled out in the middle of the playground. "That."

Gregor cocked his head to the side. He could hear Nick's heart as it pounded in his chest, a trip-hammer beat that made him sound like prey, and under that, the labored rattle of the monster's heart, failing but not stopped.

"It's not dead yet," he said.

Nick croaked out a laugh and scrubbed his hands over his face. "That doesn't help," he said. "So either I get the shakes or I piss myself. Your pick."

It was more defiance than Gregor would accept from a Wolf. He supposed it didn't matter so much from a human, and he enjoyed the crack in Nick's wary reserve and properly formed vowels.

"We should go," he said.

Nick stared at him for a second and then shook his head. He waved his hand back the way he'd come, toward the glow of a fire and the sound of giddy laughter.

"I have to go back," he protested. "Terry's still there and the other one. I have to warn people. I have to tell Jepson about…."

He looked at the dying thing on the ground, and the words dried up on his tongue. Gregor could understand. He doubted he could explain it to wolves. To try to convince humans who believed in nothing seemed impossible.

"It's too late for them," Gregor said. He grabbed Nick's arm and dragged him along with him toward the trees. "The prophets don't give their monsters free rein. They'll be here for me soon."

Nick stumbled over his own feet and nearly went down on the ground again. Gregor stifled a growl of irritation and yanked him back onto his feet.

"Sorry," Nick muttered. He rubbed his hand roughly over his face. "I can't... I think there was something in the drink."

That was why Gregor preferred to be a lone wolf. Other people—even wolves—were always weaker. He stopped and grabbed Nick's face in his hands and tucked his thumbs under the sharp jut of cheekbones to study it.

Even in daylight, Nick's eyes were so dark it would be hard to tell if the pupils were blown or not. In the moonlight it was impossible.

"You're going to slow me down," Gregor said.

"Leave me, then," Nick said sharply. He shoved at Gregor's shoulder and tried to twist his head free of his grip. "They're here for you anyhow. This all started with you. Maybe it will go with you."

No. The thought of being out in the wolf winter on his own, no pack in howling distance, no wolf to tuck himself into, no bony, beaky man dozing in an uncomfortable chair for his sake, dried Gregor's mouth and curdled in his stomach. He cringed from the weakness of it, the fear, but it wouldn't go away.

Jack had let his Dog go down into England because it was better for him. A life away from the Pack, from the Numitor and his sons, was the life that Danny wanted. Gregor should be able to do the same. He and

Jack were just shadows of each other, each pulling at the *stuff* that made them try to be whole. What one did, the other surpassed. Except Gregor couldn't let Nick go.

"You're my doctor," Gregor said. It was the closest thing to *please* he could tolerate. "I'm not healed yet."

"Considering I'm a pathologist, I'd be of more use if you were dead," Nick muttered as he let Gregor drag him farther into the trees. He kept one hand on Gregor's arm, fingers clenched onto his forearm, as they scrambled over roots and through bushes. Pain pulsed steadily in Gregor's thigh as he walked. It spread with each step with tendrils that reached down to his knee and up into his groin. The wound in his gut ached heavily, like the bloodletters had sewn a rock in there. His legs held under his weight, though, and that was all he needed.

"Len," a distant voice yelled. "Len, did you find him?"

Then, with mockery, "Doctor Blake, are you lost?"

That made Nick flinch and stumble. He caught himself that time. "When they arrived, they said they'd found your brother, that he'd been the one who hurt you."

Gregor snorted. "He'd have had the good sense to kill me."

Nick's fingers flexed on his arm, but he shook his head and pressed on with what he'd been saying. "They wanted to take you away. When we wouldn't let them, Terry radioed someone to bring your brother here."

That piece of information made Gregor pause for a second. If they brought Jack here… they'd be fools.

Gregor might hate his brother, but he knew better than to underestimate him. More likely it would be the prophets, come to play shepherd to their herd of monsters.

He glanced back over his shoulder. The glow of the flames was lost in the thickening snow, but he could smell the smoke on the air. A prophets' bone fire never heralded anything good. It was a portent of doom more reliable, if less wide ranging, than a comet.

Nick didn't need to know that. Not when his people were the ones herded to it.

"They'll come empty-handed." He pulled a branch back, cracked the coating of frost, and pushed Nick through the gap. "Prophets always do."

"Who—what—are they?" Nick asked.

"Poor guests and worse hosts," Gregor said. "If you want to know more, walk faster."

Maybe he owed whoever had dosed Nick a resentful thank-you, because Nick just sighed and did as he was told. Under normal circumstances he thought Nick would have more questions. It made it easier that he didn't, particularly if it lasted a few more hours.

Gregor had no desire to stumble over unfamiliar moors and strange roads in the dark—roads strange to him, at least.

He grabbed the tail of Nick's coat and reeled him in.

"Do you trust me?" he asked as he wrapped an arm around Nick's waist. It wasn't an easy fit. Nick was all bones and angles, sharp shoulders, and lumps in his pockets.

"I don't know you," Nick said.

Gregor snorted and tightened his grip on Nick. "That's not what I asked."

He didn't wait for a response, but he still caught Nick's reluctantly muttered yes as he reached for the Wild. It wasn't *there* like it usually was, like water to a fish. He had to strain to catch it. The wound in his spirit throbbed like his thigh, but for a second, he felt his stomach sink. This was the first time he'd tried to touch the Wild, instead of passively accepting what it would offer.

Like an adulterer who'd cringe under his mate's teeth for the chance of a bitter fuck.

The cold—very cold—shoulder only lasted for a moment. Then the Wild softened to him. The high, dry stone and heather of it washed through him and overlaid the mundane reality. Dented metal swing sets shared spiritual space with a rotted nithing pole, the empty-eyed near-skull of a sheep mounted on a blood-slathered pole. On the horizon an unfinished white and brittle ship stood at anchor on the wide gray ribbon of the sea.

Gregor had seen it before—the ship of corpse nails. It haunted the wet boundaries of the Wild, sometimes even crept up along rivers or moored itself in lakes. This was the first time he'd seen it so close to being seaworthy, almost done.

In the curve of Gregor's arm, Nick stiffened, so wire-taut that Gregor could almost feel him vibrate, and made a wet, scared noise in his throat. It could have been a scream or a question, but it wasn't willing to make itself into the world to find out.

"Go to sleep," Gregor told him. He kissed the Wild into Nick's temple, a command and a kindness, and Nick slumped bonelessly against him. His head flopped against Gregor's shoulder, and his face relaxed—still all beak and bones but softer around the eyes and at the corners of his mouth.

He could have done it before he called the Wild, but he wanted Nick to see it, to see Gregor be the master of it.

The Wild flicked him with a cold zephyr for that bit of pride. His response, like any lover back in favor, was to push his luck. He let the Wild go and followed it back, a side step out of reality.

Instead of being overlaid on the landmarks of his world, it *was* the world. Gregor couldn't just see the ill-omened cursing pole, but he could smell the rot of it and hear the dull buzz of flies that covered the skull.

First flies he'd seen since the cold snap that spread down from the Highlands. It was too cold for them in the snow, but that was science. The Wild wanted flies, and so flies there were.

"Tell Jack I'll save his ass, him and his pet Dog," Gregor said. He could feel the Wild's attention on him, vast and dispassionate, as he stooped down to fold Nick over his shoulder. "The prophets have taken enough from me. They won't take Jack's death too."

The Wild bore witness to his request, wove it into snow and wind, but that didn't mean Jack would get the message. It was only a foolish or arrogant Wolf who believed himself the master of the Wild. Gregor could be arrogant, but he wasn't a fool.

He hitched Nick up more securely on his shoulder, hooked his fingers in the back of his jeans, and started to walk. It hurt, but he could live with it. The things the prophets made couldn't follow here, and few of the prophets… but that meant some could. Besides, Wolves weren't the only thing to worry about. The Sannock—the other not-humans who used to haunt Britain, the shifters, goblins, and strange monsters—might have been killed or exiled by the Wolves in the other world. Here they still roamed and tried to lay claim to territory. Especially here.

The snow was all fresh powder, loose around his boots. He limped stolidly for the horizon, where mountains poked jagged peaks untouched by wind and time toward the sky. Either the Wild would set his feet on the path to shelter, or Nick would be the first mortal in centuries to leave his bones here.

It would be an honor of a sort, but Gregor doubted Nick would appreciate it.

A hint of something on the wind caught in his nose. Even dulled by his human nose, it was ripe and musky, with notes of blood and estrogen-rich urine piercing the scentscape. An offer from the Wild? An unlucky litter of rabbits? Gregor couldn't be sure, but it was something. He paused to cast around and sniff the air until the scent coated the back of his throat.

That way. He turned to the west and kept walking. The ache in his leg peaked and then dulled as the cold sank to his bone. After a mile, blood stained the snow behind him—a drop at first and then nearly a whole footprint, but it didn't lie long. The wind that blew down from the North, from the vast, distant forest, brushed it away under a fresh coat of snow.

Somewhere a wolf howled—a sound that ached with loneliness and threat. Gregor nearly choked on the emptiness in his throat where his answer should have been.

THE MEAT was gone by the time Gregor tracked the scent back to the source. A bloody burrow with the roof caved in was all that was left. Hooves had trampled the snow down to the mud, and the sooty black hair was caught on the rocks.

Gregor spat into the mire of it. "I hope you ate your fill," he muttered to the glutted pig. "Tonight my kin will eat the fat of you and fart your eulogy."

He dropped awkwardly to his knees and shrugged Nick off his shoulder and into his lap. Frost tipped Nick's dark hair with white and sealed his lashes. He still looked more at ease than Gregor was used to seeing him. Whatever small, neat life Nick had been content with before had been upended by Gregor's intrusion into it. Now he was hunted by monsters and breathed in the Wild by the lungful—something that would linger in the pit of his lungs until he died.

"You shouldn't have been kind," Gregor said. He cupped his hands in front of his mouth and breathed into them for a second. Then he laid his thumbs over Nick's eyes to melt the crust of frost. Water dribbled down the sharp jut of Nick's cheekbone like a tear. Gregor brushed it away before it froze again, and his hand hesitated on Nick's cheek. The monster had left livid fingerprint-shaped bruises on either side of Nick's chin, livid purple under a fine scruff of stubble, and there was a scabbed-over graze on the bridge of his nose from contact with the ground. "I never am."

He let his hand cup Nick's cheek for a second, cold skin and the soft prickle of stubble against his palm. Unconscious, without the clever mobility of his features to distract from it, he wasn't handsome.

Pretty when he was younger, probably, but the severe elegance of his bones and the delicacy of his narrow face didn't quite fit together anymore. Gregor didn't care. He liked Nick's face, and when had he ever cared what anyone else thought?

"Wake up." He kissed the order into Nick's mouth, chapped lips under his and the itchy aftertaste of whatever they'd dosed Nick with. Like a prince in a fairytale, he thought with a flash of bleak contempt as he pulled back. Even Jack, soft and sentimental as he was, had found a Dog to make eyes at.

And Nick didn't do as he was told. He sprawled awkwardly over Gregor's thighs, his eyes closed and his face lax.

"Wake up," Gregor repeated, a snarl on the edge of his words. "Nick. Nicholas. Get up."

He slapped him. The crack of his palm against the cheek he'd *just* stroked made him flinch, but Nick's eyes didn't even flutter.

The noise that escaped Gregor was somewhere between a bark and a laugh. He folded himself over Nick, his face buried in the thick, sweat-ripe wool of his coat, and maybe that was it…. Every time he thought he had something that was his—his face, his brief stint as his da's favorite pup, his wolf—it was stripped from him. Even this… brittle thing he had for Nick, had to be ruined. What reason was there to drag himself any fucking farther?

The despair settled on him like a shroud. It would be easy enough to just curl around Nick and wait. Wolves didn't mind the cold as much as humans did, but eventually it would have its way with him. What better place to die than there? The Wild had always been easier for him than the world he was meant to walk.

Let Jack have all of it.

Gregor let that thought rise through the fog of misery and self-pity. There might not be hope or much joy left in it, but there was spite. It was black and bitter, but it was all he'd ever really had, and he knew how to ride it.

Fuck the prophets. Fuck Jack. Fuck the Old Man, smug in his betrayal to the North.

It would solve all their problems if Gregor just lay down to die. So he would crawl out of there if he had to, and he'd drag Nick with him by the hair if he had to. If the world wanted to take one more thing from him, it could try, but he wouldn't just let it go.

Gregor unfolded himself, and his back ached as though he'd been slouched there longer than he thought. Snow slid off his arms as he shoved the Wild away and let the bone and meat and weariness of his body drag him back down.

THE CRISP white winter of the Wild faded away and was replaced with rutted ice and the stink of dead farm animal. Gregor wiped his face on his sleeve—ice melt, that was all—and looked around. It was too dark to see much, the heavy stone walls and rattling metal roof blocked out all but a few chinks of moonlight. But from the smell, it had been in use as a pigsty until recently.

"Fuck you for that," Gregor muttered to the Wild. Maybe it heard him. The empty socket where his wolf had been was chafed raw by his trip outside the world. He felt too raw and too tired to care.

Gregor waited for his eyes to adjust to the dark and then looked down at Nick. He was still asleep, but his heart was a steady pulse in the dark, and the close, straw-sweaty warmth of the shed had banished the icy discoloration under his skin.

"You made promises, Nicholas Blake," he said. "You don't get to make yourself a liar. If I have to drag you by the ankle to Lochwinnoch to wake you up, I will."

It was a good threat. Probably a better one if you knew the rutted, steep roads and hard, stony fields that led to the Wolves' territory. Either way, Nick didn't stir.

Gregor leaned back against the cold, knobbly stone wall and stared at the ground. It probably wasn't safe to stop there. The prophets were still hunting him, and Jack and his Dog were still captured, but even spite couldn't gall Gregor into movement right then. He closed his eyes, his fingers still idly twisted through Nick's hair, and he waited.

"Don't think dying will get you out of it either," he muttered to his unconscious companion through a jaw-cracking yawn. "I'll find you one way or the other."

He didn't want to sleep—the Wild would inevitably take him to some dark memory that he had no desire to revisit—but he did.

Chapter Ten

AS HE walked down the stairs of his childhood home, Nick knew it was a dream. He was too tall to be there, the stairs much narrower than he remembered, and the smell of stewed meat much stronger. Nick hadn't been in that house since he was eight. He remembered it as huge, but in his dreams, it always shrank around his adult frame. Besides, the last time he'd looked, he'd been drugged and about to freeze to death somewhere cold and improbable.

Dream or not, though, he stepped over the crooked stair that creaked when you put your weight on it. The house was quiet. It was always best to enjoy the silence while it lasted.

There was a dusty picture frame mounted crookedly on the wall opposite the front door, so it was the first thing you saw when you came into the house. A faded sketch of a man with a hard jaw and cold eyes stared down from it, with something about his face that suggested he wasn't impressed by what he saw.

"The Run-Away Man," Nick said. He'd forgotten about him or made himself forget. He mouthed the rest of his gran's old warning as he fidgeted out from beneath the irritated glare. "If he sees you, he'll catch you. If he catches you, he'll eat you. So run away if you see him, boy."

"…if you see him, boy."

The hoarse echo of his words made him flinch, and he spun around on his heel.

Gran crouched in the hall behind him, one finger jabbed in the direction of the sketch and her other hand on Nick's shoulder. She had a face like Nick's, with broad cheekbones, a slightly weak chin, and a mouth that settled too easily into sour. He remembered how old he thought she was back then, but her hair was thick and only touched with gray.

Her eyes were the big difference. They were an odd light brown that looked paler than her tanned face.

"What do you do?" she prodded Nick.

He didn't know what she wanted him to say, but he heard the words come out of his mouth anyhow. Some triggers were too long-buried to fight. "Run away, run home to you."

She put her hand on his head and ruffled his hair. "Smart as budgie, you are," she said. "Do you have your nail?"

He nodded. "Aye, Granny," he said and patted his chest. The twist of iron hung almost to his sternum and poked through the thin gray wool of his school sweater. No wonder the other kids thought he was weird, Nick thought dryly, even as he reached into his coat pocket. The nail was still where he'd shoved it, cold and tacky with half-dried blood.

Nick tapped his thumb against the point…

…and woke up in a prickly, stinking bed that didn't particularly cushion the hard surface underneath. His back hurt with a sullen ache that promised to do something eye-watering the minute he moved, but he wasn't cold. A warm, heavy body was tucked around him, an arm was hooked over his stomach, and warm breath rumbled against his ear.

Nick opened his eyes, squinted at the bright dust-mote-glittering beams of light that filled the space, and licked his lips. His tongue was too dry to do any good, and he waited for the terror.

His memories of the… night before?… were foggy and scattershot but unmistakably full of terrible things—things that he should dismiss as a psychotic hallucination but that were too rough and too real for that. They felt, in some hindbrain pocket, like an inarguable reality. Alternatively, he was seeing things, and that meant he was being spooned by a man who'd just murdered an innocent stranger.

He should be horrified. He should rationalize it all away. Instead he felt an adolescent "I told you so" smugness.

"You're a wolf."

"I already told you that."

"Just checking." Nick brushed his fingers over Gregor's arm, from elbow to wrist. Gregor's hand was tucked up under his jumper, his fingers spread flat over his stomach. "Are you going to eat me?"

There was a pause, and Nick felt tension slide through Gregor's body and the clench of long, heavy muscle under skin and fabric. It took him a second and the lazy flex of long fingers against his stomach to piece together that Gregor wasn't exactly angry.

"Maybe." Gregor nuzzled Nick's throat as he spoke, soft lips and a hint of teeth against tender skin. "If you ask nice."

Nick caught his breath and shifted awkwardly, his cock hard under his jeans in defiance of all common sense. He had just worked out that Gregor was a Wolf, the bogeyman that had haunted his childhood. He tried to shift his hip, but Gregor firmly wedged him back into place with his leg.

"Stop squirming. I'm not going to fuck you unless you ask." Gregor shifted his leg, and his knee bumped the hard bulge of Nick's cock. There was a dark, sticky smugness to his voice as he corrected himself. "Out loud."

Nick wanted to ask. It was hard enough to keep his distance with Gregor laid up in bed, where the white sheets and iodine were a pointed reminder it was a bad idea. But Gregor's thigh was heavy over his hip and his warm fingers were making lazy inroads on the waistband of his jeans.

"It doesn't really seem like it would be a good idea." He sounded priggish, his speech voice-coach sharp.

Gregor's low growl of amusement tickled Nick's throat. "That just means it would be a better fuck."

Despite the confidence in his voice, he moved his hand, not off Nick's stomach, but out of his jeans. Nick felt a pang of regret in his gut and a cramp of protest in his balls. He made himself ignore both. If nothing else, he needed to know what was going on before he made any more bad decisions.

"Is this a pig barn?" Apparently out of all the questions he had, that was the one his brain thought should go to the front of the line.

"I think the pigs left," Gregor said. "We needed a den, and I didn't feel like carrying you any farther."

Nick started to ask how they'd gotten there. The words got all the way to his tongue before he remembered the eerie, iced-over landscape he'd stepped into, the somehow simultaneous feeling that it was both ancient and new. He dry-swallowed the question like he used to swallow his medication. He might need to work up to some of the answers.

"Let me up." The minute he said it, he needed it. The dim light and weight made him anxious under his skin, and he shoved roughly at Gregor's leg. "I need to get up."

Gregor sucked in his breath, and, for just a second, Nick felt that cold trickle in his spine that warned of violence, and he tensed. Gregor just rolled away from him, but not far. There wasn't far to go. The awkward line of his body, his weight on one hip and leg stretched out stiff and straight, made Nick wince as he remembered.

"Sorry." He sat up and scrambled gracelessly to his knees. He'd been right, his back twinged with eye-watering pain right over his shoulder blades. The tails of his coat caught under his knees and jerked at his shoulders, and fouled straw clung to the wool. "I forgot. Did I hurt you? Are you okay?"

"You didn't. I'm fine." Nick could trace the bulge of muscle around the hinge of Gregor's jaw, and the tight line called his voice a liar. It would still be easy enough to take him at his word. It would be tempting to....

Heat washed through Nick. "I didn't mean to. I'm really sorry." He pressed his hand to Gregor's cheek in mute apology. Maybe his thumb didn't need to trace the full curve of Gregor's mouth, but he needed to give in on something. "Let me make sure I haven't done any more damage."

He felt some of the angry tension slip away under his hand. But Gregor still curled his lip in a sneer, and his attitude was nearly enough to hide the smear of sweat on his forehead and lip.

"I thought you only doctored the dead."

"You have an open wound from your knee to your hipbone and a stab wound to your stomach," Nick said. "I don't need to be a diagnostician to see the damage. Please? It'll keep me busy while you tell me what's going on."

Gregor turned his head into Nick's hand. It wasn't a kiss exactly—more a nuzzle. "If it will stop you whining," he gave in gracelessly. "Although I don't know what you think you can do about it out here." He propped himself up on his elbow and grabbed the wall with his other hand. Then he dug his fingers in around the loosely mortared old stone and slowly dragged himself up. Nick hovered nervously, his help clearly unwelcome.

"Fuck it," he muttered as Gregor awkwardly braced his leg against the slime of straw and pig filth. Nick ducked under Gregor's arm and grabbed him by the waist. He tucked his hand over the sharp jut of a hipbone and hooked his fingers in the sagging borrowed jeans. "Don't growl at me. No one's here, are they? When you tell the story, you can say you got up on your own."

Gregor grumbled but still latched onto Nick's shoulder for balance. "I'll tell 'em I had to carry you out of here, overcome with lust and fear. That's how you tell a story." He pushed his weight off the wall and onto Nick with a grunt. "And if I growled at you, you'd know it."

Neither of them could stand up straight in the low-slung byre. They had to hunch over, and brittle spiderwebs caught in their hair as they limped to the door. It hung half-open, wedged by clumps of ice and a broken bucket. Nick kicked it open the rest of the way, although the heavy drifts of frozen and fresh snow on the other side were reluctant to shift.

Outside, the morning had the eerie brittle brightness that was the winter version of the eye of the storm—a moment to catch its breath before the next wave of cold creaked down on the world. It gave the run-down farm an odd, sketch-like quality, as though an artist had drawn it in dusty crayon.

A slightly macabre artist.

The windows of the farmhouse—half old stone and half cracked render—were boarded up with bits of plywood stapled together, but the front door had been left open. A dead sheep lay in the yard, fleece all unraveled from its guts where something had eaten it, and a rusted Land Rover stood abandoned, front smashed in, at the gate. All of it was covered with a skin of snow.

"At least we won't have to explain how we got here," Nick said.

"I don't explain," Gregor said. He took a step forward and stopped. A curse ground out through his clenched teeth. "It felt better than this yesterday."

Nick absently rubbed his back. The long straps of muscle were clenched as tightly as wire under Gregor's skin.

"You slept in the cold on the floor of a barn," Nick pointed out. "I'm stiff as hell, and I'm not hurt."

Gregor stopped and turned slightly. He tucked his knuckle under Nick's chin to lift it and scowled at what he saw.

"Not for lack of trying." His knuckles grazed along Nick's jaw, but the ache of tenderness reminded Nick of the rough grip of Terry's fingers. The *smell* of the man's sweat too—sweet and meaty. "They were going to turn you into one of the prophets' monsters."

That suggestion chilled Nick. He tried to tune out the part of his brain that squinted at Len's degloved face for wound marks. There had been marks under his chin, where something had anchored its jaw before it scraped its teeth down his face. It didn't work.

"What are they?" Nick asked with sick fascination.

Gregor stroked Nick's jaw again. "The prophets' catechism says that we—the wolves—were just human once, until a she-wolf begged the moon god to give fur to the humans she suckled. Selene gave them fur and fangs, and they gave you Rome. We served Rome until we were banished here, sent over the Wall like curs, and now we serve the Numitor. No Wolf would follow a prophet, so they have to make their own. But they're not gods. They're barely wolves. So their get are twisted things."

"That's… that's what would have happened to me?"

"No," Gregor said. "I would have killed you."

He said it calmly. It wasn't a threat or some sort of backhanded reassurance, just a fact. Nick swallowed uncomfortably and stumbled into motion again. No one wanted to die, but he didn't know if he wanted to live like Len. His feet were cold anyhow, his jeans sodden down to his heels as the denim wicked in the moisture from the snow.

It only took a couple of hobbled steps before Gregor's stride started to loosen as his muscles warmed up. He took his weight off Nick's shoulder with a couple more steps, even though he still limped on that leg.

Without that heavy slouch of weight to steady him, Nick felt oddly unmoored, as though the wind could just pick him up and shake him out like a bed sheet. He should have brought that bottle of whiskey.

The inside of the small farmhouse lacked the surreal, freshly chalked appeal of the outside landscape. The walls were faded, with wallpaper that Nick—his old house fresh in his mind—could swear was the same "fever-dream rose and geometry" pattern he'd just dreamed about. The furniture was old and cast in shades of beige. Everything was covered with a thin, sepia-yellow layer from years of cooking grease and nicotine.

A pair of boots stood by the stairs with packs jammed in the top, a nod to a time when anyone cared about stinky boots.

"Here." Nick nodded to a heavy suede recliner by the window. Charred pockmarks were crusted into the arms, and the cushions had been repaired with duct tape more than once, but at least it didn't look like it was going to collapse under its own weight. "Sit down, and I'll see if there's a first-aid kit anywhere."

Gregor limped over and lowered himself gingerly into the chair, mindful of his leg. There was blood on his jeans, a dull brown stain that drooled from his thigh to his knee. It made Nick's stomach clench to think of all the things that could have gone wrong that he couldn't fix. Gregor shouldn't be able to walk to the toilet, never mind wherever they were. If Nick was going to accept monsters and wolves and that empty, ancient space he'd stepped into, he had to assume the normal rules were not applicable in other ways.

"Don't be long," Gregor said. He stretched his leg out in front of him and scowled at it as though it had let him down. "The prophets will still be looking for me. We didn't run that far."

Nick nodded and muttered agreement. He knew Gregor was right. There was no time to waste, but he couldn't help the jar of attraction that stalled him in the doorway. It was stupid. He'd seen the man naked—everything he was interested in sprawled out on a hospital bed—even if he hadn't exactly been at his best.

It didn't matter. There was something about a Gregor who looked rough as fuck in stolen clothes while daylight turned the stubble on his jaw to gold and he shoved the sleeves of his jumper up over corded forearms. It dragged Nick's attention away from everything he should do. His gran had been right—he *was* about as smart as a budgie.

He dragged himself away and went to hunt through the kitchen. It didn't take long. There was a pot, a pan, and a knife that had been sharpened into a sickle moon. Nick was briefly distracted by the coffee-stained topographical maps laid out on the kitchen table. They were marked with red circles and annotated with claims about old graveyards and burial sites. It seemed out of place set against the rest of the farmhouse.

The first-aid kid was red and hung on the back of the door, under a worn-to-fluff waxed jacket and a dangling leash for a missing dog.

Nick tapped the choke chain to make it rattle, and wondered if that was what passed for kinky with... wolves. Or Wolves, maybe. His gran had always said it so you could hear the capital *W*. His brain's brief attempt to detour him into kinky again stalled as he imagined the curl of Gregor's lip.

He flushed again—*fuck sake, focus*—and grabbed the box. It was heavy, and Nick flicked it open as he headed back to Gregor—bandages, painkillers, a bottle of whiskey, and a gun—all the essentials for a farm emergency. Nick grabbed the gun. It was heavy in his hands and somehow eager. He shoved it in a drawer with an empty roll of foil.

"All right," he said as he went back into the main room. "Neck first and who are the prophets and what exactly is going on?"

He reached for the grubby bandage, and Gregor snapped a hand up to catch Nick's wrist. He ignored Nick's attempt to yank his hand free.

"Ask," he said. His voice scraped like gravel in his throat. "I'm not a dog. Or a child."

Nick swallowed. It was a good thing he hadn't made a joke about the dog chain, huh? He relaxed his fingers and stopped trying to twist free.

"I think you already mentioned I had a terrible bedside manner," he said carefully. "Can I...?"

He waited. Finally Gregor let go of his wrist.

The dressing hadn't been changed since it was applied. The surgical tape had peeled up from Gregor's skin, and only the scab of dried blood held it in place. Nick grimaced and muttered apologies as he picked up at the edges, his head dipped close as he tried to make the most of the light through yellowed windows.

"This might hurt," he said. "Ready?"

He didn't wait for an answer. A quick yank peeled the filthy dressing off like a child's plaster. Gregor twitched at the sharp, unexpected pain and narrowed his eyes at Nick in a sour green look of warning.

Nick pretended he didn't notice it as he explored the injury with his fingertips. He remembered the ragged flaps of skin—*the frayed, dry pick of brown nails at his fingers*—and the pressure of blood as it pulsed out. Memory and a row of Copeland's neat stitches was all he had. The bloody, torn injury had knitted itself back together as neatly as a well-darned sock, with just a welt of tender, thin skin to show where it had been. Commas of scar tissue bracketed the sides but nothing like what should have been there.

For some reason, that evidence—a tangible scar that he could explore with his finger—made Nick's head swim more than the monsters.

"It itches," Gregor said.

"Umm, well, I think that the stitches can come out," Nick muttered. He fumbled for the small scissors in the kit. His fingers shook enough that he could barely hook his fingers into them, but once he got to work, they steadied. He could feel the slow beat of Gregor's pulse in his throat, the slight twitch every time the cold metal of the scissors touched him. "My gran used to have all sorts of stories about wolves, that even when they were skinside, they were still wolves," Nick said as he worked. "She said they'd have your throat out as soon as look at you either way."

Gregor made a low, amused sound in his throat. "I'm always a Wolf." He ran his finger up Nick's throat to the hollow of his jaw and paused there. Out of the corner of his eye, Nick could see him watching Nick's face as he said, "If I have you by the throat, you'll enjoy it."

Lust poured down Nick's nerves, from the hollow of his throat down to his ass. He had to stop for a second and bite his lip until the ache of it waned.

"When you get hard, you flush right across here," Gregor said. He lifted his hand and grazed his thumb across Nick's cheekbones and over the bridge of his nose. "It's... easy."

"Don't," Nick said.

Gregor scowled and huffed an exasperated sigh as he took his hand back. "If you were a Wolf, we'd have fucked already."

"If I were a Wolf, I guess I'd know what the prophets were already," Nick said. He pulled the last stitch out of Gregor's neck and stepped back. He had to resist the urge to slap the hand away as Gregor promptly and enthusiastically scratched the welt. "I need to know what's going on."

Needed wasn't the same as wanted. Nick *wanted* to lean into Gregor, to taste that stupidly pretty mouth and rough-edged tongue—a draught of bad decision to take the place of whiskey. The fact that he felt like the still heart of the storm, something Nick could count on, didn't mean he was.

Nick knew that. It was just that he didn't care. It was the end of the world. If that didn't mean you got to make bad decisions, when would you get the chance?

"The hell with it," he muttered and leaned down to slant his mouth over Gregor's in a rough, "give no fucks" kiss.

Chapter Eleven

GREGOR'S LIPS were cold, his tongue was warm, and Nick stayed in control of it for about two seconds. He wanted to laugh as Gregor's growl slid between their lips and he dragged Nick down into his lap. But there was no air left for that as Gregor scruffed the back of Nick's neck and chewed his claim into Nick's mouth.

Bruised lips and the taste of blood weren't usually on Nick's list of kinks. He liked to be in control, he liked to take his time, he liked it to be *nice*—clean sheets, a bottle of wine, languid music on the sound system to set the scene. But rough hands on the back of his neck and a mouth that wanted to *eat him* worked too, apparently. Something hot and electric pulled tightly under his skin and tugged on hidden wires that hooked straight into his balls.

Maybe Gregor was the kink.

"I still want to know what's going on," he muttered between kisses.

Gregor snorted and tilted his head back out of Nick's reach. His lips were wet and shiny with spit, and his eyes dark with an almost bleak hunger. It gave Nick pause for a second. He wasn't the sort of man someone would need that much. There was too much *fucked* inside him from his childhood, and he'd never cared enough to fix it. And it was too late. He'd rather deal with the consequences later than change his mind now.

He wanted this.

"You want to know now?" Gregor asked in a rough, irritated voice. He tightened his fingers around Nick's neck, and heat squirmed down Nick's spine in reaction. It jerked at his cock, and it took Nick a second to find his words under the sticky want of it all.

"Later," he allowed raggedly. "But you need to tell me everything."

Gregor snorted and pulled Nick back down. "I really want to fuck you," he mouthed. His lips were so close to Nick's that they almost touched. "We can talk about the rest later."

Nick cupped Gregor's face in his hands, grazed his thumbs along the high cant of his cheekbones, and kissed him inelegantly. It was all squashed noses, clashed teeth, and tangled tongues. There was no immediate deadline, no knock expected at the door, but that's not how it felt. Nick could feel the chill of it on the back of his neck—the feeling that there was no time to waste.

They moved from the chair to the old sheepskin rug in front of the cold stove in a fumble of tangled legs and still joined lips. It was too bitter to strip naked, so they explored each other under their clothes. Nick traced the long lines of Gregor's back, the taut bands of muscle tighter under his fingers, and added the texture to the image of tanned skin and black ink that he had in his hand. He already knew Gregor was beautiful. He didn't need to see it again to remind him.

Gregor bit sharp, possessive kisses down his throat to his shoulder—the sort of kisses that would leave bruises, even though no one but them would know or care. He grazed his hand along Nick's lean hip, down his leg, and then back up his inner thigh to the aching bulge of his cock.

"I want to see you," Gregor said into the hollow of Nick's throat. He tightened his fingers around Nick's cock, and Nick arched up into the touch. "All of you."

"It's freezing," Nick said. He worked his fingers into the messy tangle of Gregor's hair and cupped his hand around the heavy curve of his skull. "You'll see it drop off."

He felt the sharp tilt of Gregor's smile against his throat. "I'll warm you up."

Nick laughed and used his handful of hair to pull Gregor up for a kiss. "If I have to get naked, so do you."

"You've seen me naked," Gregor pointed out against his lips. "You've seen down to the bone."

He sounded strangely smug about that. Nick snorted, he but squirmed out of his sweater with Gregor's help. The bite of cold on his stomach made him flinch and rethink his situation. But Gregor snatched the sweater off Nick before he could untangle it and pull it back on. He tossed it over his shoulder and leaned down to kiss Nick's shoulder.

"You're so pale," he said. "You're the color of tripe."

That made Nick laugh, a hiccup of amusement that sounded loud in the small, strange living room. He shoved at Gregor's shoulder and twisted his fingers in the heavy, stolen wool. "When you see someone naked for the first time, you're meant to be nice about it."

Gregor shrugged. "If I didn't like what you look like, I wouldn't fuck you. You're still pale as something found under a rock." He dragged his thumb down Nicholas's ribs. There had never been a lot of padding over those, but Nick would admit they looked particularly sharp right then. "And you need to eat more."

He dipped his head down and swiped his tongue around the hard jut of Nick's nipple, a swipe of wet heat that faded to a chill on his skin. Sharp teeth caught the bud and bit down, just hard enough to make Nick gasp as his balls clenched up toward his body in response.

"End of the world diet," Nick said. "I'm going to write a book."

Gregor paused as his mouth found the scar that sliced down Nick's stomach. It was old and faded, a sliver of white tissue slightly indented from the skin around it. Gregor glanced up at Nick from under thick sandy brown lashes.

"You need to take better care of yourself too," he said. "You have too many scars for a doctor."

"That one wasn't on my watch," he said. "My parents died in a car crash. I nearly did too. I had to have heart surgery afterward. That's how Gran got me."

Gregor sat back, his knees braced on either side of Nick's hips. He pulled his stolen sweater over his head, and the gauze taped over the injury on his stomach came with it. Nick couldn't help but stare. The strip of scar tissue that curved down Gregor's flat, tight stomach still had the tender, pink look of fresh skin, but it looked months old, not days. Nick had seen the evidence of how fast Gregor healed. The dryness in his mouth had more to do with the heavy spread of his broad, tanned shoulders and the hard planes of muscle under his tawny skin, defined by shadows and the hard lines of ink.

"Guess we match, then," Gregor said as he brushed his fingers down his stomach.

"If my scar looked like that," Nick said dryly, "Gran would have sued."

They did match, though. Nick didn't get it, but Gregor made him feel... not safe, none of it was safe—but not alone. Considering the way he'd grown up, that was new. What Gregor got out of it, Nick didn't know. Something, though. He hadn't needed to save Nick.

"Come here," Nick said. He hooked his fingers into the waistband of Gregor's jeans and pulled him back down on top of him. "I'm cold, and you said you'd do something about that."

They tangled around each other on the heavy sheepskin rug and ignored the smell of old woodsmoke and wet sheep that had worked into the greasy wool. It took a few clumsy tries to get their jeans off, as they got distracted midtask by a bite to the shoulder or a hard thigh rubbed roughly against an erection.

Nick shivered as he finally kicked the knot of denim and thermals off his ankle. The cold nipped eagerly at his toes and ear tips. He wrapped himself around Gregor to steal his steady, unsappable body heat, hands and mouth busy on freckled shoulders and lean hips, and he protested when Gregor pulled away from him.

His complaint went mute as Gregor propped himself up on one arm to shove damp jeans down lean thighs. His cock was already hard and pointed up away from the still raw-looking scar on his thigh. The head was wet with precome that smeared over the scant hair on Gregor's stomach as he twisted to toss his jeans away.

"So, am I allowed to touch now?" Nick asked.

Gregor shrugged. "You can touch what you like." He glanced down at his cock and raised his eyebrows. "I don't think I need help getting it up."

"Maybe I just want to?" Nick laughed. He ran his finger along the raised vein on the base of Gregor's cock and watched with satisfaction as it twitched. The flicker of surprise on Gregor's face made him stop. "What? Do Wolves not like—"

"Wolves don't... fuss," Gregor faltered as he reached the end of his interruption, the word picked carefully as though there was a ruder one that was more to the point. He paused and bit his lower lip and then pointed out carefully, "You're not a Wolf, though."

Nick supposed he wasn't. He grazed his thumb over the head of Gregor's cock, which was slick and sticky against his skin, and slid his hand down the taut length of it to the heavy swing of his balls. The muscles in Gregor's stomach clenched, and he swore gutturally through gritted teeth.

The blatant hunger was satisfying. Nick squeezed at the base, the pulse of blood hot against his palm, and dragged his hand back up again. He palmed his own cock as it ached. The familiar scrape of his fingers wasn't exactly what it wanted, but it was good enough. He braced his foot against the floor and arched his hips up into his hand.

Heat settled in his balls and rolled out through his body. He bit his lip and... almost....

Before he could chase the immediate gratification of his own hand, Gregor rolled on top of him. Hands and cocks sandwiched between their bodies, Nick chewed the inside of his lip as pleasure pulsed through him like a shock.

"Gregor?"

"I'm still a Wolf," Gregor reminded him. "I like the... fuss... but I want you under me."

He kissed Nick, bit his lip hard enough to bruise, and then hooked an arm under one leg to fold it back to Nick's chest. The taut strain of Nick's thigh, from knee to ass, pulled on something that hooked directly into his dick. It made his nerves fire short, aimless bursts of pain that got confused and turned into pleasure halfway to his balls.

Gregor spat on his hand and worked wet, slippery fingers into Nick's ass. It stung at first—Gregor's fingers too rough and too impatient—but that felt good too. It was half his ass just being easily convinced by his cock that they were having fun, and half the adrenaline kick of a well-worked muscle.

"I won't break," Nick said. He grabbed Gregor's shoulders and dug his fingers into the tense knots of muscle. "Just fuck me. Please?"

Gregor laughed, and Nick felt the sound tremble in his ass. "I thought you liked fuss."

He slicked spit along his cock, his expression oddly intent, and pressed the head against Nick's ass. For a second, ingrained panic clawed its way up through the weight of lust and heat to squawk a breathless reminder in his head. *Condom.* Nick thought about it, even if only for a second, but he didn't want to stop so they could hunt for some dusty strip shoved into the old farmer's drawer ten years before.

Besides, it was the end of the world. The wolf winter had always sounded final enough that Nick supposed he wouldn't have time to regret it if he made a bad roll of the dice.

Gregor pushed slowly into him. He felt even bigger than he looked, hard enough and thick enough to make Nick's hips ache in dull awareness, even as dark bursts of pleasure went off in his balls, heavily and as hot as a fever.

For an odd, brief second, he felt a little put out at his body's sudden departure from habit. Then Gregor finally worked the full length of himself inside Nick and pressed his cock solidly against Nick's prostate, and that little resentment rattled away along with every other thought in Nick's head.

Gregor braced his arm next to Nick's head and smirked down at him.

"Worth skipping the preliminaries?" he checked.

Nick stretched up to kiss him with a quick scrape of lips and stubble. "Ask me when we're done."

Gregor laughed and reached down to grip Nick's ass. He squeezed the lean cheeks as he pulled out and thrust back in. Nick wrapped his legs around Gregor and pressed his heels against his ass to urge him deeper. At the same time, Nick reached down and grabbed his own cock. He dragged on it with each thrust that pushed him down against the rough pelt of the rug. Nick squeezed and twisted, the hard length of it hot against his fingers.

Each time Gregor's cock slid home in Nick's ass, it pushed along his prostate and milked jolts of pleasure out of it. They settled between his hips, raw and restless until he didn't know if he wanted more or he just wanted to come already.

Gregor grabbed Nick's wrists and pinned them over his head against the floor. It left his cock stiff and aching against his stomach, on the knife-edge of orgasm. "You get to come when I say."

"I need…. Gregor, please."

"You need what?" Gregor rasped. He squeezed Nick's wrists tightly enough to hurt. "Say it, Nick. What do you need?"

He didn't want to say it. The truth would splay Nick out in front of Gregor, all his soft bits on display for him to see. Nick never did that. But he *needed* this. If he didn't come soon, it felt as though his brain would melt in the backwash of lust and heat.

"You," he blurted out. "I need you."

Gregor made a smug, pleased noise and shifted position so they lay on their sides on the rug. He rocked his hips against Nick's ass in a slow, controlled fuck and reached over his hip to palm Nick's balls. Then he squeezed and dammed the swell of pleasure.

Son of a bitch.

Nick bit the inside of his cheek and tasted blood. He was almost there. He could feel the pressure of his orgasm just behind Gregor's fingers. It swelled with each slow thrust that filled him, until it ached back up into his spine. He whimpered a raw, desperate noise and reached back to grip Gregor's ass.

Finally Gregor loosened his grip, and Nick came hard enough that the world blurred over as he made a mess of the rug. He felt Gregor come a second later, hips pressed hard against Nick's as he spilled wet and hot inside him.

"Warm enough?" Gregor asked as he nuzzled Nick's shoulder.

Nick laughed and reached back to hook his arm around Gregor's neck. It was still a bad idea, and it was going to end badly, but he didn't care. Not yet.

Chapter Twelve

NICK ROLLED the bloody jeans up and shoved them into the bin. It felt pointless—whoever lived there was long gone and no one expected garbage collection until spring, but he couldn't bring himself to just toss them in the corner of the room. He wiped his hands on a dishtowel with Gregor's blood smeared over a faded picture of a castle and glanced over his shoulder.

The glimpse of a lean, hard ass and inked spine he caught through the doorway made him flush. It was stupid—literally, nothing he hadn't seen before—but it felt different.

"Do all... wolves... heal that fast?" he asked as he looked away and pretended interest in the towel.

"You want to waste an answer on that?" Gregor asked.

Nick tossed the soiled dishcloth in the trash with the jeans and turned around. He leaned back on the counter, his hands braced behind him against the cold porcelain of the old Belfast sink and watched Gregor through the door as he decided if he needed an answer. Part of him—the part that had grazed his fingers over the raised black scars where tattooed skin had dragged together—wanted to know. But there were more pressing issues.

"Prophets," he said instead. "What are they?"

Gregor sat down on the ring-stained coffee table to put his boots on. "Priests. Criminals. The worst of us."

Nick waited. Gregor tied his laces. That was apparently all the answer Gregor thought was needed. He didn't like to talk. The more questions Nick had, the shorter the sentences Gregor would dole out in answer.

"Why do they want you?"

Gregor shrugged without looking up. "They wanted me dead before. I don't know what they want now."

Nick growled under his breath and shoved himself off the sink. Apparently fucking Gregor didn't make him any more pliable.

There were too many cups in the kitchen, and he wanted to throw one at Gregor's head. He paced around the kitchen table and rolled his neck, the pop of vertebra in his neck the only satisfaction he'd gotten in the last hour since he crawled from under Gregor's sprawl.

"My gran had all these stories. *The Wolf Winter, The Run-Away Man, The Wolf Up Over the Wall.*" Others too. His gran never ran out of scary stories. "She said they were all real—wolves that walked like men, gods who would build their halls on our bones, a winter that would never end."

Gregor looked up at him. His eyes were narrowed to green slits. "I'd like to meet your gran."

"I doubt you would. No one ever did," Nick said. "She was a mean old woman, even if she was right about the monsters."

The straight sandy bars of Gregor's eyebrows pinched together in a scowl. "The wolves aren't the monsters."

"She said you'd hunt us like deer, turn cities into killing grounds, and feed our bones to the fens."

"Fenrir," Gregor corrected, his tongue curled around the last syllable. "To Fenrir. Your gran had too many stories to be trusted."

"Where was she wrong?"

Gregor rubbed his jaw. "I wouldn't let them hunt you."

The scratch of laughter in the back of Nick's throat didn't belong. None of it was funny. He pinched the bridge of his nose and swallowed it down. "So, the wolves are going to kill us all in our beds, and the prophets want to stop you." Nick took a deep breath. "I think I might be on the wrong side."

Not really. His tongue still felt scalded from the bitter drink Terry had tried to force into him, and the sight of Len's flayed, mobile face would haunt his nightmares. That didn't mean he was on the right side, though.

"Prophets don't want to stop it either." Gregor stood up and came into the kitchen. He limped. Under the scarred skin, the muscle was still damaged, but somehow he was still graceful. It occurred that he should back away and put the table between them before he got too close. Gregor wasn't human. It was self-preservation to put some distance between them. But by the time that occurred to Nick, Gregor had already cupped a hand around the nape of his neck.

"They just want to be the ones running it. That's what this is all about. When Fenrir comes, he'll expect us to be there to follow him—a pack to run with as he hunts the gods. The prophets will greet him with their monsters instead and whatever lame Wolves are willing to follow their puppet Numitor, and expect Loki's son to fall for their trick." There was contempt in Gregor's voice as he spoke. Then it dropped to a rasp, as possession licked at the edge of his words. "And the only side you're on is mine."

It was, Nick supposed, a bit late to worry about self-preservation. He rested his hands on Gregor's hips and leaned into him.

"What are they doing here, though?" he asked. "It's nowhere."

Gregor snorted. "To humans. The Numitor's territory is north of here, where the Roman legions exiled us as though we were something caught here, not brought along with them. To Wolves, this is the heart of the country. The prophets knew that we'd have to come through here to get home. They laid a trap, and they caught Jack."

"And you," Nick pointed out. He bit his lower lip. "So my friends and I are… what are we? Collateral damage?"

"Yes. That and they need flesh and blood to make their monsters," he said. "They aren't gods. They aren't even the best of the Wolves. Their monsters don't always take."

Gregor sounded confident, but something about that answer felt... weighted to Nick. He tried to shove his doubt away—after all, Gregor would know better than him—but something in his mind dragged it back out to peck at it. It wasn't that Gregor was wrong. Sometimes a corpse was wheeled into Nick's morgue, and the obvious cause of death was a mask for the real cause.

It felt like that—not wrong, just not complete.

"What about Terry, though?" he asked. "He wasn't like Len. And that drink they kept pouring down everyone's throat last night. It was...."

Gregor kissed him before he could finish. His hand tightened around Nick's neck to scruff him, and his mouth slanted roughly over Nick's. Hunger spiked down through Nick's body, straight down to his balls, and all his good intentions went out the window. Nick hooked his fingers in the pockets of the stolen jeans, and he pulled Gregor closer. The weight of Gregor's cock pressed against his stomach, the heat of it almost tangible against Nick's skin.

The taste of acetone and poison that had been scorched into Nick's tongue finally faded. It was replaced by the taste of spit and exhaustion and a hint of blood, of a night spent on the run and in an old shed. Under it all was the musky sharp taste of Gregor.

But just because he couldn't taste the booze anymore didn't mean he didn't remember it. The taste, the burn of it in his nose as he spat it out, the infant snakes that tore at each other in the snow—that was real. If all of it was real, then those vapor-serpents that steamed up off the spilled booze were too.

A jab of pain in his lower lip snapped Nick's focus back to the hard body pressed against his and the scrape of stubble against his cheek.

"Ow," he muttered into Gregor's mouth, his lower lip still caught between sharp teeth.

"I don't share." Gregor released Nick's lip and leaned back. He tapped a finger against Nick's temple. "Not even with what is in here."

Nick grabbed Gregor's wrist and pulled it away from his head. "Trust me. What's in there never goes away. Like it or not." He gave in to a sudden urge and kissed the inside of Gregor's wrist. The skin was fine there, and he felt the pulse jump under his lips. Nick felt smug for a second—whatever Gregor did to Nick, it wasn't one-sided—and then it was buried under guilt as he remembered. "What will the prophets have done to the rest of my team, when they got there and found you gone?"

There was a pause, and then Gregor very gingerly brushed his knuckles across Nick's cheek.

"Nothing I can undo," he said. "But you can help me. They've still got my brother and his Dog."

Nick closed his eyes. The guilt twisted in his stomach like wire, all the sharper because it had taken him so long to even think about anyone but himself. His eyes itched as though he were going to cry, and maybe that would have made him better if he had paid some sort of due. But he'd never been good at crying. There'd never been much point to it in his life.

"Shit," he muttered.

He felt it as Gregor stepped back and left enough space between them for the cold to slip in. "I shouldn't have asked," Gregor said, his voice gone stiff. "This isn't your problem."

Nick sniffed and tasted salt and snot on the back of his tongue. It was too self-indulgent to make him feel better. He opened his eyes and shrugged one shoulder.

"I think at this point it is," he said. "It's not about your brother. It's just that it feels…." He caught the admission behind his teeth. If he hadn't heard Gregor that first night, if he hadn't tried to interfere, if he walked Copeland back instead of going to warn Gregor—that it felt like his fault wasn't something Gregor needed to hear. He swallowed the salt in his throat.

"I guess I liked my colleagues more than I thought," he said. "But I'll help find your brother if I can. I'm not sure how much use I'll be, though. I'm not… I've never been much of a fighter."

He spread his arms as he said that, and his coat flapped open around a lean, bony body. It wasn't that he was unfit—he free-climbed in the gym, he did yoga, he hammered away on the treadmill for a full playlist of angry songs—but he was clearly built for getting away from things and not for standing up to them.

Gregor shrugged. "You're all I've got."

A startled laugh caught in Nick's throat, wadded up there like he'd swallowed a tissue. His sense of humor had taken a turn for the black since this started. Although he had always, as one of his foster parents had bitingly noted, been happy to laugh at a bad thing.

"Fair enough," Nick said. "Where do we start?"

"If I knew, that's where I'd be," Gregor said. "Don't ask stupid questions."

"No such thing as a stupid question," Nick rhymed off out of habit. Although it was usually to reassure some green-gilled young doctor, not to defend himself.

Gregor gave him a scathing look. "You're wrong."

He turned away, started to go through the kitchen cabinets, and unearthed a stash of dry-wizened onions and a damp box of cornflakes where they'd been abandoned. Nick scowled at Gregor's wide, "impervious to his irritation" shoulders. Apparently the "hungry kiss and soft touch" portion of the day was over. Not that Gregor had ever been anything but blunt and to the point, Nick reluctantly reminded himself. It was just easier to tolerate when it was about how much he wanted Nick.

"You know the prophets," he said. "What are they likely to do with him?"

Gregor crouched down to look under the sink. The back of his jeans gaped and flashed a slice of black ink and the shadowy cleft of his ass. Nick flushed and made himself not stare. He flicked through the paperwork that had been abandoned on the table. A letter was sorted in among the maps and lists of archaeological sites. It was from the hospital and urged Mr. Robbie Dewey to schedule his next scan. The way the letter was phrased suggested Dewey wouldn't have good news from his scan.

He knew the name, though. It took him a minute to place it, but then he fished the keys out of his pocket. Robbie Dewey, the nice old man. There was a hook on the wall where the keys went, and Nick hung them up with an odd twitch of satisfaction.

"Nobody knows the prophets. Maybe Da," Gregor said. He rocked back on the balls of his feet and lifted a tray of soup tins from where they'd been shoved. "They're scum. You do what business you need to do with them. Then you move on. Not talk to them."

He dumped the tins on the table. They were mostly tomato from the stripped-down store-brand value labels. The tops were thick enough with dust that it seemed more like the absent farmer's shopping habits and less like panicked winter buys.

"That's why they like their monsters so much," Gregor added. He took the sickle-blade knife from the drawer and stabbed a jagged hole in the top of a tin. "They're the only things in the world that want to be around them."

He drank cold tomato soup from the tin. Nick grimaced and looked away, not sure he was disgusted or just hungry. His stomach growled the answer.

"That doesn't exactly help—" Except it did. Nick caught the rest of the sentence behind his teeth and frowned.

Gregor wiped his mouth on his wrist and asked, "What?"

It wasn't a hard idea to explain, but Nick's mouth didn't want to let the words out. It had been easy, in a way, to accept that the world was exactly as strange as his gran had said. Despite everything—the therapy, the pills, his "she was crazy, you aren't" mantra—he never stopped believing in her. Some things were too ingrained to ever really shift.

To tell someone else that, though? Nick had tried that before, and he could attest that seeing monsters was a lot less upsetting than dealing with people who thought you were mad. The fact that Gregor was a Wolf prince in charge of the snowy Norse end of the world didn't make it any easier. It would just sting more if he looked Nick askance and moved sharp implements out of his reach.

"Spit it out," Gregor snapped.

"Girvan," Nick blurted out. "When we went there the other day, half the town was deserted. They'd all moved into the hospital."

Gregor looked dubious. "Makes sense. It's getting colder, so food will start running out soon."

"Except they wouldn't even let us in through the door to talk to them. It was weird. They were all just off. And Terry Muir was there. He's the one who came to the trailer park last night to convince Jepson to let him take you."

Gregor shook his head. "If there was a prophet there, I would have known, and they could have followed me into the Wild. Some of them, anyhow."

"Terry's son is dying," Nick said and then corrected himself. "Was dying. I saw him when we were triaging the evacuation, and I saw him yesterday. He wasn't sick anymore, or at least not in the same way. What if the prophets told Terry they could heal his son if he helped them?"

"They can't."

"What if they lied?" Nick asked. "That monster last night? His face was torn half off. He should have died from blood loss or been insensible with the pain. Instead he was up and running around. If the prophets showed Terry something like that and then told him they could do the same for his son...."

Gregor was a man who scowled a lot. It made his rare smiles look sweeter, but it also stole some of the impact from his glowers when it was his resting expression. This expression was different. There was a real, dark bleakness in the twist of his mouth.

"For the boy's sake, I hope you're wrong."

GREGOR BRACED his hands against the hood of the Land Rover and his boot against the old stone wall. The muscles clenched across his back as he pushed, and the wool of his sweater pulled tight on the shoulders.

The engine screamed under the dented hood as Nick hit the gas, one hand on the wheel and the other white-knuckled around the loose gear shift as he held it in reverse. He could smell the hot metal and burned oil as the car bucked and skewed backward.

He took his eyes off Gregor for a second and glanced over his shoulder. Through the grubby back window he saw snow spin off the tires, all white to start with and then stained with brown as the rubber reached the mud.

It inched back reluctantly, the mud and snow under it stirred into a soup until the back wheels hit the hard-packed tarmac of the yard. It lurched abruptly and Nick cursed in panic as his brain went blank on what to do next.

"Brake," he blurted at himself after a second. "Take your foot off the gas."

He did both a second too late, and the back fender of the Land Rover cracked into the wall of the stone byre where they spent the night. The impact jolted him backward, and he just about stopped himself from breaking his neck on the headrest.

"Shit." He pushed himself back and rubbed his wrists. The windshield was covered with mulch and frost. Nick needed both hands to roll down the side window. It wobbled down halfway and jammed. Nick stuck his head out and winced at the sight of Gregor on his knees in the snow. "Sorry. Are you alright?"

Gregor took a second and then grunted, "Fine." But he moved as though he hurt as he pushed himself to his feet. With one hand pressed to his stomach, he took a breath, brushed the snow off his knees, and got into the car. "Do you know where we're going?"

"Yes," Nick said.

It was mostly true. He knew where to go. The how to get there was a little more dubious. Gregor threw the car into neutral and left the engine running as he scrambled out. In the back of his head Nick tried to work out how strong that made Gregor. Obviously he wasn't Superman strong or he could have just picked up the car, but to push a Land Rover—an old one that was all metal and weight—out of the mud was still impressive.

The loot they'd cleared out of the old farmhouse was stacked up on the doorstep. Nick felt guilt nip at him for the theft, but they had need, and the farmer wasn't there. Hadn't been there, in fact, for a while. Once it was all over, if the Wolves or the prophets didn't eat them all in their beds, maybe he could pay the man back.

There was a moldy box full of scavenged staples from the kitchen, tins of cheap soup, bags of oats, a tin of Spam that reminded Nick, again, of his gran. No one ever ate Spam. It was just there in the cupboard forever. Nick had also emptied the dryer of sheets and old blankets and shoved the first-aid kit in too. Gregor seemed confident that Jack wouldn't have been hurt, but Nick wasn't as sure.

The gun was a heavy weight in his pocket. He didn't know why he took it. If it came to a fight, he was more likely to shoot himself than someone else.

He yanked the back of the Land Rover open and tossed in the first roll of sheets. Gregor limped over, favoring his injured leg, and grabbed the box of food.

"When we get there, stay out of the way," he told Nick. "You get in the way, and it will only slow me down."

"Trust me, I have no desire to get into a fight with anything like Len," he said.

Gregor snorted at him as he turned to shove the food into the back. "Len hadn't even fully changed. The monsters are much—"

He stopped and stared over Nick's shoulder. After everything that Gregor took in his stride, it was daunting to see his face blanch with shock. Nick stiffened and the crawl at the back of his neck came back. He hugged the blanket he was holding.

"What?" he hissed.

Gregor blinked, and his face tightened. He grabbed the roll of wool in Nick's grip and tossed it in the car.

"Get in the car."

"Is it the dead woman again?" Nick asked, his throat tight. "The dried-out one that came with you that night."

Gregor glanced away from whatever it was that had surprised him and gave Nick a sharp look. "Your gran had her secrets, didn't she?" he said. "Get in the car."

He backed around the side of the Land Rover, his attention focused on whatever it was, and slowly opened the door. Nick swore under his breath and made himself look. It was a pig. A big, pink sow the size of a smart car, but a pig.

It should have been a relief, a slightly cruel prank by Gregor. But Gregor didn't seem like a prankster. Nick looked past the pig and followed her tracks back toward the hill. He saw the piglets first, quick, hairy, and striped black as they trotted along the rut broken by their mother. Behind them a huge gray boar made of grease and smoke followed them down. It moved heavily, all thick muscle and effort, but it ghosted along on top of the snow without breaking the crust. If the sow was the size of a smart car, the boar could have shouldered the Land Rover off the road.

"Holy crap." Adrenaline hit him like a slap and jolted him into motion. He flinched as he slammed the trunk with a heavy thud and scrambled around the side to climb into the car. Gregor grabbed him by the collar and hauled him in when his foot slipped.

"Don't shit yourself," Gregor said. "Just drive."

Nick slammed the door and struggled with the seat belt. A quick glance through the still open window showed the boar had heard him. It turned its big head, tusks bright as bone and stained with blood, and it altered course across the field.

"What the hell is it?" Nick asked as he put the car in first. "What does it want?"

"To get laid, apparently," Gregor said.

The engine hiccupped and stalled. Nick closed his eyes in a brief formless prayer and started it again. That time it caught and rolled forward. Nick kept his eyes trained ahead as he drove through the slush and snow to the gates. Despite his efforts he could see the great shadow of the boar out of the corner of his eye as it approached the low wall. In motion it was pulled apart by the wind, the shape of it blurred at the edges, but the details snapped into place as it stopped at the wall.

It could have walked through it, never mind over it, but it seemed content to watch as Nick slid out onto the road. The rear of the car fishtailed under them as it hit the asphalt, a slow-motion attempt at a skid. It clipped a rock in the shoulder of the road and jolted over it. Nick got it back under control.

His hands were sweaty as he clenched his fingers around the wheel. The boar wasn't as terrible as the dry-peat woman or Len's placid, raw face, but it was somehow more... wrong. It gave Nick the same disoriented fever-dream fear he'd felt when he glimpsed the wide, white emptiness Gregor had dragged them through last night. That sleep-conscious assurance that something was bad news.

"Where the *fuck* did that come from?" he asked in a choked voice as he gave Gregor a quick, panicked look.

"You know that already," Gregor said bluntly. Apparently a boar made of smoke wasn't good enough to waste words on. He checked back over his shoulder and then relaxed into his seat.

Nick took a deep breath. He could taste pork, that fatty grease-thick BBQ smell that coated the tongue.

"Why—" He bit his tongue as Gregor looked at him with "I told you that already" on his face. Nick peeled one hand off the wheel and scrubbed it dry against his jeans. A scathing, well-enunciated retort was piecing itself together in his head, the sort of icily blistering remark that had earned him the reputation for being reserved. It dried out on the way to becoming actual words, and what came out was a distillation of exhaustion, frustration, and trauma. "Fuck off. What was that?"

Gregor laughed roughly and reached over to casually grip the nape of Nick's neck. Like he was a puppy that needed to be scruffed.

"No one talks to me like that," he said. Nick tensed, brought his shoulders up and tightened his hands as he waited for Gregor's fingers to dig in. They didn't. Gregor just cupped the back of Nick's head, his hand warm against the exposed skin between hair and collar. It steadied Nick more than it should. "That shouldn't be here. Not yet. There should be an order to things, and this is not how it was laid out. First the winter, then the Wild."

That just raised more questions. Nick didn't ask them because he had a feeling the answers would just make him feel worse.

"Is it going to chase us?" he asked. "Because that's not the cause of death I want written on my autopsy."

"He has a sow and a sounder," Gregor said. "His only interest in us is that we were on his ground."

That was something, Nick supposed. He tightened his grip on the wheel and leaned forward to scan through the scored windshield for signposts. All he could see were torn cardboard signs for a Christmas Market in Ayr. To distract himself he cleared his throat and tried a new line of questions with Gregor.

"If your brother is in Girvan, how are we going to get into the hospital?" he asked. "The locals have the place all locked up, and they aren't letting anyone in."

Gregor flexed his fingers and pressed down on the corded tendons that ran down into Nick's shoulder. His voice dropped down to a low rasp. "I don't need them to let me do anything."

Chapter Thirteen

THE REEK of the prophets' half-made monsters hung over the small town like a fog. It didn't have the puke-sour potency that Gregor remembered from Durham. That stink bit down into his bones until he couldn't think past the desire to rip the source of it apart. Here it was an off-putting perfume that fell with the snow and thickened in unexpected pockets around corners. It sickened his gut like gone-off meat and scraped his nerves until he wanted to bite someone just to get it over with.

He hacked out a cough and spat into a grubby patch of snow. "Do you smell that?" he asked. Out of the corner of his eye, he saw Nick pause, wipe his nose, and sniff the air.

"No," he said uncertainly. After a moment he sniffed again and changed his answer. "Maybe. It smells like a... fish tank, maybe? Fetid water and algae."

That wasn't what it smelled like to Gregor. The only thing he'd ever encountered that came close to that stench was a doe he'd cut open to reveal the fawn already rotted inside her. A bubble of rancid gas had burst with a pass of his knife.

"With that nose you'd think you'd have a better sense of smell," he said.

Nick gave him an affronted look and rubbed his beak of a nose defensively. "I slice into the dead," he said. "A too-sensitive nose isn't necessarily an advantage."

The stolen Land Rover was parked in the damp shadows under the old stone railway bridge. Frost crawled up the brickwork, smeared over scrawls of faded profanity, and picked the mortar out from the cracks. Across a scrubby field, clumps of nettles and spears of thistles were half-buried in snow, and the glass and wood sprawl of the hotel squatted. Overhead the sky was dry and raw-looking, bruised red with the promise of a brutal storm.

Gregor stood at the edge of the tunnel and watched the building. They were too far away for even a wolf's hearing to pick up much, but when he touched the Wild it felt... still, the way it got when there was nothing hot and alive to rile it.

"I thought you said the whole town had holed up in there?" Gregor said.

"Most of them." Nick cupped his hands in front of his mouth and breathed on his fingers. His heavy coat and the thick layers that thickened his thin frame weren't enough to insulate him against the cold—not when he was still. "The ones who stayed. You can't see anything from here."

"No," Gregor agreed. "*You* can't."

The snort that answered him made Gregor's mouth tilt in a brief tight smile. He could give the casual disrespect a pass since Nick wasn't a Wolf or even a Dog, and without the need to snarl, Gregor discovered he enjoyed it. It felt like the sort of easy warmth that Jack usually claimed for his own.

"You should stay here," he said.

Nick shoved his hands into his pockets and hunched his shoulders. His narrow face—pretty again, now that it was mobile—set in a frown.

"What if your brother's injured?" he asked. "He might need a doctor. I should come."

Gregor nearly choked on the growl that rattled up into his throat. The thought of Nick at Jack's bedside, all worry and soft, dark eyes for the better brother, put his hackles up. Jack had enough. He could put himself back together.

"He's a Wolf. He doesn't need your help."

"You did."

Gregor sneered his opinion. Even missing his wolf, he would have healed without stitches and bleach for his wounds. A low, brutally honest voice in his brain said, "Maybe." He remembered the dark woman Nick had talked about, although she hadn't looked like a corpse to him. It had been dark eyes, eager hands, and promises that the pinched lips never actually said.

You can go deeper into the Wild, you know. Come with me. I'll show you. Show you things he *will never see.*

It was rude hands on him and a worried Scottish voice blabbering in his ear that distracted him from her cozening.

"I'm not staying here on my own," Nick said. "I can help. I'm not helpless."

He was, but Gregor still knew he was going to give in. It was the soft crack in Nick's voice, the very small flash of fear. He didn't want to be alone, and Gregor could understand that better than anyone else.

"If you get hurt," Gregor warned him. "I'm not carrying you again. You can crawl."

The gruff warning made Nick's face go solemn. He pressed his lips together in a determined line and nodded his acceptance. Gregor sighed and gave up. He caught Nick's wrist and tugged him into a cold, wet-lipped kiss. It took a startled second, and then Nick leaned into him and tangled one hand in Gregor's sweater.

It was nothing he ever wanted before, but it was what he wanted now.

Not *all* he wanted.

"I won't leave you," he rasped out. His lips bumped against Nick's as he spoke. He slid his hand up into the unruly tousle of Nick's hair and pressed their foreheads together. "You'll like my brother. He's good at being liked."

Nick exhaled, his breath warm against Gregor's mouth. "We don't even know he's in there," he warned reluctantly. "It was a hunch."

"He is." Gregor didn't know that he knew until he spoke. Maybe it was the Wild. Maybe it was some thread of the bond they'd tried to sever since the moment they became aware of the other floating in their mother's womb. The knowledge that Jack was *here* settled in his gut like an anchor. "If we get in trouble, don't shoot me."

Nick gave a shaky laugh and reached down to gingerly pat his pocket. "I'm more likely to shoot me."

"If you need to," Gregor said. He touched the bruise that stained Nick's jaw, smeared like jam under the stubble. "Death is clean enough."

Nick's mouth twitched. "Gran said otherwise. She said death left you naked in the dark for the monsters to get."

"Your gran was a bitch," Gregor said flatly. He had a brother to save and enough to be angry about. There wasn't time to hate an old woman who'd terrorized a child, but he did anyhow. "And just because she knew some things doesn't mean she knew everything."

Nick looked dubious but let it go.

They took the long way across the field to avoid being moving targets on a white sheet and hugged close to the hedgerow and fences. The sudden rumble that vibrated through the ground rattled the branches hard enough to dislodge clumps of snow. They exploded as they hit the ground in puffs of dry powder.

Gregor looked around sharply and reached for his wolf before he remembered. It still hurt with a phantom pain like a broken tooth. He cursed and blinked red out of his vision.

"It's the train," Nick said. He pointed up at the bridge as the heavy rust-colored engine rattled across it. Unmarked cars were strung along behind it with fresh weld marks on their sides. "Twice a month it goes through here, stops here, but the men on it won't say where it's going or what's on it. They won't let anyone on it either. Jepson tried to convince them to take some evacuees down...."

The mention of the woman made Nick smell like guilt. He grimaced and stared at the train as he finished the sentence. "They threatened to shoot people. She said they meant it."

"Humans," Gregor said. "You're like squirrels, stealing from each other's hoard ahead of the winter."

"Wolves," Nick shot back. "You try to create an army of monsters ahead of the winter."

Gregor laughed softly, his breath foggy as it puffed out of his lips. It was a fair point. He took one last look at the train as it rattled along, an endless, segmented thing, and wondered where it was going that people thought would be safe from the winter.

They were wrong, of course, but maybe it would be safe enough for Nick. He was clever and braver than made any sense for someone so breakable, but he had already started to shiver and hop from foot to foot in the cold.

"How are you going to find him, your brother?" Nick asked as they started to walk again.

Smell him out had been the plan. His nose wasn't as sensitive in this skin, but he could still smell his own blood, or he could without the stench of the monsters smeared all over everything like plague shit.

"I don't know," Gregor growled. He didn't like plans. That was what Dogs were for. But he suddenly felt unprepared and nervous. It was as though the human was seeping into where the wolf's surety had lived, and it pissed him off. "Improvise."

Nick started to say something and then stopped. When Gregor turned to scowl at him, he shrugged.

"I haven't got any better ideas," he said. "Improvise it is."

The wind started to pick up as they approached the building. It whistled around their ears, cold enough to nip at the lobes, and shoved at their backs as though it were eager to trip them. Overhead, the dour red-bruised clouds roiled.

"Is this… normal?" Nick asked. He stumbled over the question, as though he were still scared to admit out loud that he knew it wasn't.

Gregor cursed as the wind wrapped around him and jabbed at his eyes. He ducked his head down into his collar and reached back to grab Nick's sleeve to pull him along.

"Whatever the prophets are doing, it's drawn down the Wild." He wasn't sure that Nick could even hear him as the wind ripped the words from his lips as though they were meant to be secret. "And now they've made it pay attention."

He felt more than heard the question as Nick pressed close to him. "Is it mad at them or at us?"

Gregor shrugged. "If ants crawl on you, are you mad at the one that bit you? Or do you just crush them all?"

The wind battered against the back of the hospital, rattled the heavy metal shutters dragged down over the window, and banged the heavy blue fire doors in their frames. Gregor pulled Nick over and kicked the doors. The heavy timber and steel locks held, but the frost-blistered wood cracked. When he kicked it again, his heel hammered into the crack, and it shattered.

Gregor pulled the splintered bits of wood away until the hole was large enough to crawl through. Inside the building, the reek of old death, sickness, and cabbage was enough to finally muscle through the stink of monsters.

He waited for Nick to scramble through the hole, splinters caught in his shoulders and hair, and then grabbed his collar to drag him to his feet.

"You're a doctor. You work in a hospital. Where would you put a prisoner?"

Nick spluttered for a second and then blurted out, "Mortuary. I guess? I don't even know if this hospital has one."

Nick muttered and shoved both hands back through his hair as he looked around. The corridor was narrow and white, featureless, and a few feet away from them, it split into three. After a second, Nick shrugged and pointed to the left.

They padded quietly through the hospital, past generic pictures of Scotland and the occasional child's smeared drawing. Other than the howling of the wind, it was silent. There wasn't even the distant sound of footsteps.

"I swear, half the town was here," Nick muttered defensively after a few minutes.

"They're not now," Gregor said. He paused for a second as he sniffed the air. The whole place stank. Misery was worked deep into the brickwork, but this was… different. He ignored Nick's "go straight here" and turned to the left instead.

The sign over the swinging doors read *X-Ray Department*. Gregor ignored Nick's question about where he was going and shoved them open. The air that rushed out was redolent with the smell that had caught his attention, and he finally identified it—old death and fresh dirt. Half the town was there after all. The dead half.

The reception on the other side of the door was sterile in surgical blue and bleach white and full of old corpses. Some had been sat up in chairs—the prophets' flash of mordant humor more than the monsters', Nick assumed—but others were just laid out on the floor or propped up against the walls.

"Jesus," Nick muttered at Gregor's shoulder. It was a small, fervent prayer, and Gregor didn't have the heart to tell him that if anyone had dominion over this sere little room, it was Hela. But maybe on some level he knew. "Why the hell do this?"

"I don't know," Gregor admitted reluctantly. He sneezed to try and snort the smell out of his nose. "Madness?"

He stepped over the dry old corpse laid out like a welcome mat at the door and walked slowly through the reception. His footsteps felt too loud as they echoed off the walls.

Death didn't bother Gregor, the hot spill of blood and the sudden limpness of meat. But the dry, still congregation of corpses the prophets had assembled made him feel… unwelcome. At some point the world should leave the dead be, and most of the corpses— jerky on dry bones in the yellowed rags of their funeral clothes—had been in the ground long enough that they shouldn't have to deal with the living.

"They must have dug up every boneyard in town," he said, baffled. "Why?"

"For the bone fire," Nick said with sharp contempt. "You can't have a bone fire without bones, can you? What would you burn?"

Gregor turned with a snarl ready in his throat. It rattled away to nothing when he saw Nick, iron straight and so white his eyes looked like holes punched in a sheet and so cold his breath didn't fog.

"Fuck off," Gregor snapped as he took a step forward. "Old dead thing."

It wasn't Nick's smile that tucked the corners of his mouth. "Dead Dog, pup prince. Or I'd not have bothered to stir myself for you. Could not have bothered."

Anger flashed through Gregor's discomfort. He had no love for Dogs, the nearly human dregs of the Scottish Pack. They were still pack, though, and their dead weren't jerky for the prophets' appetite.

"If you want burying," he said. "I'll see it done, but I have to get my brother first."

Nick shrugged. "Just old bones now, not even any skin for them to pick," he said. "Don't see it matters where they lie. The living are upstairs." He pointed at the ceiling and then shuddered and hugged himself. "Has it gotten colder in here?" he asked as his teeth chattered.

Gregor grabbed him by the throat and shoved him against the wall. He could feel the panicked pulse of Nick's heart against his palm, see the fear in Nick's eyes as they widened. It was the second time Nick had looked at him like that.

"What was that?"

Nick shoved at him with both hands braced against his shoulders. "What are you talking about? Get off me."

Gregor ducked his head to sniff the hollow of Nick's throat, where the scent caught against the tight skin, the hint of death that always clung to him, along with honey and the musty aroma of old clothes and sweat. He smelled like humanity and Nick. Except something that claimed to be a dog had just crawled inside his skin and then back out again.

"What's upstairs?" he asked.

"I don't know." Nick took a deep breath and let it out carefully. "Gregor. Let go of me now."

There was a tight note in his voice. It sounded like something that might be about to break. Gregor let go and stepped back. He watched as Nick peeled himself off the wall and straightened his coat.

Nick wasn't a Wolf, but there was nothing else he should be. The United Kingdom was the Numitor's territory from John O'Groats to the Cornish border. Even over the bridge there were only muttered rumors of anything but humans and a sense of unwelcome.

Of course this coast was where the Sannock had claimed their last sad patch of territory in the Highlands, where they made their last stand on the rocky shore. Maybe, once they realized they were doomed, they left a few bastards behind for the Wolves to deal with. No one could fault them that, not after the slaughter. It would explain why Nick could see more than he should and why his gran had been such an evil old hag.

"What the hell was that about?" Nick asked. He rubbed his throat and creased the red mark that Gregor had left when he grabbed him. "What happened?"

Tell him or not? Gregor weighed the question for a second and decided it could wait. If there was something upstairs—if the dead Dog had been real—maybe Nick needed to know. Maybe. What good would it do to tell him that he might be one-eighth something that Gregor's people had wiped out?

"Nothing."

Gregor took one last glance at the waiting corpses—less a congregation, he realized, more like a jury—and bundled a protesting Nick out the door. They'd passed the stairs two turns back, so he retraced their steps down the echoing halls.

"Stay here," he told Nick when they reached the bottom of the stairs.

Nick gave him a hard look and snorted. He stayed at Gregor's heels as they climbed the stairs. The step at the top was cracked as though something had hit it, and dark liquid had seeped down into the concrete.

The dead were in the first ward. A row of brutally twisted bodies strapped down to hospital beds. Once upon a time the sheets had been white, but they were stained with blood and worse. The metal frames of the beds were warped and twisted, almost crumpled in some places. The corpses stank but only of rot.

"Is that what happens to them?" Nick asked shakily. "The... the monsters that don't work?"

Gregor didn't know. Perhaps there were roomfuls of twisted dead from there to Durham—whole families dead to make one monster. He clenched his jaw until it ached. The smell of even the dead made him want to tear into something, and he stepped closer to the beds.

Flaps of thick-scabbed skin had grown over the straps used to hold them down, while elsewhere on their bodies it sagged over empty pockets of flesh. Some of them had popped jaws, inflamed muscles swollen and rock-hard under their skin where they'd tried to grow muzzles.

"Maybe they weren't strong enough to change their skins," he said. "Or were strong enough to defy it."

None of the dead monsters were old. Under the twisted muscles and broken bones, they had the fresh skin and clear features of well-fed youth. Most of them couldn't have been far away from adolescence, but they could pass as adult enough to live and die on their own. But the body at the end was different. There was no lying to yourself that it wasn't a child.

The boy barely filled the bed they'd put him in. Unlike the others, he wasn't strapped down, and his body wasn't twisted, so he hadn't given the prophets much time to torment him. Someone had tucked a teddy bear under his bandaged arm. The cream fur was stained with foulness, and the sight nearly choked Gregor with rage.

He leashed it back, crouched down next to the bed, and pressed his hand to the boy's cheek. There was a coat of frost on the pallid skin, as though the winter had taken pity and hurried his death, and it melted under the warmth of Gregor's fingers.

"Wolves don't believe in sin," he said. "I don't know another word for this."

Chapter Fourteen

THE SCAR zipped the boy from clavicle to breastbone. From the thickness of the keloid tissue it had been the access point to the child's heart more than once. This boy hadn't been among the ones Nick had sent away. He was grateful for that, but he probably would have turned him away if he had seen him.

"His heart probably gave out," he said. "He wouldn't have suffered."

Gregor growled. It stuck low in his throat and rattled there. "That's a lie," he said.

"It's comfort," Nick said after a second.

Gregor brushed the boy's hair back from his face with a gentle hand. "He's the one who died. Where's his comfort?"

"Nothing makes the dead better," Nick said. He stepped forward hesitantly, not sure of his welcome, and put a hand on Gregor's shoulder. "Lies are for the living."

"Who would let a prophet do this to their child?" Gregor asked. He took the bear out of the boy's arms and wiped the stains off it. Once it was clean as it could get, he stared at it in his hands. It was a cheap nylon bear with sewn eyes and an unraveled nose. "Who'd think they could buy off their guilt with a toy?"

"Gregor." Nick shifted uncomfortably and glanced around. He didn't know if it was real or just his old paranoia, but the back of his neck itched as though something had its eyes on him. "They were scared and thought this might save him like it saved Terry's son. They did their best."

Gregor tucked the bear back under the child's arm.

"When my daughter was born, we knew she was going to die," he said. "You could smell it on her. She wasn't made right. The prophets wanted to take her away into the Wild and let it have her for meat. I wouldn't let them. She was mine, and I couldn't bear the thought of her dying alone, dying cold when she didn't even know what it was."

"I... I'm sorry," Nick said, caught flat-footed. He had a lot of worn-out platitudes he used for parents. It didn't seem right to use them on someone he cared about.

"She wasn't your daughter."

Nick swallowed the catch in his throat and knelt down next to the bed. He hooked his arm over Gregor's shoulder and leaned into his side.

"Still."

"I buried her high in the stones," Gregor said, "where they'd never find her. I made sure the prophets never touched her, first breath to last. That was the best I could do. Not just hand her to them."

Nick rested his chin on Gregor's shoulder and sighed. "It was your best," he said tiredly. How many of the parents who'd wept over their dead child had turned out to have been the reason for his death? Not his killer, just the reason. "Some people, they do their best, and it just isn't good enough. Whatever they did, he's safe now."

He reached out and drew the blanket up over the boy's face. The melted ice on his cheeks soaked through the thin fabric like tears. After a second, Gregor reached up to ruffle Nick's hair and then shrugged him off.

"Safe or not, it's done," he said. "I can't imagine a Dog crawled back from Hel to tell me to look at dead children."

"What?" Nick asked with a confused frown.

Gregor glanced at him for a second, his jaw set. Then he scowled and shook his head. "Nothing. Come on."

There was a cold spot inside Nick's head. It felt like a condensed ice-cream headache, buried under the folds in the brain stem. He rubbed his forehead— nowhere near the ache, but the closest he could get.

"Wait," he said.

Gregor looked impatient. "If your town comes back—"

"Just," Nick held up his hand. "Wait."

The dead child was easy to cry over—still recognizable as a child—but the monsters had been people too. Nick turned to look at them. People didn't just up and die. There was always a reason, and seven times out of ten, Nick could get in the ballpark before he even opened up the corpse. How many times had he creeped himself out of a Tinder date by diagnosing the likely eventual cause of death?

So what had killed the monsters?

At first glance the gross and inconsistent damage to their anatomy made it impossible to diagnose. Gender in most of them was a coin toss and a stereotype based on hair or nail polish. Some of them had severe dislocations of the joints, others extensive malformations under the skin that he would have assumed were organ ruptures. When he touched one, however, it was bone that had grown spurs under the skin.

"Enough," Gregor rasped. "They're dead. What do they matter now? We need to find Jack and his Dog and get out of here."

"In a minute," Nick said. The one common symptom all the dead bodies shared were the odd patches of localized muscle wastage. It was in different places, on one the forearm, two the upper arm, one stomach. He paused as something awful occurred to him. "I... maybe you're right. We should go."

"I'm always right," Gregor said. His footsteps echoed off the high ceiling as he walked away. Then he stopped. "Nick?"

Nick wanted to turn and go with him. Rescue Gregor's brother. Never see another monster again. Except he'd pretended for years he couldn't see the things in the shadows, and they were still there. Just because he didn't look at something, didn't make it go away.

The girl on the end bed had a sunken injury on her stomach that ran from her ribs to the blade-sharp splay of dislocated hip bones. Thick patches of hair had spread out across the skin, and for a second, Nick thought that maybe this... skin change... had cannibalized muscle to produce the hair. It fit with the rest of the skeletal alterations.

He ran his fingers along the edges of the wound. The skin was slack where the flesh had shrunk away from it, but Nick could still feel the thick whorls of collagen scars under it. It wasn't a particularly unusual scarring pattern, but the context had thrown Nick.

Gregor's hand on his arm made Nick flinch. He looked up and was suddenly aware of the thin, soupy stink of cold-slowed rot. His stomach lurched sharply, and bile scalded up the back of his throat. It filled his sinuses with a sour smell and an acid stink. For a second, he thought he was going to puke over his first corpse since medical school.

"There's no time for this." Gregor yanked on his sleeve impatiently. Ink slid down his forearm and slashed three sharp lines over his wristbone.

Nick thought of the crows fighting over a bit of skin in the road. He'd thought it was Gregor's, but....

"Does your brother have tattoos too?" he asked.

Gregor hesitated, a confused frown notched between his eyebrows, and then nodded. "The same. Neither of us could gain a line the other didn't chase. Why?"

The black line could pass for decomp until you pressed on it. Then it was clearly ink instead of discoloration.

"It's a skin graft," Nick said. His voice sounded far too calm for what he had just said. "They all have them. Based on the necrosis and wastage, whatever the prophets do to make monsters couldn't cope with systemic organ rejection."

"Or the Wild rejected the prophets' corruption," Gregor said. His voice was flat with the sort of careful rage you couldn't let off the leash. "They used my skin for this?"

Nick swallowed. His throat hurt when he did, the bruise from where Gregor had grabbed him tender inside and out. He supposed he should be worried that what he was about to say would set Gregor off again. But he didn't have the room in his brain beside the horror and the fear.

"There's too much skin for that," Nick said. "I think they've...."

The word he wanted to use, sharp and clinical for an autopsy, was harvest. It wasn't something he could say to the victim's brother, but he couldn't think of a kinder word.

Gregor's jaw clenched for a second, horror dark in his eyes, and then he said it himself. "They flayed my brother and stitched him into their monsters. They tried to make their bastard things into some monstrous quilted kin."

His temper snapped as he roared the last word. He grabbed the metal frame of the bed and slung it across the room. The bed hit into the wall with a plaster-rattling crash. Still strapped down to the mattress, the sad corpse of the dead monster flopped limply against the canvas bonds.

The noise made Nick flinch, and it disturbed something else in the hospital. A raw, wet sound somewhere between a howl and a scream echoed off the white, bleached walls. It was joined by a cacophony of other voices. Some of them were still human enough to make words, even if they slurred around the edges.

"Help. Help me."

"It hurts! It hurrrrrts!"

"Dad! Daddy. Please, I'm sorry!"

A door slammed once and then again. Someone yelled. The first voice belled again, wordless and mad. It sounded closer. Gregor turned to look at Nick.

"Do you still think?" he asked bitterly. "That people are doing their best?"

Instead of waiting for an answer, he grabbed Nick and shoved him by the shoulders ahead of him. Nick spluttered out questions as Gregor hustled him down the hall.

"What about your brother?" he asked. "If he's not here, I don't know where else to look."

He twisted around to glance back over his shoulder, even though he wasn't sure he actually wanted to see whatever it was. A shadow of something big and ugly was just visible through the frosted glass on the door behind.

Its dead had given it pause.

"You don't leave a watchdog to keep the corpses from escaping," Gregor said as he yanked Nick to a breathless stop in front of a narrow door with a blank sign mounted next to the jamb. "I'll lead it away. You find my brother."

Gregor pulled the door open, shoved Nick inside, and slammed it in his face as Nick spluttered out protests to the bland Norwegian pine veneer. He grabbed the handle to let himself back out but froze as he heard the door at the end of the hall slam open.

Maybe later he could pretend it was part of Gregor's hasty plan, but right then he knew it was fear that kept him in the room. It cramped in his stomach like a hangover, sour and heavy.

He could hear Gregor's laugh jeer through the door. "Look at you. The prophets made you in their image—ugly and gelded. A fuck-poor copy of a Wolf."

The monster screamed again. Something wet slapped against the ground. It made Nick miss the start of Gregor's taunt. The last few words were all he caught.

"…still a better Wolf than you."

Nick crouched down to squint through the keyhole. At first he couldn't see anything. Then Gregor backed into view. Two long, backward strides, and then he spun and ran. If his leg still hurt, the thing behind him was an effective painkiller.

It lurched past Nick's hiding place on painfully overextended arms and broken clubbed feet. He could only see a slice of it through his peephole, but it was enough. The skin on its arms had split and peeled back from engorged ropes of muscle, so it left slick, bloody stains on the floor as it ran. Its tail was a stubby whip of loose vertebra that rattled off a frayed cord of bloody nerves. It looked like someone had taken a person and clumsily resculpted them into a child's idea of a wolf.

Nick barely had time to take it in, and then it was gone. He realized he was holding his breath and let it out on a ragged huff that misted up the metal of the handle. As terrifying as the dead woman who'd ridden Gregor had been, with her jerky-tough skin and raisin-wizened eyeballs, she'd felt like… an intact thing, not like the horrible haphazard effort someone had made of the monster.

He waited until he was on the verge of just hiding and then cautiously opened the door.

The corridor smelled of old pennies and infection. Nick grimaced and hopped clumsily over the smeared footprint of blood and meat that slid over the tiles. He wiped his mouth on his sleeve and wondered for a weak second if he could just climb out the window.

He glanced up at the tilted "taped shut to keep the chill out" windows in the roof. The straight-line scribble tracks of a bird paced through the snow that covered it. As Nick squinted, a beak stabbed down and pecked the glass. The thick rime of snow cracked and slid enough to reveal the alien white beak and black eye of the bird. The wind tore at its feathers, forcing them out at odd angles and tearing them free. Frost scabbed in the carved lines on its beak and crusted around the lid of its eye.

Nick shuddered at the reminder that anywhere he went he'd be alone with the dry, dead women and the crows, and now he'd have monsters to be afraid of as well. He sidled out from under the crow's creepy regard and then made himself return to the room of the dead.

The beds had been shoved around, slammed into walls, and the dead had been pawed at. Nick felt nearly as guilty as he had when he abandoned Copeland as he picked his way through without stopping to help them. The dead deserved dignity too.

It was easy to follow the monster's bloodstained tracks through the cracked doors and down the corridor. Nick jogged along in fits and starts, nervous that the sound of his feet would mask anything that might try to creep up on him. The steady, hollow shriek of the wind outside had his nerves raw as he waited for the storm to break.

Every now and again he heard the distinct heavy clack of a bird beak on glass or tile overhead.

Two wards he checked had empty bloody beds. One had a handful of children huddled on mattresses laid out on the floor. They had mild, incurious faces—like Len's without the ruin—under bobble hats and pink earmuffs, but they still looked human.

Nick pressed his finger to his lips in a shushing gesture. A little girl mirrored him obediently. When she smiled, there was blood on her teeth. Nick tried not to let his smile curdle as he backed out of the room.

Despite the cold, he had broken out in a sour fear sweat that felt clammy under his sweater. He closed the doors again and shoved a chair in front of them.

"Not creepy at all," he muttered to himself as he dried his hands on the sides of his coat.

Nick took a step forward and then froze as he heard the careful, distinct click of a door pulled shut behind him. A chill ran down his spine like a dozen icy bugs, and he turned around sharply. His coat swung with him and clipped his hip with the weight of the gun. Nick had almost forgotten it. He pulled it out and gripped it in both hands. It felt self-consciously ridiculous to ape some cop he'd seen on TV, but he didn't have a clue how else to hold it.

With the gun pointed nervously in front of his feet, Nick shuffled back down the hall.

It was the puff of fog through the keyhole that gave him away. Whoever it was hadn't thought to hold their breath.

Nick inhaled and shoved the door open.

The thing on the other side made his balls try to crawl back up inside him with fear. He snapped the gun up and pointed it in the general direction of the patchwork lumpy skull. His finger curled around the trigger until he felt the weight of it start to shift.

Then the monster started to cry. It folded its arms up over its head and snotted in fear between its elbows. Nick hesitated. The only thing he'd ever killed had been a rat. Other kids had dared him to hit it with a rock, and after he did, he had nightmares for years. If he shot a sobbing monster he thought it would haunt him for longer.

"G… get back," he stammered.

The thing staggered away from him. "Don't… don't hurt me," it whimpered as it huddled into a corner. "Please, I'll go back to my room."

The orange coat strained over the muscle humped shoulders of the thing, no longer able to close over its chest. Nick took a shaky breath and let the gun drop a couple of inches.

"Did we meet the other day?" he asked in a voice that felt dry and scratchy in his throat. "You're Terry. Officer Muir's son."

The monster… the boy… dropped his arms enough to peer at Nick over his clenched knuckles. His eyes were pale and bloodshot from crying.

"Jimmy," he mumbled. "Are you gonna hurt me?"

The words weren't quite clear. Since the last time Nick had seen him, his upper lip had split completely open. His jaw had been deformed too. The hinge was compromised with two painful-looking swellings.

Abscess, the doctor said. Tusks, the kid who'd heard too many stories whispered.

"I… no. I'd rather not," Nick said. "You?"

Jimmy started to laugh and then glanced at his hands. They were still hands, mostly, but the last joint of each had been replaced by thick curves of something that looked like sharp bone. Jimmy hid them under his elbows.

"No," he muttered. "I won't. I don't wanna hurt anyone. I just wanna go home."

Tears dribbled down his face.

Nick hesitated and then put the gun back in his pocket. "Is there anyone else here?"

"Doc Davies," Jimmy said. His heavy not-quite-simian face twisted miserably. "And the poor man."

The solemnity of his voice reminded Nick that no matter what he looked like, Jimmy still thought he was a little boy. Gregor was right. The only word for this was sin.

"Could you show me where the poor man is?"

Nick steeled himself. He cut open corpses and put his hands inside. He peeled back skulls. He could do this. His hand didn't tremble as he held it out to Jimmy.

"I'm not meant to," Jimmy whispered as he tried not to look at Nick. "Da said that it seems hard, but that the poor man is like Jesus. That he's gotta be hurt, but it'll be over soon and… and then we can let him go."

Nick kept his hand out. "I think maybe you know that's not true," he said. "It's not right is it?"

One last tear ran down Jimmy's face. It dripped off his nose and splattered on the black stripe still on his coat.

"You said I was going to die."

"I thought you were."

"The priest said he could make me better, that he could make us all better. All Da and the others had to do was help him." With the shifting eyes of a kid who thought he was tattling, Jimmy glanced up quickly at Nick's face. "But—I'm not meant to tell. Da said, and the priest said they were sleeping, but all the other kids are dead. All my friends."

"I'm sorry."

Jimmy wiped his face on his sleeve, sniffed, and took Nick's hand. Carefully. Jimmy's palm was warm and dry, rough like a paw.

"I'll show you were the poor man is," he said. "But you can't hurt anyone. Hurting people is bad. That's why Da's a cop, so he can stop people getting hurt."

He said it the same way Nick had told people his gran was kind. You'd been told it, you knew it wasn't true, but you couldn't wrap your head around it being a lie either.

"I don't want to hurt anyone," Nick said. "But we have to hurry. Okay? Before anyone comes back."

Jimmy limped quickly down the corridor. He dragged Nick with him rather than Nick having to follow.

"Da said they'd be gone all day," Jimmy told him. "The priest was real mad they hadn't found the dizzy lady. If they don't have the lady then he doesn't need us."

"Who's the lady?"

Jimmy shook his head without looking around. He pushed open a ward door, and Nick tensed, but behind the swinging plastic, the room was empty. One of the beds had been slept in. There were blood stains on the mattress and mud on the frame, but whoever it had been was gone.

"I'unno. She's just a lady who's dizzy. The priest knows her, but she's hiding from him." Jimmy glanced back quickly over his shoulder and confided in a sharp, angry whisper. "I don't blame her. I'd hide too if he wanted to kiss me."

Nick coughed out a laugh in surprise. "Yeah, me too. From what I've heard."

Two more turns, and then Jimmy stopped in front of a door. He pulled his hand out of Nick's and shuffled back nervously. Behind the wood Nick could hear the sound of misery—wet, labored breathing and the restless, unhappy shifting of bodies in pain.

"The poor man's in there," Jimmy whispered. "With them. Da said I can't go in. He said I shouldn't have to see."

Nick didn't want to see either, but he supposed he couldn't just wait for Gregor to find him.

"That's okay," he said. "Jimmy, when we go, I'll take you with us if you want. Okay?"

Jimmy looked down at his feet. His boots barely covered whatever his body had done to reshape them, and the stitching was blown along the sole. He shook his head.

"No," he said. "Da would be worried. Da…. Da only did this for me."

"Your da did it for himself," Nick said. "It's not your responsibility."

Jimmy just shrugged and backed away. It was always easier to blame yourself than anyone else. Nick let him go. He felt like he should stop him, but he wasn't even sure where he'd take the boy. Or if Gregor's pity for the abandoned dead child would extend to a living, monstrous one.

Chapter Fifteen

NICK CLOSED his eyes and took a deep breath. He tried to find his calm center, the place where his hands didn't shake before he sliced open a corpse and started doing irrevocable things to it. It was gone. The wind had worked its way into his head, a skirling whistle around the inside of his skull, and scattered his concentration like so many leaves.

He opened the door anyhow.

It smelled like death, the distinct odor of an emptied-out body on the slab, but the bodies there still moved and fretted. It would have been better if they'd been monsters, but they still looked like men—broken men, but men. Nick could hear the snap of fracturing muscles, and the distinct pop of a tendon unmoored from its setting in bone. Open wounds lay bare and suppurating on arms and thighs, the ulcerated flesh down near the bone black with slough. The snakes that

Nick had seen in the brew Terry had tried to shove down his throat squirmed like sharp maggots in the exposed meat.

The room was cold. Everywhere was cold, but this felt different. It was sharp enough to freeze the breath between Nick's lips, and he felt it all the way down in his fear. The dead woman, her muddy hair elf-locked with ice and icicles on the tips of her fingers, crawled out from under the bed. She dragged herself up onto her knees, blade-sharp elbows digging into the mattress, and held a finger up to her ragged lips. It wasn't her finger.

Shhhh.

Nick groped for the old talisman. He'd scrubbed Len's blood off it and hung it back around his neck, but it was buried under the layers of coat and wool. While he hunted for it, the dead woman dug her hands into the open wound on one of the monsters and dragged out a handful of the tiny snakes. She squeezed her fingers tightly around them until the scales of pus and blood they'd donned popped and their vaporous innards spilled out.

"Are you the lady they're looking for?" Nick asked in a whisper.

She smiled at him and sucked the snake slime from her fingers. Nick closed his fist around the talisman and squeezed until it hurt. Tetanus would be better than this. The rusty iron cut into his thumb, and the snakes and the dead lady wisped away. All that was left were the monsters and the ice-chill conviction that the rest of the horrors were still there, just out of sight.

Nick kept his hand clenched around the nail and carefully walked down the middle of the ward. He walked slowly and carefully, each footstep as quiet as he could make it. The monsters-to-be in their beds groaned and moved restlessly as he passed them. He wasn't sure if it was because they sensed him or if the dead woman had reached them.

Neither option made him feel any better. He wished, with a sharp, stupid ache, that Gregor were there—not because Gregor wouldn't piss himself if someone made a loud noise, but because Nick just felt better when he was there.

Idiot. There was probably a rule out there in some old wives' tale to never take food from the fey and never fall in love with a wolf.

"Doc. Doc, it hurts," one of the patients slurred out. His head rolled to the side, and he opened his eyes. They sat oddly in the sockets, the light reflected bright and red from one pupil. He looked straight at Nick, but it wasn't Nick he thought he was reaching a begging hand out to. After a second his arm dropped limply and hung over the side of the bed. "I need a drink. Y'don't mind so much…."

Nick mumbled something reassuring, his tone stolen from night-duty nurses—all reassurance and nothing to disturb the patient. He skittered by and reached the door at the end of the ward.

Treatment Room B, the no-nonsense placard declared. Nick rested his fingers on the cold-misted glass and leaned in to listen. Someone muttered on the other side, too softly for him to make out the words. Just the frustrated grumble of someone doing a job they weren't happy about.

Nick took a deep breath, lifted the gun, and pushed the door open.

Gregor hung in a bloody ruin on the wall, all raw meat and neatly incised lines. It was only the wet, labored rattle of his breath that gave away that he was still alive. Horror wrung a shocked, hurt noise out of Nick's chest, and he lurched forward one quick, impulsive step.

"What—"

A bloody hand grabbed his wrist and twisted until there was sharp pop of pain. Nick tried to keep hold of the gun, but his fingers wouldn't cooperate. It dropped to the floor with a sharp rattle, and some distracted part of Nick flinched as he worried that it would go off. A foot kicked him in the back of the knee, and he lurched forward.

It had been a very long time since he got in a fight. He only vaguely remembered the few sweaty panic-driven scraps in corners and empty rooms. The most important lesson had always been not to let them get you on the ground. That was when kicking happened.

Nick flung himself backward into, he guessed, Doc Davies. His shoulder hit somewhere between stomach and hipbone, and they both crashed into the wall. The impact slammed the door and woke the monsters. Groans and wails cut through the noise of the wind. Nick reached out blindly, grabbed the first thing he could reach, and smacked the stapler back blindly into the doctor's face.

The impact rattled a grunt out of him, and Nick scrambled away from them toward the gun. He scooped it up clumsily as he lurched to his feet, his hand numb and hot with pain when he tried to move his fingers.

It was likely a scaphoid fracture, he diagnosed himself as he tried to fumble the gun into his left hand. Before he could hook his finger around the trigger, Davies twisted a hand in his hair and shoved him forward. His face bashed against the wall, and the world smeared gray for a second. He tasted blood in the back of his throat, and dull heat spread across his eyes, which would be black eyes later.

Davies yanked him back again. Nick saw the man on the wall lift his head and struggle to focus glassy green eyes. Not Gregor, Nick realized. In his foggy state, it seemed important—a relief despite his pain. He couldn't put his finger on the difference, but maybe it was something in the set of his jaw or the green of his eyes. It would have helped if Gregor had said they were identical twins.

"Well done, prophet," Jack slurred through scored lips. "You beat up a little man. When my brother gets here, he'll eat your liver."

"I took the boy's wolf," a low, hard voice said. A cold, dreadful fear ran down Nick's back and into his legs and turned them into slush. They threatened to fold under him as he was dragged backward. "He'll find me hard chewing, with no fangs to set to it."

Jack barked out a harsh laugh. "If you think that will stop Gregor, you don't know him," he said. "He'd gnaw his teeth to the gum from spite. The Numitor's sons aren't your meat."

"The Numitor's sons were a bird in the hand." He twisted his fingers in Nick's hair and yanked his head back. His scalp was on fire, and his neck felt like it would snap with another inch. Blood and snot glazed the back of his throat as he looked up at the woman's hard, weathered face. "This is the bird in the bush we needed."

The slash of coral lipstick had been wiped off her mouth, and her hair left to grow iron gray and iron straight from the cheap perm he remembered. It was the cold-cream greasy shadow face he'd only seen at night, full of wicked stories and warnings. Still her, though.

"Gran," he said.

There should have been something else—affection despite everything she'd done to him and anger because of it. All he felt was hollow, the bottom of him knocked out by the shock. It would be all right, he thought dully. Gran would fill him back up with words, the way she had when he was little.

She pinched his chin between her fingers, thumb and index pressed precisely against the bruises smudged onto his jaw. Her teeth were sharp and crooked when she smiled.

"Look at you, how tall you've gotten," she said. There was something like genuine delight in her voice as she spoke. Not love exactly—although Nick remembered when he'd thought it was—but pride, as though he were something she made and it turned out better than she expected. "How long has it been? Twenty years? More. I've been in the Wild. You lose your place."

"Thirty," Nick answered dully. He swallowed the cotton in his throat and tried to think. "Thirty years. I thought you were dead."

She smiled. Her teeth had always been sharp. Nick remembered how she snapped them when the monsters in her stories caught the little boys. They looked sharper now.

"I told the humans when they took you away that I'd get you back," she said. "I told the other prophets that we didn't need the Dog, that you'd find your way back to your granny."

She hooked a hot, bony finger under his collar and pulled out the twisted nail. It dangled—rust, metal, and blood—in front of Nick's nose.

"What was it I always told you? Run home. Run to your Gran, and I'd keep you safe." Gran yanked, and the chain grated against the back of Nick's neck for a second and then snapped. She licked the blood off the point with a pale, swollen tongue. "And isn't that just what you did?"

Nick breathed in cold air and body odor, the smell of the Camay soap he'd always associated with her long gone.

"Gregor was right," he said. Her eyes flared with eagerness for a second, and she leaned in like Gregor might have praise for her. Nick twisted his lips back in a hard grin that he knew, and for once didn't regret, looked the mirror of hers. "You are a bitch."

She recoiled and went white with anger, her weathered skin a grayish beige as it blanched, except for a hot stripe of color that lay across her nose.

"You make this *easy*, boy." She threw him into the wall. Nick hit it hard enough to rattle him and felt the sharp crack of bones giving way under skin. Ribs probably, maybe his shoulder. He'd know once it started to hurt.

While he tried to drag himself back to his feet, Gran shrugged off the shabby duffel-coat she wore.

The skin underneath was leathered and tanned, stitched in close to her body in a patchwork of old flesh and fresh, flayed hide. Nick glanced at the black ink that slashed through a patch on her side and then at Jack. If he used Gregor's body as a template, he could map onto Jack where that patch had come from. It made it more horrible somehow. Gran reached back and dragged the hood up over her face.

Except it wasn't a hood. Nick already knew that, but he'd just hoped that he could lie to himself. No matter how horrible your gran was, you should never see a man's peeled-off face flop down over her eyes. And it wasn't a tidy job. The eyes and nose were gone, just ragged holes cut into the mask, and the mouth hung lax and open as though it wanted to scream.

Gran closed her eyes and took a quick, eager breath. There was something almost sexual in it, the satisfaction in her wet exhale, as though it were sex instead of something so wrong that Nick missed the dead woman and her dried-out eyes.

Fur appeared in thin, mangy patches on Gran's cheeks and spread down her neck. It started out red and then twisted as it hit the seams, sprouting pock-marks of black and tawny. Gran hunched over as her face twisted and reshaped itself into a horror-show mask of a wolf. Rot-hollowed teeth sprouted in her gums, and a dried-out, black ribbon of a tongue filled her mouth.

"Die quickly," Jack rasped his advice in the back-ground. His voice was brutally weary. "Save yourself the pain and me some skin."

Nick shoved himself off the wall and tried to run. He didn't get far. Gran caught him by the shoulders, buried her clawed fingers deep in the muscle, and dragged him back. He smelled her breath—rancid enough to make him gag—and then she sank sharp, filthy teeth into his shoulder and down through the meat until they grated against the bone.

Shock vibrated through Nick like a plucked wire. He opened his mouth to scream but couldn't screw the noise out of his throat. Heat ran down his arm and chest—a flood of red that startled him somehow when he looked down.

He reached back with the arm that still worked and clawed at the alien lines of her twisted face. His nails caught in the stitches that held her skin together and pulled hanks of dry, brittle hair out of her skin. He tried again, and his fingers found the sharp jut of an ear where it stuck through tangled hair.

What big ears you have. Nick choked on a copper-sharp laugh. If he was Red Riding Hood, where was the woodsman? He twisted his fingers around the ear and yanked on it. She snarled with pain, her teeth still buried in him, and the sound rattled through him like a slap. It woke the pain that shock had kept tamped down and it bloomed in a sick heat under his skin.

That time the scream forced its way out of him. He ripped at the ear again, and it tore away from Gran's skull with a wet, crackling noise. Whatever leaked from the wound was cold and viscous as it coated his fingers.

Gran shook him with a short terrier snap of her head and let go. He tried to lunge for the door, but his body just folded under him instead, and the floor came up to meet him. Heat boiled under his skin, and he watched blood spread out across the floor.

"Just let him die," Jack demanded in a scraped voice.

Nick didn't want that. He didn't want to be a monster, but more than that, he didn't want to be dead—not now that he had the horrible feeling it wasn't the end. He got his elbow under him and dragged himself toward the door, through the puddle of his own blood. It was an inch of progress paid for in pain and fever sweat. Nick wiped his face on his arm, and when he looked up, the dead woman was back.

She lay on the floor with her chin between her ragged hands and watched him crawl with bog-colored eyes. Another inch, and she stretched her hand out toward him. Her bug-chewed fingertips beckoned him, and Nick didn't know what scared him more—her or Gran.

"Kill him?" Gran laughed, a staccato hiccup of half barks, and grabbed his ankle to drag him back into the room. "Don't be a fool. He's my own flesh and blood, and just think of all the things I can do with that."

The dead woman slowly drew her hand back, and the world faded out around Nick.

Chapter Sixteen

THE LIMITATIONS of human skin and human bone gnawed at Gregor as he ran full pelt down the hall. If he were a wolf, the fight would be over. In a pack, the prophets' monsters were dangerous, but on their own, they lacked the instinct of how to fight with fangs and claws.

He ignored the flight of cracked stairs and headed for the railing instead. His palms hit the length of curved plastic slid in their own sweat, and then his weight anchored him as he boosted himself up and over.

At least he only looked human.

He hit the ground with a thud and let his legs fold under him to absorb the impact. His leg was good enough—good enough to run, good enough to fight—but he didn't want to push that until he had to. He tucked and rolled on the hard linoleum, the scent-splash of bleach and old acidic puke almost a palate cleanser after the stink of the monster, and scrambled to his feet to take inventory.

His ribs hurt with a pulse of pain on each intake of breath, and his ears still rang from a lucky backhand by a bone-thickened fist that had bounced him off the wall. Worst injured was his pride, but there was no one to see him run from the prophets' clumsy abominations, so that would recover.

Besides, he reminded himself harshly, it wasn't a status fight in front of the Pack, with rank and respect in the pot for the winner. It was a hunt, and only a stupid wolf played fair with something you wanted to kill.

Gregor spat bloody phlegm onto the tiles and jogged to the main doors. He heard the meaty thump of the monster as it crashed into the railings and the sharp metal snap as something cracked, but he didn't look back. The main doors were lashed shut with a padlock and chain, twisted in and around the handles to make a knot of tempered metal as thick as Da's head. It was drawn too tightly to get any purchase on and made well enough to give even Fenrir pause.

Gregor kicked the glass. It fractured with the first kick, and a web of safety-first cracks spread out from the point of contact but held. He kicked it again and again, and the impact jarred up his leg from his heel to his hip. The window crazed and rattled but still held.

That was fine.

Gregor finally glanced over his shoulder. Instead of going over the banister, the monster had crashed through it and brought the section of railing and a rain of shattered concrete down with it. Not that it seemed to care. It rolled to its feet, the metal railings still twisted around it, and shook the gray dust off.

Its lips were torn and rolled back like a sleeve from the raw jut of its gum and bone muzzle, but it still tried to smile with them.

"Kill 'ou, Woof," it slobbered out as it took a clumsy railing-hampered step forward. "Kill 'ou. 'Eh the Dinter is ours. 'Orld, ours."

It almost sounded proud. Gregor laughed at it. "Yours?" He spat on the ground again. "You're not the prophets' adopted get, monster, you're the abortions they'll eat before the gods get home to see the mess they made."

The monster shook its head and splashed strings of clotted slobber up the walls. It lurched forward and nearly tripped on the metal wrapped around it. The raw gape of its muzzle chewed on the words it wanted, but it couldn't get them up. There was only a shard of sanity left in it, and it couldn't muster the concepts to argue.

"Kill 'oo." It fell back and charged him. The sharp ends of the broken railing gouged the floor and tore the linoleum up in long, frilled strips to reveal the concrete underneath.

Gregor braced himself and pulled his lips back in a snarl. The growl in the back of his throat felt strange without the wolf's timbre behind it, but it still satisfied. Wolf or not, he was the Numitor's son, and he would not let a monster beat him.

The monster hit him with bone-cracking force, and he grabbed its flesh-slippery head, his thumbs jammed into the hinges of its jaw. It gnashed its teeth, and the hard bone ridges of its gums ground down on

Gregor's joints. They crashed back into the door, and the already fractured glass bowed under the impact... and held. Gregor tasted his heart sour in his throat for a second, and then the glass finally gave.

Still entangled, the pair of them crashed onto the pavement outside. Chunks of glass ground into the back of Gregor's head and his shoulder blades—not sharp enough to cut but hard enough to bruise. The wind tore at them with hard icy fingers that jabbed into Gregor's ears and made his eyes ache.

The monster, all bare skin and peeled flesh, faltered as the cold hit it. Gregor twisted and got his feet up into the pit of the thing's stomach. He twisted and yanked at it with all his strength. The muscles in his shoulders strained, and he felt a wet, hot pain in his gut as he tossed the thing off him. It hit the ground and skidded over the ice until it crashed into the long stretch of glass wall. The impact jarred a sheet of ice off the window and it splintered down onto the monster.

Gregor rolled over and up in one mostly smooth motion. The full force of the wind hit him hard enough to stagger him. It stripped the breath out of his throat and dragged at his sweater.

"You could kill it for me. You did for Jack." Ghostly pins and needles in the small of his back convinced him the Wild heard him. Apparently it was unimpressed with his demand for equal favor, because the monster pulled itself back to its fight. Snow scabbed on it where it was raw, stained pink as a butcher's freezer. It gaped its mouth open and screamed at him. Fresh bone jutted through its jaw where the skin had scraped off on the ground—a try at tusks. Gregor snorted at the Wild. "Fine. I never needed help to kill."

The monster shook itself. The tangled metal garland rattled like spines, and it charged him again. Gregor turned and ran toward the hump of an abandoned car, half-buried in the snow. His foot landed on a patch of black ice and twisted slickly out from under him. He went down hard in the snow. It was rougher than it looked—all chunks of ice and stone.

Gregor swore under his breath and staggered back to his feet. He'd lost time. A ragged croak of noise made him look around as a huge black bird, white bone beak almost invisible against the snow, stooped down over the monster. The bird canted on the tip of a wing and swept over the monster's back. A sharp jab drilled the bird's beak into the monster's heavy muscled shoulder and came up with a long, thick string of tendon. The monster screamed and twisted around to snap the bird out of the air, but the bird cawed out a laugh at the effort and let the wind toss it away with its prize.

Gregor hopped onto the hood of the car. The cold-stressed metal gave under his weight with a hollow pop. Gregor scrambled up onto the roof and crouched against the snow.

The monster snapped at the air one last time and swung its attention back to Gregor. He grinned, blood high even in this skin, and waited for it to rush him. It lurched up on its back legs and smacked what used to be a hand onto the roof. The bone claws on the tips stabbed through and tore the metal.

Gregor punched it in the face and cracked off a few teeth. Just because. He jumped off the car and onto the monster's back, his feet braced on the twisted metal railings. It thrashed and tried to reach back to get him, but its arms weren't jointed that way anymore. Gregor latched one arm around its throat, grabbed its muzzle with the other—his palm gouged with its ragged teeth—and yanked back.

A pained gargle rattled out of its pulled-tight throat, and then its neck snapped. The big, twisted body went limp and pitched backward. It landed awkwardly, and Gregor found himself pinned under it, the heat of it sickly against him.

The thing wasn't dead yet. It rolled a bloodshot eye at Gregor and snotted blood laboriously out of its nose. Give it time and its body might repair itself, the way it thickened cracked bone and turned fingers into claws. Gregor wasn't going to give it that time. He grabbed one of the railings and snapped it free from where it was welded in place.

On top of him, the monster started to twitch. He stabbed the railing through its throat like a spear and twisted it back out. The monster gave a small sigh and went limp. It smelled dead, of days-old rot and damage. But it was still better than the infected stench that had clung to it before.

Gregor dropped his head back into the snow and lay there for a second. Then the wind slapped an icy spray of snow into his face, and he pushed himself up on his elbows. He shoved the heavy corpse off his leg—the prickle of returned blood flow twitched down his thigh to his knee—and dragged himself to his feet.

The bird swooped down out of the sky. It landed in the snow and walked to the corpse with that peculiar pointed gait and hopped onto an outstretched arm. There was blood smeared on the white of its beak, rubbed into the grooves carved on it.

"Take it, then," Gregor said. He had to quash the urge to feint at the bird, to protect his kill, even though he had no use for the tainted meat. All it was good for was to make him look magnanimous. "Stuff your gullet and call us even."

The bird laughed at him—the sound rolled gleefully in its throat—and Gregor left it to peck. He stalked back toward the hospital on his way to find... who?

It should be Jack, for whatever loyalty blood and hatred earned—or the prophets, whom he owed a tally of pain.

But it was Nick he wanted. Gregor snorted to himself. He'd been in this skin too long. He'd gotten sentimental. Either that or he'd let Nick get more important than a Wolf should let a human get. Rather than find the answer to that, Gregor shook himself into a jog.

THE MONSTERS were gone, the straps unbuckled, and the bloodied beds emptied. There was only one body left in the ward, hung like meat to age on the wall with a knife in its heart.

"Jack."

The word was rough as gravel. Gregor hated his brother. He hated that they shared a face, hated that they moved the same, sounded the same, and yet, somehow, Jack was still better. He hated that Jack still had a wolf. Those were the truths that both of them understood, the foundation of brotherhood.

Hatred was as strong as love, and it left as big a hole when it was gone.

Gregor bolted over the bloody floor to his brother and hesitated, his hands at loose ends in midair as he wondered where to touch first. Strips and rags of skin had been peeled off Jack's body from his shoulders to his thighs, the raw skin underneath barely scabbed. After a second, he hooked an arm around Jack's waist and took his weight as he yanked the spikes out of his hands. Unmoored, Jack's body slumped over Gregor's shoulders. The hard bone jut of the knife jabbed against Gregor's shoulder blade, and blood drooled down his back.

Still warm.

Gregor grunted and manhandled Jack's limp body onto the narrow blue plastic bed at the side of the room. It was an eerie feeling to see yourself dead, how your face would go slack with the absence of you. Gregor licked the back of his hand and held it in front of Jack's mouth. There wasn't even a ghost of a breath to tickle his knuckles. He got the same result when he pressed his fingers roughly up under Jack's stubble-rough jaw.

"Are you this spiteful, brother?" Gregor growled. He wrapped his fingers around the stained bone hilt and braced his free hand against Jack's shoulder. "Would you really rather die than owe your life to me? I know I would, but you're meant to be the better brother."

He wrenched on the knife. The blade had been punched through Jack's breastbone, and it grated on the way out. Gregor had to brace his elbow against Jack's to hold his brother down on the stretcher, and it creaked precariously under the added weight. He finally worked the knife free and threw it into the corner of the room.

A dribble of blood welled out of the wound. That could have just been the pressure of Gregor's weight against Jack's torso. He stepped back, wiped his hand over his mouth, and waited.

"Come on, Jack." He laid his hand on Jack's flayed shoulder and squeezed down on the raw span of muscle. "I'm not done with you yet. What joy will there be in winning, without you there to lose?"

Nothing. Then another weak dribble of blood, as a sluggish heart tried to beat and then tried again. Jack sucked in a breath and opened his eyes. The usual bright green looked dusty, as though whatever the prophets had taken from him had leeched his eyes as well.

Gregor twisted his mouth in a triumphant sneer and went to gloat. Before he could say anything, Jack slung an arm around his neck and dragged him down into a damp, desperate hug. His knuckles dug in under Gregor's ear, and his breath was frantic against his throat.

"My heart hurts."

"You had a knife in it," Gregor said. His back was hunched awkwardly as he tried to preserve the distance between their bodies. "That will leave an itch."

Jack snorted. He didn't let go.

"I knew you weren't dead," Gregor said. "Like it or not, you're my flesh and blood."

It wasn't much, but it was the closest to kindness either of them had ever managed for the other. Jack nodded, his hair greasy against Gregor's cheek, and then finally let go. He slouched back on the narrow mattress and gingerly touched a raw stripe on his stomach.

"More blood, less flesh," he said. "They stripped me for leather. Let it grow back. Stripped me again."

Gregor looked away. It felt unnatural not to take advantage of Jack's weakness, but at the moment, Jack was his ally, not just his rival.

"They took my wolf."

He didn't know why he said it. It wasn't a secret. Any Wolf would know if they got close enough to see the emptiness in him. Maybe he just wanted Jack to be kind. Then he could get back to clean hatred. Of course Jack couldn't even give him that.

"You always have to try and go one better, don't you, Gregor?" Jack said. He pushed himself up on his elbow and stalled, gray and sweaty with the effort. "The prophet—"

"Can wait," Gregor interrupted. "I have to find someone first. My...."

He didn't know if there was a word for it. There would be if they were both human or both Wolves, but they weren't. Jack saved him from the struggle to work out what to say.

"The dark lad," Jack said. "With the nose. He smelled of you."

"Nick. He found you?" Gregor stared at Jack and felt his stomach sink when Jack, his murky eyes oddly hard to read, nodded. When Gregor found Jack, he assumed that Nick was lost somewhere in the hospital, locked safely behind a door. If he wasn't.... Gregor clenched his jaw in frustration. That's what came of getting attached to someone so fragile, human, and *brave*. "Where did he go? To find me?"

It took a moment, but Jack slowly shook his head.

"He went with the prophet," he said. "They knew each other, and... she'd been waiting for him to get here."

She. Gregor absently touched the scar on his throat, the sharp pressure of fangs still clear in his mind.

"How would Nick know a prophet?" Gregor asked. "He's human."

"So is everyone else here," Jack said. He finally dragged himself up and slouched forward with his elbows braced on his naked thighs. Battered hands, fingers still curled in like spider legs as the spike damage healed, hung limp in front of his cock. "Or they were. They made a pact with the prophets, Gregor, and now that debt has been called in. Besides, since when do you care about humans?"

"I don't. I care… I just owe Nick, that's all, and he wouldn't do this." Even as the words left his mouth, he felt doubt. He flicked his tongue over the back of his teeth and remembered the sharp, sour smell of poison on Nick's breath. It had been forced on him, according to Nick, but Gregor hadn't been there to see it. "He helped me. Why would he do that if he worked for the prophets?"

Jack cautiously slid off the bed and onto his feet. His legs trembled under his weight, and the soft scabs around the edges of his injuries cracked and bled.

"Maybe… maybe he didn't want to, Gregor. The people here might have entered into this deal of their own freewill, but they don't have much will left now, free or dearly bought."

The sympathy in Jack's voice put Gregor's hackles up, and he clenched his fists. He wanted to grate it back through Jack's teeth with his knuckles, to deny it was for him. It felt like weakness. It *was* weakness. He'd always known that.

"They had his pack," he said in a harsh voice. "The people he worked with. I should have known the prophets would use that against him. After all, I walked him in here for you, didn't I, and I don't even like you. You just don't expect humans to be loyal."

"No," Jack said. He reached out hesitantly. "Gregor...."

"Enough. He picked a side, and it was the side that had the wits to get out of here," Gregor snapped. "We should follow suit. We still need to take your Dog back from the prophets and get home before Da ends up as a rug."

"Yeah," Jack said slowly. He dropped his hand and then repeated himself in a harsher voice. "Yeah, you're right. What's done is done. I'm still sorry, Gregor."

JACK LEANED his shoulder against the cold metal of the locker for balance as he tried to step into a pair of khakis they'd scavenged from the sad collection of belongings the people of the town had left behind. A long smear of blood stained the chipped green paint.

"...three prophets," he said. "They took Danny, and they stuck me to the wall like a fucking trophy. After they started with the knives, I only have bits and pieces. I don't even know what they wanted."

"Better monsters," Gregor said.

"Words aren't coin," Jack said. "What do you mean?"

Jack went gray as he dragged the trousers up over his raw thighs. Gregor felt an ache in his own leg, where scar tissue darned his skin back together.

They would both need to get their rank re-inked. One of them never could have anything without the other. He didn't look forward to that itch.

"It's a notion."

"Theory," Jack said. "Danny would call it a theory."

He would. So would Nick. Gregor swallowed the pain and buried the thought of Nick down deep—down with his daughter and the name Gregor had told no one he'd given her—where no one would find them.

"The monsters are half-made." Gregor shrugged and leaned back against the wall. He hurt more than he ever had after a fight, and he felt as tired as he'd ever been—that bone-deep weariness where you just wanted to crawl into a den in the stone and lie there until you either slept or died. Grief, his da had called it. "They're a fever-mad mind's idea of a wolf. The skins of the dead give the prophets back their wolves, so what would a Wolf's skin give their monsters?"

Jack dragged a stained gray sweater over his head and shoved the sleeves back. "What did it give them?"

"Death," Gregor said. His anger shouldered his weariness out of the way and crawled under his skin. "They used children, and they left them to die afraid."

"prophets," Jack said. "When you think they can't get any lower, they dig a hole."

"And unearth a corpse," Gregor said. At Jack's curious look, he pointed down the corridor to where the dead waited. He could have shown him, but he felt—on a level that didn't need logic—that they should be left in peace. "They've emptied the grave-yards and brought the corpses here."

Jack squinted and rubbed his forehead with his knuckles. "They were looking for something," he said. "Someone? I heard them send their people out to look for the unhallowed graves of suicides. Why, though? We know they skin our dead, but what good are the human dead to them? The long-dead?"

"Does it matter?" Gregor asked. "We get your Dog, we kill the prophets, and we leave their plot to rot with their monsters."

Jack snarled with frustration and slammed his fist into the locker. The impact dented the metal and nearly knocked Jack off his still-unsteady feet. He managed to catch himself and closed his eyes for a second.

"Find Danny-Dog," he said through clenched teeth. "We have to find him before we can do anything. I don't know where they took him or why. And kill the prophets? Look at us. Your wolf is gutted, and I can hardly stand. The two of us barely survived Durham. Without the Wild we'd both be skinned and Job would have his pick which of us to wear when he killed our da."

Gregor grabbed the collar of his shirt and dragged Jack back onto his feet. He leaned in until they were nose-to-nose, even their freckles reflected across their skin. The green in Jack's eyes sparked resentfully, and he curled his lip.

"The only reason I didn't kill you in Durham is—"

"Because you couldn't."

"—because the Wild chose you to kill the prophets. If you've given up, if you want to sit here and mourn your Dog for dead while he's still up and walking, then what use are you to me or the Wild?"

Jack shoved him. He was still too weak to get his muscle behind it, but Gregor stepped back anyway.

"I haven't given up," Jack said. "I just don't know how to start."

Gregor didn't either.

"Just think," he said. "You're Da's favorite, the one with good sense. Now prove it. What is there for the prophets in this shabby little town, and where would it be?"

"I don't know," Jack yelled. His voice bounced off the bare white walls, a weak effort at an echo. "How the fuck am I supposed to know when the prophets don't even seem to know? Something dead, I guess."

It was the memory of his dead daughter and the first time his da had let him down that gave Gregor the answer. He could remember the smell of heather and the taste of bitterness in his mouth, his daughter's body tiny and twisted in his arms.

"The dead lie where they lie, and that secret stays with me," Da had said. "I wouldn't tell you even if I could, but trust me. That's no place for a wee soul."

"Da would know," Gregor said. He ignored Jack's impatient look. "But he'd never tell, not even the prophets, where these dead are buried. He wouldn't even tell me."

Realization flickered over Jack's face like a light. "The Sannock Dead? No. They wouldn't. We took their lands, their place, and then we found where they had hidden, and we killed the last of them. There's a reason that Da sealed them away in the Wild. Dead they had more ways to hate us than the living. Even the prophets wouldn't be that stupid."

They both knew that was a lie.

"They have the town doing their scut work," Gregor said. "If we find them, we'll find the prophets…

and if the Wild still likes you, maybe it will find you before they find the Sannock."

He gave Jack his shoulder to lean on as they headed out of the hospital. It didn't remind him of Nick, of the bony shoulder under his arm and the careful hands on his back, because he wouldn't let it. Like any other pain, grief was to be endured and forgotten.

The prophets would only get to endure it. He would kill them before they forgot.

Chapter Seventeen

IT DIDN'T hurt anymore. A slow throb of heat and weakness had replaced the raw screech of outraged flesh and bone. Nick wasn't going to complain about that, but it meant he had a chance to gather his wits enough to know it wasn't a good sign.

"Drink," a rough, Ayrshire voice ordered as the cold lip of a bottle was pressed against Nick's lips.

He opened his eyes. The world stayed the pink-tinged black of the back of his eyelids. So maybe he hadn't. Nick tried again, and this time he managed to peel his tear-crusted eyelids apart. Terry Muir glowered down at him, his face pinched and sour under the heavy goggles that hid his eyes.

"Drink," Terry insisted again. He tipped the bottle up so the liquid spilled over Nick's closed lips. It ran up his nose, and he felt the squirm of it in his sinuses. "It will make it easier, Doctor Blake."

There probably wasn't a lot of point in resistance, but Nick twisted his head away.

"Fine. Rot alive, then," Terry said as he shifted back and leaned against the wall of the van. He lifted the bottle and took a swig, wiped his sleeve over his mouth and glared down at Nick. "There. Now it's gone. Remember that when you want to beg."

The snakes nested on the back of his tongue in a ball and wriggled as he talked.

"You... you aren't...." The attempt to talk had been a mistake. It woke up the pain in his torn throat. Nick stopped and closed his eyes for a second and waited for the wave of it to crest. When it did, he gingerly lifted his arm and gestured weakly at himself.

He was laid out on a rough bit of stained tarp in the back of a heavy Jeep that jolted and bounced as it drove... somewhere. Frost furred the inside along the ridges of metal and rivets, and Nick could hear the rattle of hail battering the outside. Someone had bandaged him while he was unconscious. Presumably, if he died too quickly, whatever made him a monster wouldn't happen. But it hadn't done much good. Blood had seeped through the hastily wrapped gauze, dried out into a scab-brown crust, and soaked through again. He could smell it—the sweaty-penny smell of raw flesh cut through with the sweet stink of infection.

"Not yet," Terry said. He sat on the wheel well, his back hunched and his foot braced against Nick to stop him sliding when the Jeep pitched. "They still need me."

"They... will, though, do... it."

Terry ran his finger around the rim of the bottle. He licked the heavy residue off his finger. "I'm counting on it," he said. "That's what my friend promised me. Once they have, once they've fixed the Changed, I'll join them. We'll see this out together, and everyone else can freeze or burn. I don't care. All I care about is my son, and they saved him."

"Did you…." It was hard to talk, hard to do anything. Death, Nick thought, or just whatever Gran had done to him. "… ask him?"

Guilt flushed over Terry's face. He set his jaw and rejected it. "He's a child. He doesn't know what's best for him. I do. They'll fix him, anyhow. They've promised. They'll fix us all. Even if they don't… better to live as a monster than die as a little boy."

Nick could have argued. He'd seen enough bodies come over the table in his morgue to know that sometimes death, however sad, was kinder than what life had held in store, especially now that they knew there was another world laid over theirs, even if it was colder and darker than the afterlife he'd been promised when he still went to the kirk.

Instead he passed out again. Or that's what he assumed when he blinked and opened his eyes again to find that the Jeep had stopped. Disappointment curled through his mind, distant under the pain. Part of him had expected Gregor to save him again, like his personal guardian wolf. He should have known better. At the end of the day, after all the foster parents' and lovers' assurances were done, people had their own backs.

The Jeep's hatch opened to let in the cold, and his gran stood in front of it as she glared at an older man, his faded brown hair thin and tufted around his ears. He'd brought his dog with him, a big, lanky thing that slouched gray and cowed at the end of a stiff leather leash. A too-small muzzle was buckled around its head, tightly enough to mash its nose and crease an ear.

"Then you're a fool, Lewis," Gran was in the middle of telling him bluntly. "And I have no time for fools."

Lewis's already ruddy cheeks darkened. There were no snakes on him, but like Gregor and like Gran, he looked just that little bit more vivid than the background of the world—sharper edged, more vibrant.

Although, Nick supposed giddily as he licked sour sweat off his lips, that could be the fever.

"We have the Made, we have the thralls," Lewis said stiffly. The dog cringed away from him, and he wrenched it viciously back to heel. He wasn't old, not much older than Nick, but gaps flashed in his teeth as he spoke. Nick remembered his gran's teeth, scrubbed and pink in the glass next to her bed. She hadn't been old then either. She wasn't old now, somehow. "We have the dog. Maybe Job was right—"

"Another fool," Gran scoffed. "A dead fool, at that."

"We have weapons. We have the Wild," Lewis protested. "When has a Wolf ever needed more than that?"

Gran drew back and backhanded him across the face. The crack of it made Nick flinch and knocked Lewis to the ground, out of sight of Nick's limited field of vision. He got his elbow under him and pushed himself up, bile sour in his throat as pain ripped at him. It got him a glimpse of Lewis on the ground, sprawled out in the pocked snow as hail bounced off his skin.

The dog bolted away from him, its leash yanked out of surprise-loosened fingers. It was lame on its back leg, the skin raw and blistered looking, but it raced for the tree line. Terry stepped forward, big and bulky in his police gear and a lot less terrifying than the other two. He grabbed for the dog's collar and missed. Then he stamped his foot down and caught the loop end of the leash. The dog's escape was brought to a neck-jerking stop, and it flipped over onto its side in the snow. A flick of Lewis's gloved fingers made Terry back up and drag the dog with him.

"We're prophets," Gran spat. "Wolves spit on us, *piss* on us. Even the Wild looks down on us, favors them over us. We're sentenced to lick the gods' shit-stained feet, while the Numitor pretends he is above such obeisance."

Lewis blotted a split lip on his sleeve. "Above *you*," he muttered, but not low enough. Gran kicked him in the hip, and he yelped and writhed away.

"I hate him *first*. He turned on me. He made me a prophet. Do you think I hate the rest of them less? The prophets have crawled in the gods' shit for years. We're inured to the stink," she said. "If you're not, maybe you've still too much Wolf in you for this game, Lewis."

"No." Lewis scrambled back to his feet and glared at Gran. "I've crawled in as much shit as you, Rose. I'm not squeamish. I just question if it's wise."

"Job was wise, and Job was cunning. He even found out how to make us our monsters," Gran—Rose—rhymed off sarcastically. The idea that she had a name befuddled Nick a bit. He'd been too young, too scared of her when he went into foster care to imagine.

"What did it get him? Wisdom won't get you a crown, Lewis. Power does, and this will get us power enough that I will chew the Numitor's crown out of his skin myself."

She scrambled into the back of the Jeep and grabbed Nick by the bloody collar of his coat. Agony made the world go gray again, his drifting thoughts brutally anchored back in his too-hot, too-damaged body as she dragged him out of his makeshift bed and threw him out into the snow. He screamed. It was an embarrassing display of weakness, but it wasn't the first time. Lewis caught him before he hit the ground and held him up. He dug his fingers into Nick's bloody arms.

"Your own grandchild," he said as he looked at Nick. "It's lucky you're a cold bitch, Rose."

"Do you think it's easy?" Rose asked.

"You killed your daughter to get him," Lewis said. Somewhere down under the pain and the watery distance of fever, Nick clawed at that piece of information. It was important. He could tell. "I don't think you'll lose any sleep."

Gran twisted her hand in Nick's hair and pulled his head back. Her face was hard as she looked at him. Then her mouth twitched. "Then you're an idiot, as well as a weakling. It's not a sacrifice if I don't care," she said. "It will break my heart to ruin him, and that's why this will work. The gods love to watch us debase ourselves, to bleed our dignity for their favor. Now move. We've wasted enough time here already. The winter won't wait."

She yanked on Nick's hair, and he lost his balance and fell, his legs folded awkwardly under him in the snow. Gran just dragged him behind her, snow wedged in his collar and down the back of his jeans. It felt almost good against the dry heat of his skin.

Lewis limped along behind them with Terry and the dog at his heels.

Grass whipped against his face, sharp as knives with the ice layered on it as the wind tore through. Overhead, the new moon shared the sky with the low, fading sun, like an open bracket.

She reached the top of the hill, and Gran grunted as the wind caught her. She leaned into it as it whipped her hair, and she shoved Nick down the other side. He rolled down the slope in a tangle of limp arms and legs and bounced off rough-woven hillocks of grass and deep-buried rocks. Cold, rough hands caught him at the bottom and rolled him over.

"Doctor Blake." Copeland's narrow face swam into focus. Her hair was muddy and matted around her face, and there were bruises on her jaw and temple. The hands that cupped his face were raw and filthy, those neat-stitching fingers scarred and broken-nailed. Her face was battered and dirty, her mouth twisted into an angry line as she looked down at him. "What the hell are you doing, you idiot? You fell."

"Run," he told her, or he tried to at least.

Nick rolled over onto his side and tried to pull himself using Copeland's sleeve for support.

"You're hurt." Copeland peeled his fingers off her arm and shoved him back into the sand. "You need to rest. I can... I can help."

Her face softened as she focused on him. The anger slipped away for a second as a crease of worry pinched her eyebrows together and she bit her chapped lower lip.

"I can help," he repeated in a mutter.

"Leave him be." Gran skidded down the hill and grabbed the collar of Nick's coat. She dragged him onto his knees. "You're here to witness, not minister."

Copeland protested. The "something wrong" of the situation seemed to have seeped into her dazed mind, and she tried to follow as Gran dragged Nick through the audience and across the wet, half-frozen sand. Terry dragged her back, shook her, and shoved a bottle into her hands when that didn't work. She drank and scowled and tossed an angry look after Nick as she faded back into the crowd.

"What's the drink?" Nick asked.

He could hardly hear his voice over the wind and the roar of the sea. It was a mutter in the back of his throat. But Gran heard him. She glanced down and snorted.

"Still nosy," she said and shoved a man with half his arm gone, the stump wrapped and taped into a bag, out of her way. He flinched away from her and then spun to shove someone else in turn. The woman shoved back and yelled, "Fucker," in his face. The rage brewed almost tangibly between them, the anger in their words as empty and vicious as the storm. Gran ignored them. "That's your problem, boy. How many times did I tell you, the smartest farm animal is a pig, and do you think that makes it happier when it's loaded for slaughter?"

Nick coughed out blood and a mad little laugh. "Didn't realize you meant slaughter literally."

She threw him down on the sand, looked up at the sky, and shoved him around with her foot until he faced the sea and the moon was behind him.

"The bitch is blind tonight," Gran told him. "Sometimes she'll squint, and we don't want her to see this."

She stepped back and stripped off her clothes to reveal weathered brown skin with raised scars of bluish tissue, as though someone had tried to score out tattoos a long time ago. Nick looked away—stupid, he supposed, he didn't think he was going to have time to form an emotional scar—and watched the ocean. It was half-frozen as it rolled up onto the shore and jumbled slush and dead fish on the sand.

"It's just a drink," Gran said. He jerked his attention back to her in surprise. She tilted a dented silver flask his way and took a drink of it. Her eyes closed as she let it slide down her throat. "A drug that makes you... not mind so much."

"It's not. I saw the snakes."

She snapped her eyes open and gave him a startled look. Something that might have been doubt—in someone other than his gran—flashed through her yellow eyes and then was shoved toward satisfaction instead.

"It's true and it's not. It's both. The gods gave it to the prophets as payment once, when we had humiliated ourselves for them past all expectations. They say it was milked from the venom-blisters on Loki's face, half poison and half some strange new offspring of the Trickster. It can help a Wolf see farther, deeper." She glanced around at the audience. The scattered crowd had been urged in as she spoke and now huddled in a circle around them. Most of them were still human, with burned lips and dreamy eyes, but a few of the monsters squatted clumsily on the sand and watched

Gran with empty, adoring expressions. "They get into a human's heart and eat all the bits that care about things. They turn the weeping pigs into angry cattle, and then I turn them into monsters. It doesn't always work. Some of them have things hooked too deep in their hearts to budge, but in most, the Change takes... easier."

"I'll drink it now," Nick promised, his voice cracked and... it didn't feel like he was crying, but he could taste his own tears. "I promise, Gran, I promise I'll take my medicine."

"Too late," she said. "You'll need to mind this. That's part of it."

She stepped back. Her bare feet sank into the sand as she walked, almost to the ankles. She stared up at the sky for a second, spat, and gave the moon the finger.

"Let's get this over with," she said and crooked her fingers impatiently. "Bring her over."

Jepson was too stubborn to scream. She struggled the whole way over, but it didn't do much good. Lewis just dragged her by the elbow, her hands lashed behind her back, and kicked her feet out from under her to put her on her knees in front of Gran.

The dog started to bark frantically, half-throttled sounds as it twisted the end of its tether. Terry had to grip it with both hands and drag it backward. It stood on its back legs, nearly as tall as Terry as it thrashed.

"You—"

It was the same bone-handled knife that Nick remembered from his childhood, the same "no wasted motion" slice of his gran's hand. Jepson's voice faded into a shocked gargle as blood spilled down her chest.

"She has to mind too," Gran said. She kicked Jepson over on top of Nick to bleed out on him. He stared into her brown eyes and mouthed frantic apologies as she coughed her life into his shoulder. It didn't take long. Gran was good with a knife. "Open your mouth."

Nick knew he shouldn't. Defiance was all he had, but he really wanted to not mind what had just happened. If his gran had taken pity on him, he'd take it. He opened his mouth, and a cough caught in his throat as the cold hit and Gran fed him a handful of black feathers and sharp bones.

He choked and spat, but she shoved them down his throat with hard fingers. He retched up bile, but she clamped his mouth shut and pinched his nose between her fingers.

"Be a good boy, Nicholas," she crooned to him. Gran hadn't been kind often, so he remembered when she was. "Hurry up and die."

Chapter Eighteen

IT WASN'T cold. Nick stood on warm, dry sand in his bare feet with the dead woman and watched the tide come in. Even here it was Scotland, and the water looked gray and cold.

"I was scared of you," he said.

She knew that, he supposed, but she didn't seem to hold it against him.

"Am I dead?"

In the back of his head, Nick heard Gregor grunt, "Stupid question." He felt a jab of pain at the thought and rubbed his shoulder. He would have liked to—he didn't know actually—say goodbye, maybe, or at least see him again.

He sat down in the sand. It was more sand than shale, the grains like powdered sugar when he dug his fingers into it.

"This is going to go to shit in a minute, isn't it?"

The dead woman just stared out to sea. Nick took that as a confirmation. He supposed he wasn't surprised.

"Are you my mum?" He sniffed back a salty clot of snot and tears and looked up at her. Death stripped away all the individuality from a face, blunted the nose and thinned the cheeks. Nick didn't know what his mother had looked like. He hadn't realized it still mattered to him, now that he was a grown man instead of a little boy. "Is that why you're with me?"

The dead woman brushed her dry hand over his cheek and then walked away from the shore. Her feet left no tracks in the sand. Nick tried to follow her, but he couldn't. A leash he couldn't feel tethered him to the spot—the bloody spot. Red seeped up through the grains of sand. It coated his feet despite his attempts to avoid it. He looked up in time to see the dead woman crawl into the dunes and pull the sand down over her just as a black-cross shadow swept over the sere grasses. The raven screeched, white beak wide to show a split tongue, and flipped its wings back as it dove toward Nick.

He choked on a mouthful of spit and bones, black pin-feathers dusty and hard on his tongue. It did no good to spit. More just filled his throat. He clawed at the mass in his mouth with hooked fingers to try and clear them. The raven hit him before he could and knocked him back into the raw red pain.

JEPSON'S BODY was still warm on top of him, a coat of ice already formed over her pupils like cataracts. The blind gaze felt like an accusation. Nick coughed and squirmed under her weight. It wasn't fair.

How many times did he have to die? The dog hadn't stopped barking, but it sounded hoarse and exhausted.

"I told you," Gran snapped to Lewis. "The boy just needed a minute."

They grabbed Jepson by the feet and dragged her corpse off him. Gran left Lewis to that and crouched down next to Nick. She cupped his face and turned it toward her. She was still naked, with hail in her hair and half-melted on her shoulders, but she barely seemed to notice the cold.

Something about the scene tickled some strange dark weight that settled in Nick's mind. It wedged a snigger into his throat that he couldn't understand.

"Where are the dead?" Gran asked.

The laugh escaped Nick. "Look around," he said. "Look behind you. The dead aren't hard to find."

She tightened her grip and pressed her thumbs down hard on his cheekbones. Her eyes were sharp and unamused. Maybe she didn't get the joke. Nick supposed he didn't either, but the dark thing in his head wriggled in delight at it.

It wasn't something new. Nick had always felt that black cackle in the back of his head, the bleak humor that laughed at bad things. It had just moved to the forefront.

Gran gave his chin a rough shake to focus him.

"Not the new dead, not the winter dead," she said. "I want the salted dead, the slain dead."

Nick didn't know what she meant. Apparently his mouth did, though, and the cackle answered for him. "The Sannock Dead."

He saw them as he said it, corpses on the shore—not quite human, not quite other—blood on the stones, and meat in the pot. The cackle felt nothing, but Nick's throat ached with pity.

A mirthless smile folded Gran's mouth, and she gave Lewis a triumphant look. "Yes. I need their skins, boy, so I can stitch their power into my people. I need the bitch that killed him so I can drink her down. Where are they?"

"Look where you left them."

That pinched the smile off Gran's face. She dug her nails into Nick's jaw until the skin split. That was the first thing that the cackle didn't find funny. It flinched and pulled itself back into the folds of Nick's brain, like a snail into a shell.

"We have dug up every graveyard and burial site, every holy place and haunted hollow," she snapped. "Our thralls have worked their skin raw to dig up all the dry old bones on the coast. Our monsters dulled their bones as they pulled out old stones. None of them were Sannock. None of them were wolves."

Nick writhed in distress. His body felt pulled apart, strung together by tender nerves and heat. Sand grated against the raw meat of his shoulder, worked down under the folds of the bandage, and it felt like Gran's fingers scraped his jawbone. The thing in his head squirmed deeper into his skull, eager to avoid the question, but Nick had nowhere to go. It wasn't his knowledge, but it lived in his brain.

"Where you left them," he repeated. His voice trailed off in a scream as Gran shook him again. "He never moved them. He moved *it*."

Gran sat back. Her iron-gray hair blew around her shoulders, ice matted into the tangles. Her face was blank, and her jaw moved as she had to chew on what he'd said to get it down.

"He never moved them," Lewis parroted Nick incredulously. "All these centuries, all this fucking work, and the bastard left them where they fell?"

"Of course, he did." Gran let go of Nick's jaw. His head dropped into the snow and sand with a crack. It was harder than it looked, wet sand. The bones in his shoulder twisted and jabbed each other under the torn skin as they tried something new. "We thought he'd done something clever, something cunning as a fucking bird, but he'd just swept it under the rug."

"Job was there. He never said."

"Of course he didn't," Gran snapped. "He wanted us to follow him. Why tell us what other options we had? You should have heeded me from the get-go."

Lewis held out her coat. "You won the leadership, Rose. You came back and beat him down in front of us all."

Gran grunted in disgust and pushed herself to her feet. When she turned around, Nick saw the old scars that ran down the backs of her legs, razor straight and raised like varicose veins. They clipped the hollow of her knee and slashed down to her ankles. Someone had tried to hamstring her once but lacked the will to cut deep enough. She dragged the coat on over wiry arms but left it unfastened as she impatiently rolled the cuffs back from her hands.

"Yet he still thought he knew better," she said. "Thought if he couldn't lead the prophets, he could lead the wolves. I should have pinned him to the wall and strung his guts out on a spool. Eventually either the augury or Job would have given in and told me what I needed."

"And you could have spared your grandson," Lewis said.

His voice was low, muttered into the wind. It made it hard to tell if he was being sympathetic or cruel. Nick felt his lungs crackle as he tried to breathe in ice-cold air. The world around him was a blur of real, not, and don't know anymore, and his head was heavy with something sullen and unhelpful. He voted for cruel.

Gran barked out a laugh at him. "Aye? And what, walk up to the Sannock Dead with our tits in our hands and beg them for help." She put on a shrill voice that whined down her nose, nasal and snide. "Och, I know the Wolves slaughtered you all and hung ya like pigs, but bygones, aye?"

"You can't keep the bird here."

"Can for as long as the boy lives," Gran said. She looked down at Nick and poked his hip with her foot. "Did you think I infected him with our curse for shits and giggles, Lewis? He'll live for as long as I need 'im. Maybe less him than he used to be, but a good boy wants his gran to be happy, right? And when I finally let the bird go, he'll do."

Nick reached out and tugged weakly at her ankle until she looked down at him.

"I think seeing you naked retroactively made me gay," Nick wheezed out.

Gran laughed with him. It was a warm, low, and oddly sweet sound. "I hate to disappoint you, Nicholas," she said. "But you're not going to goad me into killing you. Give it a few days. Soon you'll love me so much you'll accept your pain as the price to serve me. Just like when you were a wee lad and I gutted you to make room for the gods."

She tapped her finger against his stomach, and he felt the old scar twitch on his skin—the one that matched Gregor's where they'd carved the wolf out of him. He supposed he should have thought of it before. Gran was a Wolf after all, and he could see things that he shouldn't.

"They thought the Dog would work," she said. "That it not being a wolf would make it smaller somehow, leave enough room to cram the bird in. I knew better. You can't make a god lie down with a dog."

She laughed at her own joke.

"That's why you killed her," Nick muttered. The cackling thing in his head gave him that the same way it had given her the Sannock Dead. A girl with a fat belly who screamed as her car went off the road. It was too dark to see her face, no matter how hard Nick strained, but he could see her hands white and bony as they twisted on the wheel. He saw Gran, the old scars fresh and raw where her ink had been scraped away, drag her out of the car and cut her open. "My mum. To get me."

He hurt too much to even enjoy the flash of pain on his gran's face. "Broke my heart that, boy," she said. "But it was her fault. If she'd listened to me, she'd have lived to raise you up instead of leaving it all to me. Lived for a while."

"Why?"

She licked her dry lips and looked as lost as he felt. "Because hate's like a god, my bird boy," she said. "Sometimes you have to cut out everything else to give it somewhere to live."

The kiss she pressed on his forehead stung. Then she turned her back on him and jabbed a finger toward Terry's grim shape where he lurked in the tense crowd.

"You, get your people and collect the dead," she ordered brusquely. "Bring them to me at the cave."

"And then," Terry said. He was red in the face from fighting with the snarling dog, the leather lead wrapped so tightly around his hands that flesh bulged between the straps. "Then you'll be able to make us like you, to make my son like you? Not…."

He didn't gesture at the monsters, but then he didn't need to. Everyone looked, even Gran.

"Your children could be worse off than monsters," she pointed out slyly. "They could be dead."

Nick wondered how many of these people's children were already dead, their bodies slaughtered by skin grafts they couldn't absorb. Terry probably knew, but the only sign of any guilt was a muscle that twitched in his jaw. Lewis limped over, his boots heavy in the sand, and took the dog back. He brought it to heel with a yank of the lead and the crack of his knuckles on its head.

"Your son will be fine," she said. "Your son will be special."

Nick laughed and rolled onto his side. The pain hadn't lessened, but he felt stronger. When he tried to brace his hand against the ground, he saw black scabs scaled over his knuckles, and his index and middle fingers had twisted over each other like roots. He tried to straighten them, and pain jabbed down into his palm like fire.

"She'll love him like a grandson," he croaked out. "Look at what you can do with that."

"Bring the dead to the caves," Gran said. "After that, you'll never have to worry about your son again."

Terry had to know what stewed under those words—the poisoned subtext. He chose to take it at face value as he thumbed his radio to crackling life and barked orders.

GRAN TOOK the dog and Lewis with her—through, Nick assumed, the sharp-edged landscape of the Wild—and left Nick to travel with the dead. He huddled in his ruined coat on the floor of the second van, hemmed in by the stiff, dry dead and a raw-skinned monster with restless hands, and wondered what it said that he considered it the lesser of two evils.

He'd spent his working life around the dead. They'd done a lot less damage than his gran.

"It's still cold." Jepson stood with her feet in the guts of her own corpse, like a peculiar flower, and hugged herself. "I always thought it would be warm after, or scorching."

He side-eyed her. Death became her. She looked… not younger, but lighter, as though there had never been any reason to frown or any problem to purse her lips over. Also lighter in that she was just air and shades of color.

She wasn't like the dead woman. Jepson was just the specks of herself not made of meat.

"Not sure I should talk to you." The monster lifted its head at his voice and stared at him with wet red eyes that bulged under broken brow bones. Nick ignored it. His teeth chattered as he tried to talk, so it was probably cold. All he could feel was the sour heat of his half-cooked body, his flesh softened by its own grease to make it easier to reshape. "Are you...."

There were so many things he didn't want her to be—scared, angry, disappointed in him—that he couldn't get the question out.

Jepson tilted her head. Her hair was huge and faded off into nothing at the ends. "I still have a job to do."

"You're dead."

She looked down at her corpse. "I can see. Duty isn't marriage, Doctor Blake, it's not until death did us part."

He held his hand up. The muscle had wasted, and the dead skin hardened into black, charcoal-textured sticks. He'd seen similar wastage before, usually on homeless, usually nameless, corpses in the winter, or on the occasional unfortunate diabetic. It shouldn't hurt—the flesh was clearly dead—but it still did.

"I don't think I'll be much help," he said.

She stared at him and then faded out of sight. The black cackle that lodged in Nick's brain fluffed itself with disappointment and a sharp curiosity about what Jepson would taste like. As bizarre as it would be to indulge those sorts of thoughts about women at this stage in his life, Nick almost wished it were a sexual thought. Instead it was a sharply predatory sense— no words but the curl of a split tongue and the filmy sharpness of a life in his throat.

The black cackle in his head or the monster halfway through shedding his skin? He didn't know.

The van hit something in the road. The impact lifted the vehicle and then sent it into a skid. Jerky-and-bone corpses tumbled out of their roughly wrapped packaging and clattered onto the ground.

Fragile joints parted ways from their moorings as they landed, and the bodies and spider-bony limbs rolled in opposite directions.

Heavier bodies, waxy and embalmed, hit the ground and tangled around each other. A man wearing the top half of a three-piece suit, tie neatly knotted around his throat, with boxers and socks, rolled into Nick's legs. The fixed, tranquil expression some assiduous worker had sprayed on his face looked deeply inappropriate to the situation.

Nick shoved him away. His legs cracked and sent spikes of pain up into his hips as he moved, as though they'd been trying to do something he'd interrupted.

"Shit," the driver yelped as the van jolted to an abrupt stop. The monster had braced itself against the skid, but the sudden stop threw it into the wall of the van. The impact cracked its head at a sharp angle and dropped it limp and twitching on the ground. "What the hell was that?"

"You hit something, idiot," his passenger snapped. "Or do you think the van can fly?"

They shoved roughly at each other for a second across the handbrake, a flash of temper away from a punch. Before it got that far, they scrambled out of the van to see what was going on. The other van pulled over, and Nick could hear them yell at each other. He couldn't make out the words, but when the second van drove away, the driver grabbed a rock and lobbed it after them.

Nick cautiously stood up. His body felt wrong. There was something in his joints and the itch under his skin, but that didn't matter... or it wouldn't soon. He had to get away, had to tell Gregor what his gran was going to do.

What Nick had helped her do, like it or not.

The thought of that conversation made Nick shudder. Gregor might think he'd lied. He wouldn't understand that Nick hadn't been strong enough to not tell Gran what she wanted.

Then the inaudible tangle of noise resolved itself into words as the two men shuffled back over to the car.

"Fuckers."

"Shut up and fix the tire. If we aren't there on time, maybe the prophets won't want to Change us."

"What the hell did we hit anyhow?"

Nick limped over the dead to the back of the van. Still sprawled on the floor, blood puddled under its nose, the monster watched him edge past. Its big bony knuckles twitched. Nick reached for the release on the door and flinched as the sight of his ruined hand reminded him of what else Gregor would think—that he was a monster, that he needed to die.

The last pulse of his self-preservation made him shudder, but then it faded, and he wondered if death would be so bad. If he'd just gone with the dead woman in the hospital, maybe none of the pain and betrayal would have happened.

In his head, the black cackle thought that was a marvelous idea. Why wait, though? Do it now and they'd both be free.

Nick bit his lower lip and felt the hard plates of callused skin that had formed. He didn't want to die, but the cackle seemed very confident that it was a good idea. Just as the lock finally clicked, something hit the side of the truck hard. Nick pitched forward, hit the door, and toppled out into the dark. He fell to the ground and rolled. When he finally stopped, he had a noseful of snow and he'd taken a layer of skin off his ribs.

His hands were fine, even though he'd used them to block his fall. The hard, fleshless skin was tough. Nick huffed out a ragged breath into the snow, melting a few flakes, and struggled onto his knees.

The monster had been flung out with him and a handful of corpses. It lay in the snow, surrounded by the dead like some sort of Gothic diorama and dug its bone-spurred heels into the ground as the nerves tried to knit in its spine. Before it could make it back up, a familiar man stalked from around the car and pinned it down with a foot to its chest. Gregor flipped a tire iron in his hand and brought it down in a short, vicious arc that shattered the monster's skull. There was no anger in the murder, but there wasn't any regret either.

The dark thing in Nick's brain wanted to go. There were lots of ways to die in the Highlands in the winter—an endless list of options.

Nick wished he could go along with that plan. The last thing he wanted was for Gregor to see him as a monster that couldn't even hold its tongue. It didn't matter. He wanted to see Gregor, and that desire locked his knees and held him in place as Gregor turned around.

He recoiled a step when he saw Nick. That hurt. Everything hurt—from the bones of his skull to the tendons in his feet—but the flash of disgust on Gregor's face hurt worse. It felt like a knife to the heart.

Maybe he'd know exactly what that felt like in a minute. He raised his hands out of some ingrained, TV-learned habit. Of course, he realized when Gregor scowled, his hands didn't look too reassuring right then. He dropped them and hunched in on himself to try and hide what he could.

"I...." It was the sort of moment when Nick would have expected there to be too many words. Instead he had none. He couldn't even smile properly. His lips were too stiff to bend. "You were right. Gran's a bitch."

He fell over. At least he knew the thing in his head appreciated his joke. The ragged cackle followed him down into the dark.

Chapter Nineteen

GREGOR SLAMMED Jack against the side of the van—once to make his point, and then again in case it made him feel better. It didn't. The driver of the van, sprawled on the road with a bloody face and broken leg, flinched at the impact.

They had followed the dead from the hospital and cut across the gorse and rocky hills to beat the vans to the turn at the bottom of the hill. The hot, almost sexual thrill of the hunt had almost made Gregor forget his lost wolf and his grief. What he couldn't forget, however, he worked out on the prophets' servants.

Now all that satisfaction was gone, punctured by the fact that Nick wasn't dead, and he stank like a monster.

Gregor didn't know what he felt or how to deal with it, so he slammed Jack against the van again.

"You said he betrayed me. You said he went with her."

There was a gray cast to Jack's face. With the wolf still under his skin, he would heal faster than Gregor. It probably didn't feel that way right then, though. He wasn't recovered enough to change skins, and Gregor had anger on his side.

"Went. Took. What does it matter? He was as good as dead." Jack roughly shoved Gregor back. He pushed himself off the side of the car and glanced at the ragged leftovers of Nick with bleak pity. "Look at him, Gregor. Whatever he was—to you, to himself—is gone. Now he's just the prophets' creature."

Gregor stepped back. The wind whipped sleet along the road, sharply enough to sting as it hit his face. It carried away the loose snow they'd piled over the cement block they dragged into the road to sabotage the car.

"If I'd gone after her—"

"She infected him with her curse in front of me," Jack said. He grabbed Gregor's arm to keep him from walking away. "His arm was barely attached. I could smell the taint take hold. There was no hope for him, and the prophets have Danny. They have my mate, Gregor. Danny is pack. What's one human—however much he helped you—compared to that?"

It sounded reasonable when Jack said it. Things always did. The words always did what he wanted. Gregor had never had that knack. Words always turned on his tongue, but this time he only needed the one.

"Mine," Gregor said flatly as he took his arm back. "He's mine."

This time the pity in Jack's eyes was for Gregor. It made Gregor want to wipe it away with his fist.

"He's gone," Jack said.

"No." Gregor wished that the prophets had taken just a bit more of what made him a Wolf—just enough so he could believe his own lies. "Not quite yet. Find out where the dead are going, Jack. Then go to hell."

He turned and stalked away through the snow.

"If she's found the Sannock Dead," Jack told his back. "We're all going to hell."

Gregor clenched his jaw against another unpleasant truth—that he wasn't sure he cared. He left Jack to interrogate the bloody-faced driver and joined Nick by the side of the road. Nick perched on a weathered rock with his hands held under his arms and his chin tucked down into his collar. The wind flapped the ragged tails of his coat like wings, the shadow sharp and desperate to escape on the snow.

He almost looked human, if Gregor didn't look too hard and didn't breathe in at all.

"Did you know?" he asked. The voice that came out was harder than he meant it to be as the unreasonable anger the monsters roused in his gut just by their existence escaped his tongue.

Nick glanced up. His eyes were black and red, blood blisters puffy and bright on the whites of his eyes. Hard skin callused his lips and froze his expression in place. Gregor didn't know what hurt more, the memory of how soft those lips had been against his skin or the loss of Nick's vivid, mobile expressions.

"That Gran was a bitch?" Nick's voice was hoarse and raw. It was hard to tell if that was from pain or from some change in the structure of his throat. He tried to smile, but the skin at the edges of his mouth tore. "I knew that. Might not have wanted to admit it, but I knew."

Gregor snorted. "You know what I meant."

"No. Maybe I should have, but I didn't." Nick closed his eyes and tucked himself down into his coat. He looked like he didn't want to be seen. "Gregor, I'm… I'm sorry."

Gregor stared at the back of Nick's neck. The bony ridges of vertebrae showed through pale skin and the close-cropped dark fuzz at the back of his skull. It wasn't a wolf's submissive posture, but it was sharply vulnerable, and Gregor felt an uncomfortable urge to… be kind. He just wasn't sure how or if he could be kind to a monster.

"Why?"

Nick hunched harder, his shoulders like spikes under the stained wool and bandages. His hoarse voice dropped to a mutter that was barely audible through his collar.

"She always said I was weak, that I needed her," he said. "I was never strong. I was never brave. Smart, but nothing else."

Gregor cupped his hand around the nape of Nick's neck. He hadn't known he was going to do it until he did. Under his palm, Nick's skin was dry and painfully hot.

"What did you do?"

The tendons under Gregor's fingers went tight as Nick tensed. It felt as though they didn't move properly anymore, as though they were anchored to the muscles in a new way.

"I told her where they were, the Sannock Dead," Nick said. He hiccupped out a bitter laugh. "I knew that I shouldn't, that she'd only do something bad with it, but she hurt me, and I told her anyhow."

Gregor had already worked that out. It was the only thing worth the effort the prophets had put in. It still jarred him to hear it confirmed. Even in the Pack, the Sannock Dead were only talked about in whispers, to give the weak-minded nightmares and the thoughtful reason to fear the Numitor.

"You couldn't know where they were. No one does."

"He does." Nick forgot to hide as he tapped a black, talon-like finger against his temple. He tapped hard enough to leave a mark on the pale skin. "She trapped him in my head and then she hurt us, but I was the one who told. I told her where they were."

The bird. Gregor remembered the span of black wings and the carved beak of the raven. If the gods' roast pig had escaped to roam the hills, why not the raven who found the fresh dead to eat the pork.

Odin's bird, Muninn, who found the slain. None of the Sannock Dead had gone in their sleep.

"Where?" When Nick didn't answer quickly enough, Gregor gave in to the sick temper squashed under the surface and shook him. "Where are they?"

"I don't know." Nick cringed away from Gregor as he answered. "I don't know what they are. I don't know where it is. Just that he never moved them. They're where he left them. The where's what he moved."

Gregor scowled. "That makes no sense."

"Gran knew what it meant," Nick muttered. He finally opened his eyes and glanced sidelong at

Gregor. "When I was a kid, Gran used to tell me about the Run-Away Man. She said if he caught me, he'd take me somewhere no one could find me, no matter how hard I screamed. I could stand in the middle of Glasgow Cathedral and scream as he ate me alive, and people would just go on about their day. They'd never know what happened to me. They'd never care."

"The Wild. You think the Sannock Dead are buried in the Wild?"

"That's where you buried your daughter isn't it?" Nick asked. He folded his twisted hands back under his armpits. "Somewhere high and stony, where no one but you could find her, where you knew she'd be safe."

No one knew that, not even his da. It felt like a threat. Gregor tightened his grip on the back of Nick's neck. He could feel the bones under the skin, and he knew just how hard he'd have to twist to snap them.

"Just do it," Nick said. He took a deep breath and squinted his eyes tightly shut. "Please."

Gregor snatched his hand back as though he'd been burned. He wouldn't have done it. He needed to believe that. "What the hell, Nick?"

"You have to kill me," Nick said calmly. "Gran needs me—or the thing—for something. If I'm dead, I can't help her. It's okay. I don't mind."

"Shut up." Gregor grabbed Nick's sleeve and dragged him to his feet. "You don't get to just give up, to not mind."

"You don't get it," Nick said. "I'm not… whatever she put in my head? It's trapped there until I die."

"Fuck it."

Gregor didn't care if it was Muninn with his wings clipped to fit inside Nick's skull. He wouldn't care if it was Fenrir—the last god the Wolves trusted, whose winter they'd bring down on the world—caged in there. Nick was one thing the prophets were not going to take from him. He was all Gregor had.

"You don't get it," Nick said. His new rough voice cracked miserably. He stepped closer to Gregor and raised his chin so there was no way to avoid seeing the curse at work. "This is what I am. This is what I was meant to be. Gran took me when I was a child, and she made me into a trap."

Gregor squashed the revulsion that roiled in his stomach and cupped Nick's face in his hands. He rested his forehead against Nick's. It was hot enough that he felt fevered by contact and breathed in his curse-sour breath. He didn't care what Nick was. All that mattered was that he was Nick.

"The gods made us all for something. They have a plan for us all," he said. "Fuck the gods. Fuck your gran."

Nick's breath hitched in a disgusted snort of laughter. "Please, don't."

"I'll fix this," Gregor promised.

"You said you couldn't," Nick reminded him. He touched Gregor's cheek gently with a dry finger, and Gregor steeled himself not to flinch. "It really hurts, Gregor, and not just my bones. I can feel it in my head. I can feel bits of me rotting out. What will you do when there's nothing left except the monster?"

There was only one answer. Both of them knew that. Gregor pressed a hard kiss against Nick's forehead.

"I'll bury you with my daughter," he promised. "The prophets won't touch you again. But not yet. I'm not ready."

"Me neither. I don't think that matters," Nick said. He sighed. "I'll wait, but not for long."

THE DRIVER cursed them for dogs and their mothers for bitches. His eyes were glazed with viciousness, and if they had a match, his breath could have lit a fire.

"Wolves," he spat. It arced through the cold air and then splatted down onto his leg. "More like foxes. More like... like rats. You hide in our houses, eat our garbage but think you're sommat special."

Jack laughed at him. "Our da owns four hundred acres of the Highlands, and Wolves from here to Cornwall acknowledge his rule. I don't need your bins to fill my stomach."

Gregor kicked the broken leg that bent the wrong way and in one more place than it should. The man shrieked and writhed like a fish on the shore. He preferred a more direct approach.

"Not much of a snow angel," Nick said.

The croak of his voice made Jack glare briefly his way. He thought Gregor should have killed Nick and called it mercy—or pragmatism. He didn't really care.

"Where were you taking the dead?" Gregor asked. He booted the broken bone again and waited for the whining to stop. "Where are the prophets going?"

Sweat ran down the man's face in greasy rivulets and froze in his beard. His skin had the sallow undertone of aged wax.

"The prophets are going to replace you," he gritted out through clenched teeth. "Upgraded. Improved. We will inherit the earth."

"For whom?" Nick asked.

The man shot him an impatient look. "For us. For our children." He wiped his forehead on his arm. "The prophets told us. This is the Flood returned, and we're the beasts on the Ark."

Gregor grimaced. He had spent less time in human society than Jack had—the hours his brother spent stuck in school he'd spent hiding from their da in the crags—but some things you couldn't avoid. The prophets must have decided that it wasn't enough to whore themselves to only their pantheon.

"Your children are gone," Nick said. "Dead."

The flatness to his voice made Gregor uncomfortable. It wasn't cruel, but there was no kindness in it either. It could be the injuries that filled the air with the smell of fresh coppery blood and sour infection, or it could be that a monster wasn't often kind.

The man laughed harshly. "Don't try and threaten me. The children are safe. The prophets are going to make them—"

"They're dead," Nick repeated. "When did you see them last? Hear them?"

For a second the man looked uncertain, and vulnerability cracked through the aggression. After a moment he shook his head in rejection and reached into his coat for a plastic soda bottle. It was empty. His hand clenched around it and collapsed the plastic.

"My kids are okay."

Nick limped forward and leaned down so the man couldn't avoid his sweat-shiny, half-twisted face. "Do I look okay?" he asked. "She's my gran. I'm her only living family. If she could do better than this, don't you think she would have?"

The man's face crumpled in on itself like the bottle. He muttered a denial, but it was obvious he didn't mean it.

Gregor caught the back of Nick's coat and pulled him away so Jack could move into the space.

"I don't care about your people. I just want Danny back," Jack said. He crouched down next to the man and gripped his shoulders. "Tell us where they're going. You owe me that, don't you?"

There was a hard edge to Jack's voice as he said that. It made the man look more miserable.

"I don't know."

"It's the only way you get to be there," Gregor pointed out. "What if, whatever the prophet is going to do for you, it can only be done then?"

The man licked chapped lips and twisted the empty bottle between his hands as he tried to decide what to do.

"The sea caves," he said. "We started digging there. There was nothing there, just gull bones and old dogs, but she said to go back. So we go back."

"And the dead?" Nick asked.

The man shrugged. "She told us to do it." He glanced at Jack and then frowned down at his hands. His throat jerked convulsively as he swallowed. "We'd done everything else she said, so we did this too. What else could we do? We have to trust her. If we don't…. We have to trust her."

Gregor grabbed his collar and dragged him onto his one good leg. The man screamed and swore, his skin gray and his eyes wild as his broken leg jarred.

"You're going to take us there," Gregor said. The man started to shake his head, but Gregor closed his fingers around his throat and pushed him against the side of the van, into the dent he'd already made with Jack's shoulder. "Drive us. Or I leave you here to freeze. Unless you think you can crawl all the way back to town."

"He can't drive with a broken leg," Nick pointed out.

Gregor glanced down at the awkwardly pointed foot and snorted. "He can if he wants to avoid another broken leg."

The acrid stink of piss suddenly filled the air. It spread down the man's leg in a dark stain.

"I'll drive," Jack said. "He can navigate."

The sleet had gotten heavier. It came down sideways, caught on the harsh wind, and clouded the air like mist. The temperature had dropped again too. The already cold air was suddenly arctic. On the man's thigh, the piss-stain froze into his trousers.

"What about the dead?" Nick asked.

Gregor remembered the cold, old voice the Dog had put into Nick's throat. He didn't know what corpse belonged to the Dog or how to find out. Wolves were inked at birth, but Dogs had no rank.

"Leave them," he said. "We can give them a proper burial later."

THE SLEET had turned to a freezing rain by the time they reached the beach. It froze as it fell and glazed the narrow dirt road the van bumped along. Jack cursed and hunched over the wheel to see through the narrow crescent of glass the laboring heater had managed to clear.

"Can you turn your skin?" Gregor asked. His tongue felt stiff and resentful as he said the words, his pride brutally aware of his own lack.

Jack steered the van through a skid and into the fence that carved out the road. It raked down the metal for a long minute until Jack corrected. Once the tires were back on the road, he straightened up and stretched for a second, the heel of his hand pressed against his breastbone.

"If I need to, I can," he said grimly. His eyes flicked up to the mirror. The doubt in them grated all the more for them being Gregor's own damn eyes. "Can you...?"

Hope was stupid, but Gregor still reached for his wolf. He knew the feel of it under his skin, the dense coat and the heavy, musty smell of a healthy male predator. Instead he dug into the scabbed cavity it had left behind in his spirit, an abscess of loss and resentment under the barely healed crust.

Pain sliced through his brain, a claw that ripped from behind his eyes to his spine, and smeared gray around the edges of his vision for a second. He clenched his jaw through it.

"No. I can still fight."

The corner of Jack's mouth twitched. "I remember," he said.

In the passenger seat, the prophets' man was hunched up against the window. He was flushed, and his skin looked tight on his flesh. His leg was swollen and smelled of marrow, but he seemed more troubled by the empty bottle. He fumbled at it anxiously.

The Wild always felt strange near the sea. It ebbed and flowed like the tide, and ripples of it were dragged out to sea with the salt. As it waxed, Gregor could see the blisters just under the man's skin, the flesh on his temples and around his mouth pocked and sloughed with dead flesh.

Snakes, Nick had said.

"It's not the fight I'd have picked," Jack said as he hunched back down. His hands flexed absently around the wheel. "We're outnumbered."

"We're not at our best," Gregor added. It felt better to drag Jack down with him.

"Gran called them pecking hens." Nick's voice drifted from the back of the van. It was a relief to Gregor after the patient, suffering silence, but Jack grimaced at the reminder. He already had the window cracked down to let the smell out, and his shoulder and sleeve were coated with frost from the chill. "She said it ate all the good bits out of them."

The man in the passenger seat stirred. "It makes us strong. Kills the pain."

Gregor cuffed him around the ear. "Don't interrupt."

"When Gran did this…." There was a pause. Gregor didn't look. It was easier to remember it was Nick when he didn't see what the curse had done to him. "Half the town was there, and they could hardly stand next to each other without a brawl. I think the drink makes it easy to control them and hard for them to control themselves."

Gregor rested his chin on the back of Jack's seat and frowned. If what Nick had said about the origins of the drink had any basis in truth, that made sense. Loki was a fractious god, and his children inherited the trait. If any of them could control themselves, the world wouldn't be ending.

"If they want to fight," he said to Jack, "we should give them something to fight about."

Jack reached over and jabbed a hard finger into the passenger's shoulder. "How much farther?"

The man stirred and leaned forward. He scrubbed the windshield with his hand and scraped away the ice that had formed on the inside. It didn't make it any easier to see.

"There's an old rock spike in a couple of miles," he said. "Spray paint all over it. You can't miss it. Turn left at that, and you're right there."

Jack nodded and put his foot on the accelerator. The engine coughed and rattled under the hood, and the van bounced like a kangaroo, and then it sped up. Gregor could feel the ice under the wheels as they raced the skid down the road.

IT WAS a small parking lot, the asphalt corners of it hidden under drifts of snow and ice. An ankle-height metal fence marked off the boundary between it and the beach, and it glittered like glass in the scant moonlight and reflected shards of red flame from the bonfires that guttered on the sand.

They burned blue from the salt-soaked driftwood used as tinder, with bright flicks of sky in the depths of the flames, and belched dark, greasy smoke as the dry bodies of the dead were tossed into the maw of the fires. The snow cringed back and left a ring of dark sand and scorched rocks around the base of the bonfire.

The prophets stood naked on the gray stone-pocked sand, their skin mottled red and white from the heat and the ends of their hair singed and curled as the wind fanned the fires higher. The sparks and smoke were drawn up and across until they met at the apex and spun together.

On the other side of the fires, against the back-drop of ice-glazed grass and rock, shadows of things that weren't there anymore were cast on the sand. Child-sized figures with large ears and too long hands massed at the edges. A long-legged silhouette of a man stretched over the uneven sand, the suggestion of horns fading into the dark. The profile of a heavy-shouldered dog with loose jowls and cropped ears paced back and forth. It stopped, shook its head, and mummed a mute snarl. Flat cutouts shouldn't have held so much rage.

The Sannock. Relics of what used to rule the British Isles before the Wolves came and were just better bastards. They were pushed to the outskirts, left to eke out their existence on the rocky slivers of the coast, and then murdered—not all of them, but those who'd been foolish enough to linger there, where they butted up against the Wolves' territory.

There was a greed that Wolves took from the Wild. Not the gray wolves or the timber wolves, not beasts that ate to fill their stomachs. The greed came with the ability to turn your skin like a coat. It was the hunger for the Numitor's praise or his position or for the few things that the Wild hadn't given them freely.

So brew a broth from a Black Dog and see death haunt men's shadows. Crack the bones and clean out the marrow of a Green Man and know what the Wild whispered.

Of course, you'd also be a fucking monster. Even to a people who had little truck with disgust and none with shame. His da had killed the Wolves who'd done it and left them with the Sannock to rot. Too late for amends, but they'd been forgotten. Even the story wasn't howled to the moon, only muttered during the dark of the moon to scare pups.

"More," the woman—Nick's gran—yelled. The wind stretched her voice out like taffy. "Stoke the fucking flames till I tell you to stop."

Gregor scratched his throat. Under the scruff of a week's stubble, he could feel the hard lines of a scar. Maybe he always would. He owed the evil old mare for that.

The people of Girvan dragged tarps of dismembered dead through the rocks and across the sand. Arms and legs were used to stir the embers, heads tossed up by their hair into the heart of the bonfire It flared around the dry old bones, and the assembled crowd—the prophets' congregation—roared their appreciation.

On the other side of the gate, the Sannock shadows drew back from the sour smoke, but not far enough.

Nick's gran kicked the sand with rage and yelled for more. But the tarp was lighter, the jointed corpses fewer and smaller.

"Now," Gregor said as he tapped Jack's shoulder. "Before they start looking for us."

Jack grinned and hit the gas. The bald tires spun on the slick-as-glass concrete and then caught. The van roared forward and hit the low metal fence with a crunch and a jolt. Jack swore, his breath visible, and clenched his hands around the wheel. The tendons stood out in his wrists as he steered through the impact and down the rocky hill onto the sand.

It was frozen hard enough that the wheels didn't foul on it. Jack spun the wheel hard, and the ass of the van fishtailed on the snow. He steered out of the skid and aimed at a bonfire as people yelled and scrambled to get out of the way. Even the prophets, their eyes wide and white-ringed as the headlights hit them, threw themselves to the side.

Jack drove straight into the bigger of the two bonfires. Driftwood and bones went flying into the dark with a shower of bright firefly sparks, and Gregor heard the tires burst under them.

"Shift if you can," he told Jack shortly as he hefted the tire iron in one hand. "I'll hold them off."

The prophets' people picked themselves up off the sand where they'd scattered. Boots kicked the van, and angry fists battered at the thin metal sides. It rang like a discordant bell.

"What the fuck were you doing?"

"You could have killed us!"

"Bloody nutter!"

They shoved at the van and rocked it on its melted wheels. They were more of a mob than a congregation as self-preservation, and the hot satisfaction of self-righteousness, dethroned the prophet-demanded piety. Someone smashed at the passenger-side window with a rock and grabbed at the passenger. His shrieked excuses went unheard as they dragged him out.

Gregor scrambled over the corpses that hadn't been ejected back on the road. He grabbed the screwdriver wedged into the back doors as a makeshift lock

and glanced at Nick, who huddled back against the
far side of the cab. The light of the fire still burning
on top of the van glittered in eyes that were too round
and too black.

"You stay out of the way," Gregor said. "You're
not a fighter."

Nick tried out a stiff and difficult smile. It was still
oddly wicked. Gregor still liked it.

"I know that better than you."

Gregor yanked the screwdriver out and kicked the
doors open. The mob fell back. One man spat blood
where the door had caught him in the face, and Gregor
jumped out onto the sand. He swung the tire iron in
short, vicious arcs and jabbed the spiked end at angry,
puffy faces.

The Wild was so strong there that he didn't even
have to try to see the effects of the prophets' venom.
He saw rotted-out bone, skin slack over collapsed hollows in their skulls, and when he broke their bones,
snakes squirmed out of the wounds like maggots.

Not that they cared. If the pain did anything it just
made them angrier. Gregor swayed to the side out of
the way of a telegraphed rock to the head. Luckily it
didn't make them any more skilled. There were still
too many of them, though, and he couldn't dodge or
block every blow. Clawed fingers slipped past his defenses, and the woman dug her ragged nails into the
side of his face. She missed his eye by a hair and the
instinctive jerk of his head. He kicked her feet out from
under her and left her to be trampled by her neighbors.

The wind blew bitter rain in from the sea. It froze
on the ground and on their skin. Gregor felt it crack
around his mouth as he snarled.

"You should have run when you had the chance, boy," Nick's gran yelled from the still burning fire. "Now I'll kill you like I did your brother."

Gregor laughed, and Jack launched himself out of the back of the van. It was bitter to see *his* wolf on Jack's back, the same pattern of guard hairs just as they had the same constellations of freckles, but the satisfaction when the prophets screamed in rage was worth it.

He could see the gaunt hollow under Jack's ribs, the dullness of his coat. The wolf wasn't any more over what the prophets had done than Jack was. But what the mob saw were sharp teeth and sharper claws.

"Kill them," the prophet ordered. "Now."

The monsters scrambled down the cliffs where they'd been perched. There was nothing graceful about it. They moved like things with broken bones and ruined tendons, but they moved—five of them against a cripple and an ailing Wolf.

Gregor peeled his lips back from his teeth. If they planned to fight fair, those were terrible odds.

The first monster to reach them was almost wolf-like and obviously a favorite. Her hair had been braided back from her face, and the long points of her ears had been pierced with gold rings. It somehow made the thing sadder. Bad enough to find yourself a monster, but a pet?

It went for Jack. He ducked under the slash of the ragged bone claws and snapped at her face. Blood splattered the snow, and the monster flailed as her eye burst. Gregor dropped his tire iron and grabbed one of the mob by the arm. He grinned into the man's ape-angry face and threw him to the monster.

Gregor had no idea if the monsters were clever enough to understand allies or if all they had was blind obedience. Either way, the only one she seemed to sense was something coming in on her blind side. She grabbed him out of the air and smashed him down into the sand with enough force to break something important.

Behind her Jack dodged a charge from a hulking, bull-like monster, and it crashed into the mob. People howled as it trampled them under hook-clawed feet, and the mob turned.

Gregor wiped his bloody face on his sleeve. He doubted that seventy or eighty humans, even drugged on Loki's own poisoned sweat, could take down five monsters. It didn't matter. They fouled the monsters and slowed them down, and none of them cared about Jack or Gregor anymore.

He stooped to grab the tire iron and turned to look for the prophets. Jack slunk up next to him, ears flat and a low snarl rattling around his chest. After everything she'd done to him, Gregor knew he wanted her dead nearly as much as Gregor did.

Nick's gran stared at him from under the patchwork calico skin of a dozen Wolves. Her dried leather tongue panted in the air, and her lip curled back from rotting fangs. The other prophet, still in his own scarred skin, grabbed at her arm. Whatever he had to say, it didn't convince. She snatched a rope from his hands and gripped it as it stretched out taut into the sea. It was slick with ice, and she had to struggle to hang on to it.

"You think you've won," she said. Her borrowed jaws chewed on the words before she could spit them out, ragged edged and slurred. The laugh that gargled out of her barrel chest sounded even worse. "You think you're stronger than me? Well, I sacrificed the things I loved most. Can you?"

She wrenched viciously on the rope, and, barely audible over the wind and the sea, a dog yelped.

A Dog, and they still had Danny.

The prophet waited until she was sure they understood. Then she let go of the rope. It sliced through her fingers and was gone before they could even start to grab it.

"I guess we'll see."

Jack nearly tripped over his feet as he stumbled to a halt. He stood stiff legged for a second, torn between duty and his Dog. Gregor kicked him out of the way.

"Go," he snarled. "Get Danny. I have my own score to settle with this prophet, and I don't want to listen to you whine for a year."

It wasn't kindness. Gregor just wanted to be the one who got to kill the prophet who'd taken his wolf, who'd hurt Nick. That was all. Jack flashed him a grateful look out of the wolf's green eyes, and then launched himself toward the sea.

He howled as he hit the water and chased the answering whimper out into the breakers.

Gregor turned back to the prophets and flashed a cold smile.

"Not much I love."

"No," Nick's gran said. "And nothing loves you."

She grabbed the male prophet by the scruff of his neck and dragged him through the gateway with her, into the Sannock Dead. He screamed once, his voice shrill like a fox, and then laughed as the angry shadows cringed back from him.

Gran turned back to spit at Nick and then took off at a loping run toward the cliff face. The male prophet hobbled along behind her on ruined legs.

Gregor cursed and went after him, but when he stepped through the portal, the dead didn't cringe. They mobbed him with fists and fangs, and centuries of rage clawed into his skin and bones. He screamed with raw fury and tried to push through, but there was nothing for him to hit or tear.

Teeth met in his leg and ground down on the bone. The cold that spiked into his marrow and crawled up through his body made the winter wind feel balmy in comparison. He felt slow and tired, and somehow he found himself on his knees.

A shadow danced forward and swung a paper-thin blade of darkness at him.

Chapter Twenty

NICK GRABBED Gregor's shoulders and yanked him back from the bonfire. He tripped over his own feet—the joints and tendons not quite lined up as his body expected—and spilled them both onto the ground. The heavy weight and warmth of Gregor sprawled on top of Nick felt briefly, inappropriately silly and sexual, as though there would be a kiss and a laugh before they got back to the fight, on a promise for later.

It lasted long enough for Gregor to inhale, grimace, and scramble away from Nick. Not that Nick could blame him. Even without the stink that made Gregor's nose wrinkle around the monsters, Nick wasn't exactly kissable right then. His skull felt loose, as though the growth plates had unsealed, and the back of his throat tasted like kidneys. The heat of the fever that made the world swim around him, a stone of nausea that rolled between his gut and bowels, melted the ice on his skin as he cooked from the inside out. He wouldn't kiss himself.

"Why won't they let me through?" Gregor rasped. He staggered to his feet and grimaced as his leg threatened to fold under him. It didn't show any sign of injury—no blood, no tears in the fabric of his jeans—but he held himself as though the teeth that had sunk home in his calf had been solid. "They let that old bitch through."

For a moment the eight-year-old that Nick had been bristled in automatic defense of the gran he loved. He *had* loved her back then. So not only had he been an unappealing coward as a child, he hadn't been too bright either.

He swallowed the bitterness of that and glanced at Gregor.

"You can't see them?"

Gregor shot him an impatient look. "Of course I fucking see them. The Sannock Dead—shadows with teeth." He kicked a spray of slush and sand toward the smoky gateway and yelled at them in frustration. "Do you think that the prophets are going to do you a good turn? The prophets led the slaughter. They braised your gods' damned meat."

"Not them," Nick said. Although what he saw of the Sannock and what Gregor saw didn't sound the same. "The others."

"What others?"

On the other side of the smoke, the dead guarded Gran's flight toward the cliffs. Every corpse she'd stolen from the clay and the peat was there, their bodies newly cast in smoke and salt. They were still dead, their ribs staring through torn flesh and lips peeled back from their yellowed teeth, but that was in their favor. It meant they didn't care what insults were visited on their dried-out bones, and they were still strong enough to bar the Sannock from Gran's heels.

"All of them," Nick said. "Every one of the dead she burned are tied to her now. Fifty of them. More. The others—the Sannock—can't touch her, so they'll take it out on whoever they can."

Gregor looked grim as he absorbed that. He limped back two steps and glared at the smoke as though the dead might be intimidated into letting him see them.

"Can they get out?" he asked. "The Sannock?"

The no was confident when it started in Nick's head. By the time it got to his tongue, it had a few doubts. He watched the Sannock—not shadows to him, but still clearly dead—as they picked and sniffed at the greasy smoke.

Was the faded man—with his empty eye sockets over cheekbones that really could have cut someone—a little less faded? Did the big black dog's massive paws sink a bit deeper into the sand?

"I don't know," he corrected himself. "What should we do?"

A laugh caught in Gregor's throat and rattled there. He paced the short distance between one bonfire and the next with long, restive strides. The layer of ice that coated his sleeve and leg cracked with each step and then resealed as the water sank into it.

"Put the bonfires out, and we'll close their grave back up, but with your gran and her plans still free...," he said. "If we let it burn out, maybe I can get through to get her, but maybe they can get to us. What's worse, Nick? Your gran or them?"

He jabbed a finger toward the Sannock. They snarled back at him, and somehow—in that cold spot in his brain—Nick could feel the bleak destruction of them. Anger had passed them by centuries before, and resentment had lingered but eventually dried up and blown away. All that was left was the habit of hatred and the ability to kill. Anything that survived the winter, they would kill—wolf, human, or pig thing—it wouldn't matter to them.

It didn't matter. The answer was still the same. "Gran," he said. "At least with them, they'd leave you be once you died."

Gregor grimly shook his head.

"You aren't a Wolf, Nick," he said. "You don't know what we did to them, why they're so angry. All your gran wants is power, but they want weregild that's gone unpaid for generations. And a pound of flesh won't even these scales."

He was wrong. Gregor might have grown up with tales of the Sannock, but Nick had grown up with Gran. The Sannock would kill and be sated, because anger was a thing you could satisfy. Nick had never seen Gran content. She'd never felt *full* of anything, never looked at a job well done and felt happy. She wasn't angry or afraid or resentful. She was empty. All of this— the death, the worship, the sacrifice—was poured into a hole so insatiable that, if it ever got close to full, it would vomit up the glut to make room for more.

...*duty*.

The memory fluttered through Nick's head, almost hidden under the noise of lost function and fear, and he barely caught the tail of it. But as long as it had taken him to believe it as a child, not everyone was like Gran, and not all ghosts were angry.

He stared into the pale flickering flames for a second and was almost sure it was the fever's idea. Even if it were, what did it matter now? It was the only idea he had.

"We need more." He dragged himself away from the fire and staggered toward the van. The brutal scuffle between the venom-drunk people and the monsters had eddied around and away from it, leaving the dead and injured where they'd fallen.

Copeland, eyes wild under hair frozen into tangled knots, screamed as she brought a barnacle-covered rock down onto the well-broken head of a dead monster. Her voice sounded like it belonged to a ghost, a raspy whisper of rage. Maybe it would soon. Ice glazed her face like a mask and cracked around blue lips and a dark-nipped nose.

She should be dragged away to warm up and sober up, to blankets and coffee and safety. Nick liked to believe he'd have made that happen for her if he could. Since he couldn't, he grabbed her arm and dragged her off the dead thing. She coughed out an infuriated attempt at a yell and swung the rock at his head.

For a second Nick wondered if it might be a solution—not to everyone's problems but at least to his.

Gregor grabbed Copeland's wrist before Nick had to decide one way or another. He squeezed until she dropped the rock.

"Not yet." He hung on to Copeland with both hands as she struggled and kicked at him. "What do you want with her?"

"Another pair of hands." Nick leaned against the door of the van and tried to muster the last bits of himself. He took a deep breath and forced Doctor Blake's voice out through his rough larynx and over his aching tongue. "*Doctor Copeland.* We have a trauma situation. Pull yourself together."

It wasn't magic, just habit ground into her bones over years of sleep deprivation, shifts, and no time for the breakdown you've earned. It jerked her out of the cycle of rage that was eating itself and vomiting up more rage to eat. She sucked in a harsh breath and jerked away from Gregor's hold. Her eyes were still hot with barely controlled anger, but she was sane enough to speak.

"Fuck you," she spat at Nick. The anger was a wire twisted through her body, her shoulders hunched aggressively, and her lips peeled back like a dog's. "You aren't my boss, you aren't my friend, and I don't have to do what you fucking say."

"Please?"

She looked baffled. Her cold-chapped lips opened and then closed again as she tried for words. Nick left her to it as he dragged a dead man with Gran's infected stigmata torn into his face away from the van. The doors swung open, and he stared at the dead, given pause by the shadow of professional responsibility he'd just conjured.

Respect. The corpse on the slab was just meat, organs, and evidence, but once upon a time it had been someone. So you treated it with respect, like the clothes your dead dad left hung up in his closet.

"If I got this wrong, I'm so sorry," he muttered as he grabbed Jepson's ankle and dragged her heavy, unwieldy corpse out of the van. She was stiff and cold, gray had spread like lichen under her skin, and her ghost didn't make an appearance to tell him one way or another if it was what she wanted. He touched her jaw. "If I got it right, I'm even more sorry."

One of the monsters had seen them. It struggled free of the brawl of enraged humans that tore handfuls of flesh and muscle from its bones. The venom didn't make the townsfolk heal any faster, but they didn't seem to care about the wounds that lay open on their skin. It had to tear them off and slap them away before it could lumber up the beach.

"Shit." Nick struggled to get Jepson up into his arms. "I need—"

"I'll hold it off." Gregor bent down and unearthed his tire iron from under a pile of bloody snow. His mouth twisted in a snarl. "Go and do whatever you're going to do. You can't make this any worse."

He gave Nick a quick nod that could have meant a lot of things. Then he stalked down the beach to intercept the monster. It screamed at him with bloody frost caked around its gums and lashed out with a bony-clawed hand. Gregor dodged the blow—although he didn't get out unscathed, Nick saw blood fly and freeze like crystals in the air—and stabbed the tire iron into the monster's armpit.

Nick dragged his attention away from the fight while it looked like Gregor was winning.

"Help me get them to the fire," he told the sullen Copeland. "Come on. Hurry."

She scowled at him. "Why the hell should I? We're going to be fucking superheroes." She grinned at him with more teeth and gum than a smile could justify. The ice cracked on her face, and so did the skin underneath. "I'm going to live forever."

Or not. She was half-drenched, and her hair was frozen, and frigid water had scabbed over the bloody cracks around her lips and nose. They'd barely been acquaintances back in Glasgow, but she'd been the closest thing to a friend he had here.

"That's why we need to burn them," Nick lied to her. "Like before. Gran told us to before she left. Help me."

Copeland hesitated, but it was easier to believe him than try to think. She shoved him impatiently out of the way and grabbed for an ankle in the tangle of corpses. Nick left her to it and staggered up the beach with Jepson. At some point her ghost appeared and matched his stride. She disappeared when he looked directly at her, smeared away like a fever dream, but the footprints stayed.

Nick supposed they could have been his from earlier. Just because the supernatural was real, that didn't mean everything was real. It didn't mean this was going to work.

He staggered up to the bonfire and stopped. On the other side of the smoke, the faded man was barely faded at all anymore. He didn't look so much like a man either. All the relevant parts of humanity were there—the eyes, the mouth, the cheekbones like two knives under his skin—but it didn't add up to a person. His mouth moved exaggeratedly in some sort of mimed threat.

It was a wasted effort. Nick could feel the hate in his head and the fear under it, the cold almost welcome against the soupy heat in his head. The Sannock didn't know if it would work either.

Nick heaved Jepson off his shoulder and pitched her body into the flames. The brittle pyramid of charred sticks and bones fractured under the weight of her still-almost-alive body. It fell in on top of her as her clothes singed and the ends of her hair withered. She was dead and didn't feel it, but Nick still had to look away as her skin blistered and smoked.

She burned wetter than the older corpses. The smoke was dark and greasy, as though it would leave a skin of itself on anything it touched. It mixed with the salt smoke of burned driftwood and shells and pulled itself together against the wind.

Copeland staggered up to him. She had a corpse by the wrist and ankle. Between them they shoved it into the fire, went back for more corpses, and added them to the smoke. The monster was hobbled, its rib cage crushed and the point of the tire iron jabbed into its shoulder as Gregor ripped its bone-armored leg off its body. Some of the townsfolk had joined him—a makeshift pack that harried and picked at the monster to divide its attention.

Nick choked on the smoke as he shoved the last corpse—a man with a birthmark on his elbow that he remembered noting in an autopsy—into the flames. Fat spat and popped, overheated bones creaked, and the pall of smoke thickened into ghosts.

Jepson's pulled itself together on the other side. She was pale and see-through, more a reflection than a ghost as she stared at Nick through the haze. After a moment she nodded at him, and the slash under her jaw gaped like a mouth. There was no forgiveness in her face, but he hadn't expected any. There was just expectation.

She wasn't the only one who had a duty. Nick's had always been to the dead. The dead that Gran had told him to make proud, the corpses on the slabs who'd hoped never to become his patient, even his dead gran herself.

He could feel the thing Gran had put in him. It pecked and clawed to get out, but the monster just put him back together again. It was trapped. He was trapped. The Sannock were trapped.

Gran had a lot to answer for.

Habit made him reach for the amulet until he remembered he didn't have it anymore. He bit his thumb instead and folded the old scar tissue between his teeth.

"Sucking your thumb now?" Copeland asked irritably. She hunched into herself as she started to feel the cold again. Her hands were swollen under the coat of ice. "Is this going to work?"

"Tell Gregor—" Nick hesitated. He wanted her to tell Gregor he loved him, but what he felt was sharper and hungrier and stranger than that—nothing like he'd felt before. "I told him I couldn't wait forever."

He lunged through the smoke. It crawled into his nose and down his throat and then swirled sour and greasy in his lungs. On the other side, the air felt thinner, almost threadbare, and the cold had a pure, sharp feel to it. The beach was long and clean, the stones tumble-rounded and the sand white. No graffiti scrawled up the cliffs, and the singed van was gone.

The bonfires were still there, but the flames were brighter, and the bones picked clean and stacked higher.

The Sannock were on him before he could see anything more. They knocked him down and tore at him with teeth and fingers and roughly carved stone knives. Cold slashed through his body, stark against the fetid heat of the infection. His blood oozed out into the pristine sand and stained it a gory scarlet that was as bright as a crayon. The monster scrabbled to fuse fractures and knit torn skin back together, to keep Gran's trap intact. It couldn't patch him as quickly as the Sannock tore him apart.

Each splash of blood, each wound left to leak while something more important was sealed, fed the dead. Jepson wasn't a ghost of grubby smoke anymore, and she didn't wear her death on her skin. The edges of her body were sharper than Gran's slaves, her colors more solid, and her eyes sharp and full of Jepson.

There was more to her than bones and obedience.

It spread to the other ghosts—not all, but some. Nick could feel them in his head, like a cold bundle of needles pressed against his brain. It sank into them and made them more vivid, as though someone had turned up the vibrancy.

As... not life, but awareness... dawned in the dim, dried-out eyes of the dead, they turned on their former allies. Skeletal fingers dug down into soft flesh and into the marrow. They tore the enemy dead apart until all that was left was a scatter of salt and a cloud of smoke with no structure to hang off, and then they turned on the Sannock.

They couldn't hurt them, any more than Gran's dead could, but they pulled them off Nick and drove them back. Nick sprawled out on the ground, his injuries packed with ice and sand, and thought it was probably too late.

"No!" The desperate snarl pierced between the bonfires, and then Gregor was there. He dragged Nick up off the sand and into his arms and buried his fingers in the matted mess of Nick's hair. His face was bloody and bruised, his eyes so green and fierce that Nick wondered if Gregor could hold him there by will alone. "You idiot. What the fuck are you doing?"

Nick wanted to explain, but his throat and his tongue wouldn't cooperate to get that many words out. He just sighed and felt the liquid bubble in his chest.

"Go." He shoved weakly at Gregor's shoulder.

"No." Gregor set his jaw and shook his head. "You don't get to leave me alone, Nick. That's not a choice."

"Your brother."

"Fuck him," Gregor snapped. He tightened his grip on Nick, as though he could squeeze him back together. "I never fucking liked him. Stay. Just do as you're told for once."

"Go," Nick repeated. He barely had breath left to carry the words, but Gregor bent down close so he could hear. "Don't let Gran win. Promise."

"Promise to stay."

Nick wanted to laugh, but there was nothing left.

Chapter Twenty-One

DEATH WAS impossible to deny. Nick was still pliant and warm—too warm, his skin fever hot—in Gregor's arms, but he was gone. The nerve-scratch stench had faded from his skin, and his body was still. Nick was never that. He was always restless in his own skin.

The knowledge didn't make it any easier to let go.

Gregor knelt on the sand and snow and bent over Nick's dead, ruined body. He didn't cry. He wasn't sad. Grief was useless. It took the legs out from under the mourner, left them to keen to the moon—as if that bitch would ever listen—while there was work to be done.

Anger was what Gregor needed—that old, bitter companion that gnawed his soul to rags and filled the hole with the reminder that this wasn't *fair*. What right did the world, did the Wild, have to give him Nick and then take him away? Jack would pull his half-drowned

Dog out of the water, and Gregor would put Nick in the ground.

It had a heartbeat of its own, rage. Gregor could feel it against the inside of his skull—a throb of heat that drove out everything else. He pressed his face against Nick's shoulder, against the stained, worn wool of his coat, and fed it every moment of kindness, every touch of clever, careful hands, every glint of dry humor and want in his black heart.

There should have been more, and Gregor nearly choked on how unjust that was. His temper bubbled over, sour as acid, and spilled into even the rotted cavity where the prophets had excised his wolf.

Gregor sucked in a lungful of cold air through his teeth and carefully laid Nick out on the snowy sand. Placed against the blanched sheet of white, the prophet-driven changes made Nick look even more like a bird. The scabbed prow of his nose jutted out harshly, and the torn tails of his coat spread out like ragged wings. Even his hair, blood-matted and messy, looked like fluffed-out feathers. The sleet soaked him and froze, coating him in a glaze of milky ice.

"I'll kill her," Gregor rasped out. His throat felt twisted, more suited to a snarl than words. "Then I'll come back and take you somewhere better."

He scrambled to his feet. Whatever Nick had seen on the beach, to Gregor's eyes, it was empty except for the shadows of the Sannock and the swiftly filling-in sets of footprints in the snow. They had drawn back or been pushed back by whatever Nick had done. The ragged remnants of a remnant people. Gregor spat at them.

"If I could kill you again, I would," he said flatly. "Since I can't, I'll just leave you here in your miserable graves. Enjoy the rot."

The shadows surged forward. It was a silent charge, but Gregor *felt* their howl press against his ears until they popped. Halfway to Gregor, the Sannock were thrown back toward the frozen shelf of the incoming tide.

Gregor snarled a smile at the show of impotent force. It wasn't enough, but it would have to do. Besides, the Sannock were only the knife. It had been the prophet's hand behind Nick's death.

He turned his back on the shadows and followed the footsteps up the beach before they disappeared.

ROCKY SAND turned to icy rock under Gregor's feet, and the faint tracks disappeared. It didn't matter. He could *smell* their destination on the still air, smoke, grease, and a sourness that had sunk into the Wild and stained it. When the Numitor turned the Wild into a grave for the only shame the Wolves had, it had trapped the moment here to fester.

Gregor had heard the stories. No one had told him, but a pup with sharp ears and a lot of resentment paid attention to whispers in corners. The cliff looked seamless. It was a jagged shelf of Scottish rock. Even the gulls didn't nest there. Gregor had to pause for a second and squint at the stone before he could pick out the suggestion of a narrow track that switchbacked down the cliff.

There was a foothold there, barely big enough to brace his boot on, and a crack he could wedge his fingers in if he jumped. The ice-sharp stone sliced his fingers as he hung there for a second, his broken ribs like a grater against his lungs, and then hauled himself up onto the thin trail. If it wasn't the Sannock's secret path, it was scant enough that it could have been made by rabbits.

It would have taken a careful man an hour to climb the trail. The track was so narrow he would have to walk heel to toe, and it was completely absent in spots, so he would have to scramble across jagged stone like a spider. Gregor wasn't a man—even if he never went furside again, he was still a Wolf, and he didn't care to be careful. He used the track as a map and just headed straight up the cliff. His foot slipped off ice-covered outcrops twice, and his hands were torn to ribbons by the time he got to the crack that led into the Sannock's cave.

It looked like a dark striation in the rock until you were close enough to touch it, and it looked too narrow to fit through. Gregor hesitated for a second as he stared into the dark. He didn't care for tight spaces, low ceilings. It had never stopped him before, but there was usually someone there he had to prove something to. Without that, the dislike felt closer to fear, a damp cloth over the hot roil of anger in his chest.

Stupid. The worst thing likely to be in there is you.

When that didn't work, he thought of Nick—of how human he was, how breakable, how stubborn. He put himself in danger to help Gregor, and he let the Sannock kill him to get Gregor there. Now Gregor was going to let that go to waste because he was scared he'd get stuck in the crack like a sheep in a stile?

The mixture of anger, guilt, and shame was enough to make him move. He squirmed through the entrance sideways, with the edge of rock pressing down on his back and chest, and fumbled his way blindly through the fold in the stone. He could taste his own breath as it panted back from the wall in front of his nose—hot and ripe with panic—and hooks of rock caught in his jeans and scraped the back of his skull.

He wanted Nick to be brave for. Or Danny so he could refuse to be shamed in front of a Dog. Fuck it, he even wanted Jack. Hate him or not, at least Gregor wouldn't be alone in the dark if he could hear his brother's heartbeat.

In the end, it was the sound of the prophet's harsh laugh that dragged him the last turns, hatred like a hook in his throat where she'd torn it open.

"Leave the bones," she spat. Her words echoed off the stone, so at least Gregor knew the cave opened out soon. "We're making war, not stock."

The male prophet's voice was lower, harder for Gregor to make out.

"Take it…. We don't have the time to do a neat…."

"Will you put them in your pockets? Will you stick them up your ass? How do you plan to get them out of here intact? Skin them. We can mend them later. The grafts might not have taken on the monsters, but they work well enough for us."

Gregor's thigh, still a web of numb scarring and fresh skin, ached at the reminder of her knife. He swallowed hard and felt an unwelcome flicker of sympathy for Jack, who'd felt the slice and rip of it more than once. Another reason to take his pound of flesh from the prophets—the fact that they made him give a damn that his golden brother had finally fallen in the sewer.

"Work faster," Nick's gran urged. "We have until the bones burn out. Then the Sannock will have their way with us. I'm going to look for her."

Gregor squirmed around into the last sharp-angled corner and saw the golden glow of firelight dance on the mossy stone. The reek of the place was almost tangible, a cloud of sourness that he had to force himself into. He picked his way carefully to the end of the tunnel and stole a look around the corner into the cave.

Tarnished bronze hooks were screwed into the un-even ceiling, and slabs of unskinned, rot-grayed meat hung off them. Copper pots were hung over the black cinders of long-dead fires, the heat-stained, belled sides coated with wax that drooled down to hardened puddles on the ground. At the back of the cave, the old ovens had been relit or had never gone out, and the dull glow of hot metal and flames cast flickering shadows on the walls.

The male prophet was at work in the center of the room, a flensing knife in hand and a bag of salt at his feet. His legs were drenched in blood as he worked the knife between the hide and muscle of the gutted dog carcass. The black hide crackled as the prophet peeled it off the muscle and meat.

Gregor squirmed through the narrow gap and into the cave. He reached up and wrenched one of the hooks off the ceiling. The metal was unsettlingly warm and sweaty against his fingers, and the rattle as he yanked it off the chain made the prophet turn around.

The narrow face under a clown's frill of faded hair wasn't familiar. Nick's gran had called the prophet Lewis, but he wasn't a Scottish Wolf. Gregor didn't know his face or his scent. When he saw Gregor, his murky brown eyes widened in shock, and he opened his mouth.

"Rose!"

Gregor swung the hook. The point caught in the prophet's throat and turned his warning into a shrieked gurgle. It pierced him like a fish, and the prophet choked on his own blood. Gregor yanked it forward and ripped his throat out in a spray of blood and cords. The prophet made a strangled croak of noise and staggered backward, his hands pressed to his throat in an attempt to hold it together long enough to heal.

He tripped over a bundled salted skin on the floor and fell backward. A desperate clutch for balance grabbed the raw, slick leg of the dead Sannock and set it swinging. Gravity dragged blood out of it and splattered it over the floor.

Gregor dodged around the bloody pendulum and swung again. This prophet didn't seem to have a stolen skin to fall back on, just whatever nastiness had seen him sentenced to piety. It wasn't enough. He blocked the first blow with his forearm. The bone snapped with a distinct, muted sound, and the prophet tried to scrabble backward on the uneven floor.

"You'd have been better with the wolf." Gregor stamped his foot down on the man's shoulder and leaned his weight on it. "I'd have enjoyed it less."

He swung the hook underhand, and it punched through the soft wattle of flesh under the prophet's chin. It crunched through his jaw and up into his skull. Death gave him a moment longer than it had Nick. He blinked twice, and then a film of blood glazed his eyes.

Gregor waited for satisfaction, but the anger left no room for it. The prophets needed to die, but *this* prophet wasn't the one he wanted to kill. But he still gave the dead man a kick in the ribs. The limp body flopped over on the floor and leaked a mixture of blood and pale fluid down his nose.

The hook was wedged into his head, caught in the seams of his skull. Gregor wrenched at it briefly, but it wouldn't shift. It didn't matter. There were plenty of others.

He had just grabbed the nearest one—the body of something long and slimy stitched onto it like a worm set for bait—when Nick's gran stalked in. A bloody skin dangled over her arm, freckled and with closely shorn bright red hair. It didn't look Sannock.

"What is it—" She stopped midword. Her eyes flicked from Lewis's body to Gregor, and she folded her lips in a tight smile that didn't show her teeth. "I see. For once he actually had something important to say."

Her washed-out brown eyes met Gregor's with blatant challenge. It made the short hairs on the nape of his neck bristle and his lip curl in a snarl.

"You almost convinced me that Da was involved," he rasped out. "But this? Da might murder his only sons, he might let you make monsters out of the humans, but he'd never rouse the Sannock."

"Are you sure?" The prophet peeled the bloody skin off her arm and folded it like a ma with a school shirt. She laid it on a scarred wooden table, next to dusty loaves of flat black bread. "Really sure? The list of what your da would do seems longer than what he wouldn't do. Maybe there's a lot he'd do that you don't know about. Maybe there's a lot he did that explains everything *I* do."

The curse-ruined lines of Nick's sharp, clever face flashed through Gregor's mind, and he tasted bile. He could remember the conflict in Nick's voice when he talked about his gran, that under the fear and anger, he still wanted to believe that she'd done her best.

"No," he said flatly. "There isn't."

The prophet laughed and then rolled the sound back behind her lips. She tilted her head and mugged regret at him.

"Is this about your wolf?" There was a jab in her voice, a lilt of mockery she couldn't bite back. "The wolf I sliced out of you, the way your da sliced mine out of me? Turnabout is fair play, boy, but fair enough. Except I have mine back."

She smiled at him for the first time, her gums still inflamed where her canines had been as though she'd worried at them all these years. She pulled her stolen fur over her, and it sprouted in discolored patches—black and gray butted up against tawny and fawn. It grew in the wrong directions, whorled like a guinea pig's ass, but it still wrapped around her.

It was instinct to try and follow suit, a deeply buried urge that bypassed the part of his brain that knew it wouldn't work. His body tried. He could feel the heat of it in his bones and in the hot pulse of blood, but his spirit just spasmed around the emptiness where a shape should be. For a second, the pain of it left him undone, hung from the hook he'd grabbed as surely as any of the butchered Sannock.

The prophet laughed, and her arms popped out of joint as her shoulder blades spread to accommodate the span of muscle.

"You have no idea how long I've waited for this." The words twisted in her mouth, half her voice and half the slurred attempts to shape words with her wolf's death-dried tongue. "No idea how satisfying it'll be to kill both the Numitor's bastards."

Gregor swallowed the blood and bile in his throat and dragged himself back to his feet. His knees felt wet, but he forced them to lock.

"So far you've failed to kill either," he said. "Trust me. I've tried to drown my brother. He can fucking swim."

The prophet hunched her patchwork shoulders as she settled into the twisted, half-skin form that Job had worn—the world's first calico Wolf.

"See if you can breathe," she labored out, "wi'out your lungs. Save your brother and his Dog for later."

She lunged for him, the claws on the ends of her fingers so filthy with blood and shit that it screamed of disease. No healthy wolf would let itself sit like that. Pain still vibrated through Gregor as though a raw nerve had been plucked, but he threw himself to the side. He hit the ground and rolled, the uneven floor rough against his back.

It wasn't quick enough. A blow from her paw caught his leg and tore his calf open from knee to ankle. He bit down on his cheek to stifle a scream, hard enough to rip the tender flesh open. The sharp taste of copper mixed with the hot flare of pain that spread down into his toes and up his thigh.

He grabbed the bag of salt the dead prophet had brought with him and flung it into the prophet's face. She yelped and staggered backward as she shook her head and pawed at her salt-chafed eyes.

Gregor hauled himself back to his feet. He grabbed one of the hanging dead and shoved it toward her. She lashed out blindly as it banged into her and fouled her claws in the emptied-out hollow of its guts, and she cursed, eyes still red and wet from the salt, as she wrenched herself free. The strung hook creaked, and the rock it was buried in cracked as she fought with it.

"Do you really think the gods will come, look at you in your sad dead skins, and love you?" Gregor asked. He grabbed a mallet from where it was propped against the wall, the serrated ends of it soiled with dried gray bits of meat. "They're *gods*. They don't love anyone."

The prophet scraped the last of the salt out of her eyes. She shook her head and limped toward him on legs that weren't entirely her own.

"You think I did this? Think I sacrificed my own flesh and blood over and over again, so I could lick the shit from the feet of the gods?" She backhanded a horned corpse and made it spin. "These were gods once or thought themselves so. Now they're stew and hide for my boots. When the gods come, I'll stitch Selene's glowing white skin to my fucking ass. Wolves shouldn't serve the gods, boy, we should *be* gods."

She spat the words out and lunged at Gregor. He swung the hammer, and she didn't even bother to block it. The heavy metal caught her in the ribs and caved them in. Her side collapsed, hide torn to show scarred prophet skin beneath, but the skin mended, and the ribs popped back out. She grabbed Gregor by the throat and picked him up off the ground.

"You're pathetic," she slurred out. An attempt at a smile twisted the corners of her mouth, the flaps of her face trying to shape a gesture that a canine jaw wasn't meant for. "No wonder Wolves hate us. They look at us and see you."

Gregor clawed at her hands, tore off chunks of skin and dry hair to no avail, and tried to suck in air that stank of death and corruption. Even being close to her invited contamination. He grabbed her wrist and dug his fingers into the meat down to the bone. The glow of the untended ovens smeared over her stitch-scabbed face and wet the infection that brewed around her eyes.

"You tortured your own grandson, ended your line," Gregor forced out of his compressed throat. She tightened her hand and pierced the skin with her claws, drawing blood that trickled down into his collar. But her ears were pinned flat to her skull. It was as though he'd hurt the wolf, but not the prophet. "That sorta shit is why you hate *you*."

The prophet peeled him off the wall and tossed him across the room. He hit the ovens and smelled the scorch of wool and skin, the raw scrape of injured nerves before they went numb. The metal clung to him as he tore himself away from it, leaving melted fabric and patches of curled, freshly cooled skin on the curved sides.

"I'd gut you and make soup," the prophet threatened, "but I don't have the time. After this is over, though, I'll come and find you. Wherever you end up, wherever that sad, jealous nugget that passes for your soul slips into the Wild, I'll come for it, and I'll—"

Gregor laughed. He hunched over in front of the ovens, his blistered hands tucked against his stomach as blood puddled around his foot, and sniggered until it made him wheeze.

"What... you think I'm joking?" the prophet spluttered. She kicked the dead man on the floor out of the way. The hook Gregor had embedded in his head scraped sparks off the floor as he rolled, and she stalked toward Gregor. "When I'm a god, I'll skin your soul twice a day and you'll never die. I'll stitch your carcass to—"

"Oh, shut the fuck up."

Gregor grabbed the pot that had simmered on the heat since the Sannock were gutted, since the Numitor ended the Wolves who'd done this. It scalded his hands as he gripped it, and the tendons pulled tight as they cooked. The stink of hot, rendered fat rose up from the greasy mess in the pot.

Fear flashed over the prophet's face, and she stepped backward. Before she could take another, Gregor tossed the hot liquid contents of the pot at her. It hit her in the face, and the borrowed skin sloughed off her bones as it fried. It splashed in her eye, cooked it white, and blistered the prophet tongue under the dead wolf's.

"Little bastard," she moaned out as she doubled over. "Won't stop me."

"Yeah. I know." Gregor ripped the sleeve of his stolen jumper and shoved it into the fire. It lit sluggishly and then burned eagerly. The dry wool and lanolin were bright and smoky as the flame spread up the weft of it. "This will."

The hot fat had splashed everywhere. It glistened on the naked flanks of the Sannock Dead, soaked greasily into the dead prophet's hair, and cooled to a white film on the tables and clumsily made chairs.

It was good to see fear in the prophet's yellowed eyes. She stripped the wolf off and shrank back into her skin, and the blistered eye and burned face came with her.

"Wait." She held her hands to stop him. Her fingers shook. "Wait. What do you care about the Wolves, boy? Your father always favored your brother didn't he? Always saw too much of himself in you. I can…. Come with me, and you can rule them. We can see your potential."

The flames licked around Gregor's fingers. He'd already done enough damage that he could barely feel it—just a faint wash of nausea at the smell of his own cooked skin.

"You don't have anything I want."

She licked her lips and stepped forward, her hands still out. "Don't I? I can give you the wolf back."

He hated that he hesitated, but he did. "Not my wolf."

The prophet shrugged. "A wolf. Better than none. Better than human. Or even better." She jabbed a finger at the greasy table, at the plate of flat black bread that moldered there. "You know what they are. You've heard the stories. Bone for flour, blood for milk, that's what the black bitch baked with."

There was a greed in Wolves. Gregor glanced at the Sannock bread and wondered what blood and bone would taste like on his tongue, what it would fill the cavity with. He still wouldn't have his wolf, but he'd have something.

"You'd give me anything, wouldn't you?" he asked.

She nodded and smiled and edged closer. "Anything. Your heart's desire."

Gregor tossed the burning wool into a puddle of fat and grinned as it flared and spat. It spread from puddle to puddle, a fast, smoky burn that found enough tinder in the dead and the skinned to spread. It caught on the prophet's stolen hide and crawled up her hair. It clung to her face and spread when she tried to slap it away.

"You should have offered that before you killed Nick," Gregor told her. "You can't give him back."

The prophet snuffed the fire out on her face and glanced around desperately, a glimpse of bone visible through the char-black skin. Fire had claimed the corpses she'd come to render down to skin and power. She lunged past Gregor and grabbed the folded skin from the table, the fire bright between her fingers as she brushed the sparks and cinders off it.

"You should have taken my offer," she said. "We won't make it again."

She hugged the skin close to her chest, her arms folded around it, and fled through the fire. It licked at her legs and caught in the stitched seams of her tailored skin, which came apart in patches and burned eagerly, like paper, as it fell to the floor.

Naked and blistered, her hair on fire like a comet, the prophet threw herself into the narrow tunnel. She was skinny and wasted enough to squirm through easily.

Gregor knew he wasn't going to catch her. His leg was a bloody mess, his arms and hands blistered and numb. It would be easier to stay and die there, instead of trapped in the twisted chimney that was the Sannock front door.

On the other hand, if he knew when to give up, he'd have accepted years ago that his da preferred Jack.

He dragged himself through the tight folds of granite, his nose and throat filled with smoke. As he fumbled along the walls with his raw hands—he'd left half of his palms caught on rough stone—they still hurt.

Halfway. If he was right about how many turns he'd taken on the way in, he was halfway out when the smoke and the pain were too much. He sagged down as far as the narrow space would let him, and he waited for Nick's dead woman.

Chapter Twenty-Two

DEATH SUCKED more than Nick had expected.

He walked along the empty halls of his old hospital. There was no other sinner there, although the beds were turned back as though people had just left, and charts had been abandoned midnotation on desks, but the sound of his heavy boots on the scrubbed tiles still made Nick feel self-conscious, as though he should apologize to something.

Apparently being dead was just like being alive, only quiet and more boring.

The minute he thought that, Nick knew it was stupid. He hunched his shoulders and glanced around as he waited for a door to bang or a howl to echo. Nothing. He waited for a minute. When nothing happened, he started to walk again.

After his second round of the ward—nothing ever moved, but if he left a room and came back, things *had changed—he realized he was wasting his time. If there was any point to this, it would be downstairs in the morgue.*

He walked to the elevators first, pressed the button, and waited. It wasn't until the doors slid open to reveal an empty stretcher and dropped defib pads that he decided he'd rather take the stairs, just in case.

It was a long walk down, and there was nothing at the bottom. The morgue was as empty as the rest of the hospital. His chair was there, though, and a coat that wasn't his was slung over the back. The seat had the same odd wobble when he sat down on it and stretched his feet out in front of him.

He smelled burned meat first. People said burned flesh was burned flesh, but you could always tell when it was human in Nick's experience. There was just something slick and greasy about it that raised the bile in the back of your throat. Somehow your body knew it was tainted.

Nick straightened up from his slouch and heard something tap from inside one of the lockers. Tap, tap, tap. It rattled the metal doors and left sharp dents in them.

"Shit."

He hunched in his chair and wondered if he could just ignore it—not for long, in an empty hospital where he felt as though he'd just missed everything.

Tap, tap, tap.

He pushed himself up and walked to the locker. The door rattled and jounced in its hinges as he struggled with the latch. He could feel the force of the impact against his hands. The clip finally slipped loose, and the door slapped open. It slammed against the locker next to it with such a crash that Nick had to bite back the habitual sorry on his tongue.

Someone had shoved a huge black bird into the locker—a bird bigger than the humans Nick usually shoved in there, because its wings were jammed against the sides. It stared at him with black eyes over a scored bone-white beak and cackled at the look on his face.

No noise came out of the gaped beak, with its split, wagging tongue, but Nick heard it in his head.

"Oh, it's you," he said. "I thought you left."

The bird fluffed itself and locked down. Its breast feathers were bloody and ragged. They stuck out at odd angles from its skin, and a lump of raw flesh lay between its scaled feet.

It wasn't a gift. There'd be a price.

Nick could smell cooked flesh and hear the ragged sound of someone who'd almost given up on breathing. He didn't know who it was, but it had to be Gregor. Who else mattered?

"I don't want to be a monster."

The bird shrugged because Gran had gotten it wrong. Nick rubbed his chest and felt the old, almost forgotten seam that ran down to his sternum. The way to a man's heart wasn't through his stomach. It was with a saw and retractor through the sternum wall. Luckily enough, he had access to them in a morgue.

He gingerly reached for the heart, and the habit of a lifetime made him convinced the bird would peck or flap as he picked it up. It felt like a stone in his hand, heavier than it should be but still warm and wet.

"Whatever you want," he said. "I'll pay it."

NICK WOKE up, and he couldn't move. He couldn't even open his eyes. For a nauseating, claustrophobic second, he thought that was the price. That the bird's heart had been like the monkey's paw—be careful what you wish for.

He tried again, desperately that time, and heard something crack. Something cold slid between his lips. Ice. It had frozen over him like a colder version of Snow White's glass coffin. His breath melted it from over his mouth and nose, and Nick kicked his way out of the rest of the casing. He huffed on his hands and rubbed his eyes until the seal of frost melted from his lashes and he could open his eyes.

The bonfire had gone out, but the dead were still there. They stood with the Sannock and stared at him with expectant faces. Waiting.

Nick licked his lips and swallowed the snow melt. He searched the faces of the dead until he found Jepson's. She dipped her chin.

"Thank you," he said aloud. "I think you can go now."

He felt the release like an exhaled breath. The dead faded and fell apart. The smoke and salt of them unraveled and diffused. All that was left was the smell of burned wood and the Sannock. Nick wiped his hand over his mouth—sick with relief that it felt like a mouth again, that he had fingers to press against chilled lips—and scrambled to his feet. The world was slick with ice around him, a milky glaze that poured down the beach and into the sea. It looked eerie and alien, like something from a nightmare.

The Sannock told him *Wait*. It was a silent, communal instruction in his head. He didn't know for what, or if they even knew he could hear them.

Either way... "You can fuck off," he told them. The Glasgow boy was thick in his voice.

He turned his back on them and picked his way gingerly up the shore. The ice was thick enough to skate on, slippery and uneven underfoot. In the back of his head, the black cackle of *presence* mocked his slow progress.

It felt different from before, the roots of it more anchored in his brain, woven into the synapses. He pressed his fingers against his chest. It didn't feel tender, but he could feel his heartbeat, and it had an echo.

There'd be a price. Nick glanced up and saw smoke eddy from the cliff, black and thick like a grease fire on the hob. He swore and scrambled faster up the scrubby, sharp-edged dunes toward the cave. Grass snapped under his feet, brittle as glass. He'd pay any price, but only if he got Gregor back.

The bird in his brain clacked its beak at him. That wasn't how it worked.

"You can fuck off too," he told it flatly.

That sent it into creaky paroxysms of amusement. He ignored it as he slithered down the other side of the dune. When he reached the bottom, he saw a smoldering figure land at the base of the cliff and roll in the snow. It wasn't Gregor. He could tell that from here.

His gran pushed herself to her feet. The flames had sizzled through her hair and given her the tight perm he remembered from his childhood. She was blind and burned, her skin red where it wasn't black and charred, but Nick still couldn't make himself care.

She shuffled forward, her hand out cautiously in front of her as she squinted eyes that were puffed with blisters like a frog's. But they were still sharp enough to make him out.

"Nicholas?" she said.

What was worse, the guilt that she sounded so happy to see him or the fear at the undertone of smug possession? Nick couldn't tell.

"Gran," he said.

She smiled. "Look at you, boy. I never thought it'd work so well. You have to come with me now."

He shook his head. Then he realized that she probably couldn't see him. "No."

"Don't be stubborn, Nicholas," she said. "I might not be kind, but I've always told you the truth, haven't I? You have questions, don't you? I have the answers."

There was always a price. Nick didn't need the bird to know that. And he didn't know if he was willing to pay whatever tally his gran had set up for him.

"You'll tell me now? Here?"

She huffed and shook her head. Her fried hair bounced on her shoulders. "We have to go. I'll answer all your questions, Nicholas. You just have to do as you're told."

Nick guessed he did know how badly he wanted answers—not enough.

"No."

There was something clutched to her chest, a singed bundle of pale, freckled leather. Nick felt a wan pang of disgust. He'd been a coroner. He'd seen worse than a bit of flayed skin. There was a bright tickle of hungry interest in his head as the bird used his brain to wonder if the skin would taste like jerky or crackling. That was gross.

Gran sidled another step forward. "You have to come with me, Nicholas. You have to show the others that I was right, that we can wear the gods like our skins."

He laughed at her. It was the first time he'd ever really done that, let out a genuine blurt of mocking amusement that briefly made her flinch.

"That's what you think?" he said. He thought it was more like the god wore him. "No. I won't come with you. I need to find Gregor."

Blisters popped and leaked as Gran grimaced sourly. "I didn't ask you, Nicholas. I told you."

"I'm not a child."

"I don't care." She reached back and pulled the singed, patchwork wolf back over her. It spread raggedly over her but left patches of Gran's own skin bald where the fire had eaten too much of it to patch. "Don't be stupid, Nicholas. The Wolves won't want you. If they did, wouldn't they have come to take you off me before?"

She lunged for him with a clawed half-wolf hand. Nick flinched at the memory of teeth in his shoulder, the sharply alien sensation of something that scraped over his bones. Panic caught in his throat, a bubble trapped against the back of his throat, and he felt like his skeleton collapsed under the weight of it. He felt a weightless slip as he dropped and then….

The bird didn't want to be *rude*, but it was easier to ask forgiveness than permission—not that it had ever done either. It croaked a laugh into Gran's face and spread its wings to catch the wind, cold and sharp with ice under its feathers.

Shock flashed over Gran's twisted half-and-half face as she saw the huge bone-beaked bird where her grandson had been. She'd thought her... graft—it picked the word from Nick like a shiny thing from a stream—had taken, but not that well.

The bird stabbed its head forward and pecked at the fold of leather that Gran hugged so close. It punched a hole through the untreated skin. Gran yelped in protest and slapped at its head. The bird croaked a laugh at her and beat its wings to take itself up. It stooped over her head, close enough that it could have snatched hair from her scalp, and let the wind spin it into the air.

Laid out below it, the world was both flatter and sharper than it had been in Nick's head. It blurred at the edges and lacked contrast but was striped in colors that Nick had never seen. The flutter of movement on the beach caught its attention like a flag, and it felt the urge to chase.

In the back of its head, it felt Nick's worry, and it huffed to itself. When it was Nick, it knew that it wasn't that annoying. With a last, tempted look at the things on the beach, it gave in and flicked a wing tip to head for the cliff.

The smoke caught under its wings. Hot air battered it with changes in pressure, but it was used to that. Fire was common enough on the battlefields it had spread its wings over in the past. It aimed at the cliff face and let its feathers flip back to meat and muscle just before it hit.

Nick felt the wicked humor of the bird sink back down into him just as he slapped face-first against the rock. He grunted out a lungful of air and scrambled for a handhold to steady himself. A quick glance over his shoulder revealed his gran in flight up the coast. He felt… concerned for what she was going to do and, despite everything, concern for her. He hated it, but she was his gran.

"Gregor," he called as he edged toward the ribbon of smoke.

There was no answer. He folded his lean frame through the crack in the cliff, thankful for once for his wiry build, and squirmed through. Inside he was blind, what night vision he had brutally compromised. He quashed a bubble of panic and fumbled his way through the dark until he reached the body slumped in the ready-made coffin halfway through.

"Gregor." He fumbled his hand over Gregor's shoulder and up to his face. "It's me. Come on. Don't do this to me. I came all the way back. Don't let me have missed you at death's door."

There was no answer, not even a groan. Nick leaned up and felt a tickle of breath against his cheek. Relief nearly left him slouched against the wall next to Gregor, but the heat building in the tunnel left no time for that. He dragged Gregor's arm over his shoulder, the slack weight of him heavy as ever, and pulled him back toward the entrance.

Once outside, he had no idea how to get them both down. The bird in his skull pretended it was too lofty to deal with that, but Nick didn't think it had any answers. Nick dragged Gregor as far along the narrow path as they could get and then slid down to the ground to wait for rescue. He hung his legs over the side and cradled Gregor in his lap.

There were bruises on his lean, handsome face, and burns pocked his cheeks and jawline. His hands were clawed, his palms rough with thick burns and blisters. They would heal. Nick had seen him heal from worse.

He bent down and pressed a kiss against Gregor's mouth, and the taste of smoke mingled on their tongues.

"I came back for you," he said. "You don't get to die."

Gregor's mouth curved under his lips with that smile that still caught Nick off guard with its uncharacteristic sweetness—and opened eyes green as glass.

"Second time you saved me," he said in a smoke-raw voice. "Now you can't leave me, not till I return the favor."

IT TOOK an hour—maybe, nothing seemed to change in the pocket of the Sannock's grave—before the man who looked like Gregor found them. He was drenched, his salt-heavy clothes frozen on him, and a lean, dark man with a myopic squint shadowed him.

Nick had picked up that Gregor wasn't always fond of his brother, of *having* a brother, but there was a flash of unadulterated relief on Jack's face when he saw Gregor alive. He cupped his hands around his mouth and shouted.

"Can you get down?"

"I don't need your help," Gregor tried to yell.

"Yes we do!"

Gregor let a growl roll in his chest, but he didn't argue. His pride wouldn't let him ask for help, apparently—although his hands were still locked in burn-tight fists—but he'd take it if it was forced on him, even if it was from his brother.

After a quick discussion with his lover—a hand cupped around the back of his neck, a rough kiss that spoke of fear—Jack scrambled up to their perch.

"The prophet?" Gregor asked. There was suspicion in his eyes when he looked at Jack.

"Gran," Nick said. He wasn't going to lie about her. Even when he thought she was crazy, he hadn't done that. It only made things worse when people found out. "She got away."

Gregor begrudgingly rolled off his lap and, using his legs and with his shoulders braced against the cliff, pushed himself up.

"Without her prize," he said, "the Sannock will stay here."

Nick hesitated because Gran had gotten away with part of her prize, hadn't she? He was going to mention it, but maybe it didn't matter. What was one torn, charred skin going to do for her? Besides, before he could say anything, Jack and Gregor snarled at each other about the best way down the cliff.

In the end, Jack slung Gregor over his shoulder and easily scrambled down to the waiting... dog? Nick supposed he'd need to ask about that sometime. He followed more cautiously, and it only occurred to him as he reached the bottom with trembling legs and sweat frozen under his arms, that he could have flown.

The bird laughed at him.

NICK SAT vigil over another patient, and Gregor had already snarled at his disloyalty. It turned out that Gregor was supposed to be the only person Nick cared about, and Nick had to admit that it surprised him a little that it wasn't true. The bird in his head certainly didn't, and it resented the boredom of the watch.

Copeland lay in the narrow hospital cot with her bandage-mittened hands folded under her chin. She wasn't as flawlessly pretty as she'd been, but her scruffed-up face was still better than Nick had expected. Whatever the prophets' venom had done to them, it had provided some physical protection—not enough, but some. Copeland would never be a surgeon again, but she'd be *something*. That was good enough for Nick. He hoped it would be good enough for her one day.

"You don't have to go," she said. "Nobody blames you."

That was kind, but not true. Even Copeland looked at him with wariness, his blood too obvious in his face. He looked like Gran, apparently, or so they said. Nick didn't know how he felt about that.

"I could stay," he said.

"We need you," Copeland insisted. She raised her hands gingerly. "People are hurt. People are… there has to be a way to undo what she did."

Nick leaned over and patted her leg. "You'll find it," he said. It certainly wouldn't be him. Since the bird moved in, he could smell the rage-inducing wrong of the infected. The Wolves wanted to kill them, had seen it as a kindness—even the curse-touched children—but Nick had convinced them to let the locals decide their own fates. Danny—who might one day forgive Nick's crack about thinking he was a real doctor—had backed him up. "I need to go, Copeland. She needs to be stopped."

Even the indirect mention of Gran made Copeland blanch gray under her dark skin and avert her eyes. She searched the corners of the tent—full now with Girvan townspeople as they sweated out slick poison—as though Gran might be hidden in a shadow. Nick knew that fear.

"Did you ever hear her talk about what she had planned?" he asked.

She scratched her nose on her wrist and grimaced. "I don't know. I wasn't... nothing seemed to really matter, you know? They talked about an army. She talked about some man."

"Who?"

Copeland scratched her nose again. Nick *tch*ed at her and pulled her hand down. "Leave it be."

She pulled a face at him but wormed her hands under the sheets. "I don't know. She said he'll regret that he'd picked someone else. He'll see who the real wolf is. Well, he would once she had it."

"It?" Nick pressed. He saw the raw, neatly folded skin his gran had clutched, her skin blistered to protect it from the fire. "Not them?"

Copeland hesitated but finally nodded. "The man said 'them,' but she wanted something particular. Sorry."

"Me too," he told her. "I should have come back for you."

She grimaced. "And Harris? Jepson? What would you have done, carried us all away over your shoulder? I'm alive. I'm me. That's down to you, I think."

Nick didn't know that. He hoped so.

"You'll be okay," he told her. "If you get a chance, go home. Forget about what happened here."

She dragged her eyes back to his and searched his face. "Will you?"

"Too late for me," he said. "Always has been."

She looked pitying. He didn't know if he wanted that, but he doubted he could convince her otherwise.

"I'll miss you, Copeland."

The startled smile that spread over her face made her beautiful again. "You know, my name's Fiona."

"I probably knew that," Nick said. "Be safe, Fiona."

"You too, Nick," she said. Then she wrinkled her nose and stuck her tongue out. "That didn't feel right."

"Be safe, Copeland," Nick corrected himself dryly. "Go home."

That time she just smiled and nodded. He peeled himself stiffly out of the uncomfortable chair and left the tent. It was quiet outside for once. The world looked clean and white and safe. It wasn't, but it was still beautiful.

Nick shoved his hands into the pockets of his long coat and headed back to his caravan.

"That's a good stick," the bird noted. It jacked control of Nick's eyes and made him look at it. He could use that stick.

"I don't need a stick."

That was obviously wrong. Everyone needed a stick. To poke things. To pry things. To give to someone who needed a stick. That was a good stick.

Nick gave in and picked up the long, broken branch. He jabbed it at the ground as he walked and drilled holes into the snow ahead of him. He wished he could puncture his worries about what his gran had planned so easily.

She'd planned it his whole life. It couldn't have begun and ended with the Sannock. Nick glanced up from the ground and glanced sidelong at the forest. It was just the black dog today, hollow eyed and hungry as it wove from puddle of shadows to puddle of shadows.

It *hadn't* ended with the Sannock.

That was something else he should probably tell the Wolves. So why hadn't he? Because there was nothing they could do? Or because Nick was scared he—whatever he was—was more akin to the Sannock than the Wolves?

The stick would fix it. The bird was blithely confident about that. The bird was blithely confident about many things. Nick… wasn't so sure, yet he still ducked into his trailer and grabbed his duffel bag from the hook. There wasn't much in it. It daunted him a bit to realize how little he had that actually mattered.

Gregor mattered. That was the one thing Nick *was* still sure about. Well, that and the fact that he mattered to Gregor.

So he shrugged the pack on, hung on to the bird's stick, and struck out toward the woods where the Wolves—and the Sannock—waited.

Epilogue

GREGOR MET him as he left the road and hooked an arm around his neck. He pulled him close, his hands healed enough to use despite the tight stripes of scar tissue, and pressed a roughly possessive kiss against the corner of Nick's mouth.

"Took you long enough," he grumbled against Nick's cold skin.

Not that Nick felt the cold like he used to. The bird refused to even admit that it was cold. It was used to far harsher and far wilder.

"Nick," Danny said. He sounded... careful, as though he wanted to be friendly but regretfully knew it was a bad idea. Even after everything Nick had seen—after the prophets turned his body into a bird-shaped prison—it was still hard to accept this soft-spoken man had been the big gray stray. He squinted shortsightedly at Nick until they drew closer. "We weren't sure you'd come."

"Neither was I," Nick admitted.

"Maybe you shouldn't have, then," Jack said. His voice rolled out of him like a growl as he came up to hover protectively beside Danny. It was disorienting for Nick to see dislike aimed at him out of Gregor's green eyes and distrust on the handsome, stubborn planes of his face. He had to brace himself against it. "You aren't a Wolf. There won't be a warm welcome for you when we get to Da's den."

Gregor tightened his arm possessively around Nick. "Fuck Da, then," he said. "He tried to kill us, if you remember."

"Said the prophets," Jack pointed out. "Nobody but a fool trusts a prophet." He didn't look at Nick. It was obvious that he didn't look, but he might as well have given in to the urge.

"I'm not a prophet," Nick said. "I don't know what I am, but I'm just me. My gran… I haven't been on her side for a long time. I've seen nothing to change my mind recently."

His assurance softened Jack's face but obviously didn't change his mind. "I know," he said. "She's still blood, though. I've spent years expecting to kill Gregor, but I'd still back him against anyone else. So if you aren't sure whose side you're on? Stay here."

"I know whose side I'm on," Nick said.

THE LONG, segmented train was the only thing that moved through the snow-quilted landscape. It rattled along the ice-covered tracks with a skeleton crew of engineers and drivers with more to worry about than if they'd picked up hitchhikers along the way.

Gregor stood at the door and watched the Wild thicken and clot around the narrow wood and metal car he'd commandeered when they hopped the train. That far north, the Wild had peeled back the surface of the world to reveal itself, and the train that punched through it was an irritant—a foreign body.

Time would tell if the tracks had been there long enough to embed themselves in the landscape's idea of itself. If it had, the Wild might accept it in some form. If not, it would callus over the infection with ice and time. Either way, by then, Gregor hoped, all four of them would be healed enough not to need the lift anymore.

The black bird stooped out of the sky and skimmed alongside the train. Its shadow skipped along the frozen ground, black and sharp lined against the hard-packed white.

Three of them, Gregor corrected himself as he stepped back and pulled the door open.

Snow flurried in through the gap and settled on the stacked boxes and scavenged bedding—whoever was at the terminus of the train line would be disappointed in their fresh crated quilts—to settle in drifts and clumps. Gregor focused on the cold as the bird skimmed through the gap, and not on the cramp of jealousy as the bird landed on bare human feet and straightened up into Nick.

"No sticks?" Gregor asked dryly as he slammed the door shut again. "Doesn't the birdbrain love me anymore?"

Nick laughed and shivered. The bird didn't feel the cold, but naked and vulnerable pathologists still did. He tumbled into Gregor's arms to steal some of his heat. His skin was cold enough that it felt like frost, as though his pale skin might melt under Gregor's hands.

"None worth your time, apparently," Nick said. "Where are Jack and Danny?"

"Hunting."

Nick tucked the sharp point of his chin into Gregor's shoulder. The cold-spiked crest of his hair smelled sweet and faintly of fresh death—a hint of carrion eater. Probably not the cologne he'd pick, but Gregor didn't mind it. "I could let the bird out more," he said. "Try to roost or whatever it is birds do."

The offer didn't come with any explanation. Neither of them needed it. The topic had been talked to death, to Nick's face and behind his back, until the only option was avoidance or bloodshed.

"Let them curl up in the snow," Gregor said shortly. "If it doesn't kill them, it'll harden them."

That had always been Da's favorite saying. Broken bones or broken hearts either hardened you or killed you, and Da had never seemed to care which.

"You can't blame them," Nick said.

"Watch me." Gregor peeled Nick off his shoulder and waited until Nick looked up at him. His eyes had always been dark, but now they were true black and faintly alien in his very human, bony face. "Let them freeze. I like your company more than theirs."

Worry still pinched the corners of Nick's mouth while something as human as guilt scrawled those solid black eyes. So Gregor cupped the back of his head and dragged him into a kiss. His mouth still tasted like Nick, the supple compliance of his lean body as sweet as the first time. It just took less time to get him naked.

He reached down between their bodies and roughly groped Nick's cock. It lifted eagerly into his touch, and Nick paid him in a groan that spilled between their lips. Gregor smirked and nudged Nick backward toward one of the still-sealed metal crates. He grabbed a handful of Nick's ass and lifted him onto the top of the box.

Nick yelped as his thighs came into contact with the metal. "Fuck, that's cold," he gasped. Gregor kissed the protest into silence as he yanked his jeans open and shoved them down. As the denim slid down to his knees, he braced his arms against the crate so Nick's legs were hooked up over his forearms.

It spread him out for Gregor. Nick's cock nudged up against his stomach, and his lean, tight cheeks spread to show the pucker of his ass.

"My hands are busy," Gregor pointed out.

A pale flush washed up through Nick's face, which caught Gregor by surprise. It oddly delighted him. He liked it, although he didn't usually appreciate prudishness. There was just something satisfying about being able to slide so easily through someone's defenses, as though they had none against you.

Nick leaned his weight on one arm and reached down to press a spit-wet finger against his ass. He squirmed as he worked himself wider, and the color that flagged over his cheeks had nothing to do with embarrassment anymore. He was all spare flesh and long, elegant bones, beautiful in a way that Gregor appreciated because he knew not everyone saw it. It made it his.

The ache in Gregor's balls thickened and tightened as the lust set. His cock felt *heavy* with it as it twitched and hardened, the skin taut around the thick shaft. Nick didn't see that. He had closed his eyes and folded his lower lip between his teeth as the muscles in his forearms clenched and loosened with the work of his hand.

"Look at me," Gregor rasped out, and Nick's eyes popped open. "I saw enough of my brother when we shared a womb. So let him sulk in the snow. It gets us some privacy."

He freed one hand to guide his cock, skin fine and sweat slick against his fingers, into Nick. Pleasure pulsed up his cock as Nick's body folded tightly around the thickness of it and the squeeze of it ached sweetly back to his balls.

Nick grabbed a handful of his sweater, hooked his fingers through the wool, and pulled him in for a cold, sweet, breathless kiss. He still had doubts—they'd talked that to death too and picked fucking instead of avoidance—but he let them go unsaid.

The rattle and jolt of the train set Gregor's rhythm for him. He gripped Nick's hips in his hands to hold him in place as he thrust into him in pursuit of the hot pulse of pleasure that he could feel throb somewhere between his tailbone and his asshole.

Sweat slicked between their bodies despite the cold. Nick wrapped his legs around Gregor's waist to urge him on while he skimmed kisses against the corner of Gregor's mouth and down the tight cords of his throat.

If he'd been a wolf, he'd have sunk his teeth in. Gregor missed the sharp pressure of teeth digging into his skin and the slippery spill of blood, but instead he had Nick's ragged gasp against his neck and the sharp itch as his nails dug into his back.

Not to mention a fine collection of sticks.

He laughed against Nick's shoulder, the sweat salty and sharp against his lips.

"What?" Nick gasped out as he clung to Gregor's shoulder. His mouth found the pad of scar tissue where his gran tried to rip out Gregor's throat. Gregor could tell because he couldn't feel it. There was just a dim pressure and a numb itch along his nerves.

"Nothing," Gregor said. He bit a possessive kiss into Nick's shoulder. There was no blood, but the red-and-purple bruise would last longer than it would on a Wolf. "I just like you."

Nick leaned back and caught Gregor's face in his hands to tilt it back. "Yeah well," he said. "I love you, so I win."

"I know," Gregor growled.

It was Nick's turn to laugh, which made his ass flutter around Gregor's cock. Gregor would have explained—that love was sweet, but the more important thing was that Nick was *his*—but his mouth was otherwise occupied as Nick twisted his fingers in his hair and kissed him.

Gregor drank it down, eager as always for Nick's open offer of affection, and buried himself deeply inside Nick. He came with a stutter of his hips, his fingers tight enough that he knew he'd leave bruises. Nick swore with his tongue tangled around Gregor's and tightened his legs to pull closer. His cock rubbed slick and hard against Gregor's stomach as he ground against him. He muttered a second "I love you" as he spilled himself stickily over their stomachs. The rich smell of their come hung in the air, ripe and metallic and potent.

They stayed there for a minute, held up by one another as they recovered. Gregor wove his fingers through Nick's hair and admitted, "I love you too."

It might be weak, but it was true.

The world ends not with a bang, but with a downpour. Tornadoes spin through the heart of London, New York cooks in a heat wave that melts tarmac, and Russia freezes under an ever-thickening layer of permafrost. People rally at first—organizing aid drops and evacuating populations—but the weather is only getting worse.

In Durham, mild-mannered academic Danny Fennick has battened down to sit out the storm. He grew up in the Scottish Highlands, so he's seen harsh winters before. Besides, he has an advantage. He's a werewolf. Or, to be precise, a weredog. Less impressive, but still useful.

Except the other werewolves don't believe this is any ordinary winter, and they're coming down over the Wall to mark their new territory. Including Danny's ex, Jack—the Crown Prince Pup of the Numitor's pack—and the prince's brother, who wants to kill him.

A wolf winter isn't white. It's red as blood.

Now Available at
www.dreamspinnerpress.com

Chapter One

WINTER HAD fallen like a hammer. The cold tasted like needles, and the wind knotted snow in Jack's hair. The wind shoved at him like a hand, trying to push him back up the hill. No one could remember a harsher winter—bearing in mind his family had a long memory—and the calendar had only reached September. Strange weather. Wild weather.

His boots slid on the ice that glazed the beaten dirt of the old track, and when he cut over the moors the frost-brittle heather crackled like small bones. By the time Jack got to the old stones, his T-shirt was stiff with frozen sweat, and the cold had crept down to his balls. If anyone from Lochwinnoch saw him they'd think he'd run mad. Gods knew what they'd make of the scene on the loch.

The old man stood bollock-naked in the dark water, six foot from the rocky shore. The tattoos covering him from hips to shoulder blade, ink faded from black to blue with age, stood stark against chill-paled skin. The rest of the family crouched on rocks or sat cross-legged on the ground, waiting.

For him.

Jack's brother stalked out of the crowd, shoving their kin out of his way roughly. "You're late," Gregor said, breath misting around his lips. He jabbed a finger against Jack's chest. "You ignore a summons again, and I'll break your legs. Can't walk far then."

Jack grinned at him, humorless and toothy. "Touch me again, and I'll—"

"Boys. Enough." The voice sounded thin, the usual timbre stripped by the wind, but it still scruffed them both. Mouth set in a sneer, Gregor backed off. Jack nodded to the broad, scarred back.

"Da."

The old man turned around, ice crackling around his knees as he moved. He must have been standing out there for hours, letting the water freeze around him.

"Jack." The old man dragged his hand down his face, wiping the frost out of his beard, and jerked a thumb over his shoulder. "D'ya see?"

Not well. The snow was like a blanket, with only glimpses visible through the weave. If Jack squinted, he could just make out a string of lights crawling out of town. They were heading west, to the road.

"They're leaving."

"Aye." The old man sounded smug. He'd no real grudge against the humans that lived there, but the settlement had offended him on the day the humans built it. "Evacuatin'. They sent us a letter too."

Everyone laughed—a low growling roll of amusement.

"What does it mean?" Jack asked.

His da scratched his beard. With the cold snap, they'd all spent more time in fur than not, and the old man's nails were sharp enough to shred the gray and black bristles. "The great winter is here at last. Our prophets were right. Mad bastards, but right."

A ripple of excitement ran through the crowd. Eyes glittered black and eager as they whooped and clapped, smacking hands against their thighs. They'd all been waiting for this day for a long, long time— ever since Hadrian had turned on the monsters he'd found in his legions and banished them over the wall. Rome had turned its back on them, but in the old, high places up here they'd found gods who shared their fangs, and their hunger. Gods born of cold lands and bitter winters, who'd promised to one day give them the world to eat.

Now that day had come.

So why did Jack feel in his marrow that something bad was coming?

The old man waded out of the water, absently waving off a wee lad with a blanket, and walked over to the brothers. He was hairy as a boar, gray thick over his chest and shoulders, and so broad with muscle that he looked short until you found yourself looking up at him. Habit made Jack pull himself up straight, and out of the corner of his eye he saw Gregor do the same.

They were the same height, the same way they wore the same face and the same eyes and the same sandy-fair hair. The only thing they didn't share was the twelve-minute head start one of them had gotten on life, although their ma would never tell them which had come first. Even on her dying day, she'd eaten that secret.

Ignoring their automatic posturing, the big man dropped a hard hand on Jack's shoulder. "And it means something else, boy. I'm heartsore over it, but it means you ain't one of us anymore. You have to go."

For a second Jack didn't feel anything. Maybe the chill had gotten deeper than he thought. The pronouncement of his exile cramped dully in his gut, a feeling of loss as unavoidable as gravity.

Gregor laughed, a startled blurt of triumph. Their da backhanded him, slapping the sound back into his mouth and laying him out on the ground.

"Losing one of us is nothing to gloat over," he growled. "Not at the best of time, not now. And you, boy, you didn't win the toss by some grand margin. There wasn't even twelve minutes in it."

Propping himself up on his elbow, Gregor wiped his mouth sullenly on the back of his hand. Blood smeared bright as a crayon over his knuckles. His eyes were dark and bitter under the straight line of his eyebrows.

Both of them wanted to know. Jack asked first.

"So what was it, then?" he asked, the dullness giving way to anger. "If he wasn't older, or better, why exile me and not him, Da?"

Annoyance crimped the old man's mouth, lips bleeding white, and he looked away. "You know why. I take no pleasure in this, but if you will not change your ways, then you have to leave. It's how things are."

"What things?" Jack asked. He knew—he'd known when he got the summons—but he wanted to make the old man spit the fucking words out. "If there's not even twelve minutes in it, Da, then why does Gregor get to stay, and I have to go?"

The old man shook his head.... "It's the end of the world, boy. Too late for any of us to change now."

"What. Things," Jack growled, voice rasping in his throat. If it had been *fair*—if he'd been weak, or ailing, or if he'd lost a challenge—he could have accepted it. Strength was the rule that ordered all their lives. Except he was a good son, a good wolf, and this wasn't fair. He shouldered into the old man's space, smelling the dander and musk of him on the air. "If you're going to exile your own kid, have the balls to say why, Da."

Hooded, stony eyes met his. They held grief, and pity, but no regret. When the old man *still* didn't say anything, Jack's temper bubbled over into stupidity. He shoved the old man, punching the heels of his hands against heavy shoulders. His da stepped back, and everyone gasped. It had been thirty years since anyone had laid hands on the Numitor, and then it had been Jack's ma in a temper.

Buoyed on the hot rise of his anger, Jack thought about it for a second. Challenge the Numitor and win, and it wouldn't matter what the old man said anymore. It wouldn't matter what anyone thought—

Jack didn't even see the old man move. One minute they were glaring at each other; then the old man's hand closed around Jack's throat. His thumb, callused to leather from work, pressed against the fast throb of Jack's pulse.

"I don't answer to you, boy," his da said. "I've told you my ruling. That it's my fucking whim is all the words you need to know."

Jack cast his eyes over the crowd, seeing kin and friends he'd known for long enough it didn't seem like there was much difference. All of them avoided meeting his gaze. He twisted his mouth in a hard smile, because why pretend anymore? "So it's the length of a dick, is that it, Da?" he said, feeling the word squeeze past his da's thumb. "If I'd just fucked some girl from town every now and again, you'd have let me stay?"

The old man let go of him. Jack stumbled back, swallowing hard and resisting the urge to rub his throat. He wanted to cower, to beg, but he kept his chin up and met his da's glare defiantly.

"It ain't in you to change," his da said. "And it ain't in you to serve. All that's left is leaving, boy. It can be as hard or as easy as you like, but you *will* go. Or I'll send you for a priest."

That threat made Jack flinch, breaking eye contact in a mute admission of defeat. He wasn't a coward—he had taken beatings before—but the thought of a priest's fate scared him.

Mutilated. Castrated. Hobbled. No, he'd rather take exile than that.

Jack bent his stiff neck, swallowing pride that scraped like rocks, and submitted. "I'll go."

The old man turned his back and walked away, snatching the blanket off the hovering lad and throwing it over his shoulder. Left alone, Jack looked down at his brother and, on a whim, offered him his hand. When she'd been dying, their mam had begged them to stop fighting, damned them for fighting like dogs even when they were inside her. Well, now they had nothing left to fight over. Gregor had won.

Rage twisted Gregor's face into something ugly, and he slapped Jack's hand away, knuckles bashing. He scrambled to his feet, spitting a wad of clotty blood into the ground. "I didn't need him to *give* me this. I could have taken it. I *would* have taken it, and my face and my twelve fucking minutes back."

Jack relaxed back into the familiar enmity, a sneer curling his lip. At least their da had given him one last gift. "Except you didn't, did you," he said. Leaning forward, he murmured in his brother's ear, "And now that's what everyone will remember. That you didn't take it, you just… got it."

He left his brother with that, holding on to the smirk until the dark blocked the pack from view. Then he let it hit him, shoving the air out of his lungs in a desperate gasp. He staggered and dropped to his knees on the hard ground, scrubbing a hand over his face. Exiled. Alone. Just thinking about it made his chest crack with anger and a hot, sticky fear. In his whole life, he'd never been alone. He didn't even know how you went about it.

The bitter cold masked the smell, but the frozen ground was no friend to stealth. Jack heard the crunching shuffle of someone approaching in time to pull himself together. He staggered to his feet, growling at the wind that shouldered him, and turned to face the intruder.

He hoped to see his da, come to change his mind. He *expected* it to be Gregor, back for one last fight. Instead a prophet limped into view, scarred and shabby in heavy layers of winter charity.

"What do you want?" Jack demanded. He retreated a step, then made himself hold his ground. "Why did you follow me?"

The prophet grinned, showing the gaps where his incisors had been wrenched out of the gums. "Things change," he said, spitting Jack's words back at him. "Your da's wrong. The end of the world changes everything. If you want it to. Do you want it to, Jack? And are you willing to pay the price for it?"

In the end, no. He wasn't.

Chapter Two

THIS TIME of year, the streets of Durham were usually full of people. Tourists heading up to the Castle to get a glimpse of where they'd filmed Harry Potter, students looking for secondhand text books in the Oxfam shop, and residents just trying to live in the middle of it all. This year, the streets were empty, and the shops were boarded up. The only people left were council workers, slogging through flood water in waders as they tested foundations for subsidence, and the few poor souls who'd not found anywhere better to go.

Danny stood in the doorway of St. Chad's, shivering and rubbing cold-raw hands together, and watched the old Land Rover crawl its way out of the pea-soup fog that had come in when the storm slackened. It jolted and clattered over the battered cobbled road, wheels hitting the frost-cracked ruts and gaps. The driver was a local farmer whose son had talked him into helping out with transport after they'd closed off the motorways.

"Al," Danny said as the jeep pulled in next to him. He ducked his head to peer through the window. The air inside, blasting out of the vents, was hot enough to make his glasses mist as it hit them. He whipped them off, giving the lenses a quick polish on his sleeve. "We appreciate this. These are the last of the students. Thank God they reopened the train line this morning."

"That's one bit of good news, then," Al said, pulling his hat off and wiping a gloved hand over his sweaty scalp. He pointed to the windshield on the passenger side, a spiderweb of cracks shattering out from a golf-ball-sized hole. "Hail last night did that. Took out most of the windows in the farm too. Mad fucking weather."

"Can't keep it up *much* longer," Danny said. It was the party line, rote response to any commentary on the weather. So far the weather had kept it up for two months, and the words were starting to sound a bit empty. "You okay up there?"

"For now," Al said grimly. "I've been thinking I might lock the place up and head down to my sister's in Birmingham. It's not been hit as bad."

Danny grimaced his uncertainty about that, not after some of the news reports, but it wasn't his job to keep Al on the farm. It was ground; it would be there when he came back. He slapped the hood of the car instead. "Keep her running," he said. "I'll get your passengers."

He headed back into the building, feet crunching in the half-frozen puddles that filled the foyer. There were twelve students left, sitting on suitcases and the plastic-sheet-covered chairs. He hustled them outside and into the cab.

Larry stalled at the curb, shoving his hand through his shaggy hair. "Maybe I should wait a couple more days, Professor Fennick," he said. "If the weather lets us, they've said they might open the roads up to Scotland back up. I could head home."

"If the roads open up, your mum will be coming down to her sister's," Danny reminded him. "That's what she told you when she called, right?"

Twisting his mouth, Larry admitted, "Yeah," but didn't move.

"I'm heading for Cornwall," Rhiannon said, tossing her backpack in and shoving past him. "I heard there were surfers catching thirty foot waves off the beaches there. I'm gonna make the most of it."

"We'd rather like you to come back when the university reopens," Danny said dryly. He shoved Larry into the Land Rover, and the rest of the students scrambled in after him. By the time mousy little Neil squeezed in, clutching his laptop like a talisman against missing months on his thesis, the Land Rover looked like a clown car. Somewhere over Durham a clap of thunder grumbled disconsolately through the clouds.

"What about you, Professor?" Alison asked, rolling the front passenger window down enough to stick her nose out. "Aren't you leaving?"

"Once I get you guys safely away, I'm locking up and heading home," he said. "Don't worry about me. Travel safe."

He stepped back, shoving his hands in his pockets and shuffling his feet restlessly on the pavement. Al honked the horn—just in case—and pulled away from the curb slowly. The Land Rover lumbered away in the direction of the train station, damage-pocked rear end disappearing into the fog like a retreating dinosaur. Danny waited until he couldn't hear the engine, then went back inside to grab his bag and lock up. He hesitated, ducking his head to settle the heavy satchel over his shoulders. The tiled floor in the entrance was muddy and cracked, the cardboard tacked up over the broken windows sodden and leaking damp down the wall. It felt like he should do more than just lock the doors, but with no one here anything he did would just be a Band-Aid. Besides, one thing no one had ever called him was handy.

He huffed out a breath, tasting fresh rain in the air, and let himself out, locking up behind him.

The wind had picked up while he was inside. The tattered festival banners strung from lampposts rattled and flapped, the ones that hadn't already ripped belling out like sails. Danny ducked his head and walked into the wind, clutching his satchel close across his body. He felt like a mime, at least he did until the rain came on like a tap. Then he just felt like a drowned rat. His hair plastered itself down over his face in sodden, matted tangles—the length of it reminding him he'd been meaning to get to the hairdressers—and he spluttered on the pelting water hitting his face.

Tucking his chin down, he broke into a loping jog past the shuttered-up Waterstones and into the Market Place. The wind caught him from a different direction, making him stagger, and he caught the taste of ozone on his tongue a second before the lightning struck.

Dog Days

It hit Neptune's upraised trident, shattering the stone into blackened shards. Danny cursed breathlessly and threw his arms up over his face, yelping as the shrapnel hit him. His forearms took the brunt of the biggest bits, but what was left scattered wasp-sting pinpricks of pain over his forehead and jaw. He was still blinking away the glare spots burned through his field of vision when the next bolt struck, agitating up enough static electricity to make his hair bristle even through the rain. Then again, and again.

Forks of lightning staggered across the square like a drunkard's walk. It left charred patterns on the stone-paving slabs and shattered windows. Small fires spat and caught in the grass and behind glass, guttering stubbornly against the battering wind and rain.

In the middle of it Danny stood frozen, gaping openmouthed like an idiot. He knew he should run, but some atavistic instinct froze him in place. As if the lightning was a predator, and he just had to avoid catching its attention.

Besides, in a totally terrifying way, it was beautiful.

The growl broke the paralysis holding him in place, the guttural, hollow noise making him flinch and look around. A wolf stared back at him, hunched and sodden in the rain. It was quite clearly a wolf, from the green-eyed broad head to the muscle-coiled haunches. Only an idiot would have thought it was anything else.

It was looking at Danny.

He sucked in a startled breath, but all he could smell was stale water and ozone. "Oh hell." Danny turned to run, feet sliding on the wet stone, but the heavy weight of muscle, flesh, and fur hit him first. The impact threw him off his feet, breath hiccupping out of his chest, and sent him crashing into the window of the abandoned Cafe Nero. It had been boarded up, but the sodden plywood cracked easily on impact, and Danny and the wolf fell through into the store.

Chairs and tables went flying as the two of them landed on the floor. Danny grabbed the wolf's ruff, digging his fingers in and locking his elbows to keep the white, white teeth from his throat. Slobber drooled on him, and the wolf snarled into his face, flews wrinkled back tight from long fangs. It wasn't like the rangy, tired wolves you saw at the zoo. This was an old Scottish werewolf, big as a pony and muscled like an ox. The weight of it on Danny's chest made his ribs creak, his lungs compressed.

He growled back. "What the fuck is wrong with you?"

Green eyes in a dark mask of fur blinked at him, and then a naked man was straddling his waist, hands braced against his chest. He was all sculpted lines of heavy muscle, tattoos of rank curling down his ribs and low across his stomach. His hair was short, tawny blond, and Danny's hands were still buried in it. Flushing, he moved them quickly.

"Me?" the wolf asked, voice burred with a Highland accent. Straight brows arched over those rare green eyes. "I wasn't the one dancing with the lightning. Do you fancy yourself a priest now? Were you looking for augury in your cooked brain meats?"

"Go to hell, Jack," Danny snapped. "And get *off* me."

TA MOORE genuinely believed that she was a Cabbage Patch Kid when she was a small child. That was the start of a lifelong attachment to the weird and fantastic. These days she lives in a market town on the Northern Irish coast and her friends have a rule that she can only send them three weird and disturbing links a month—although she still holds that a DIY penis bifurcation guide is interesting, not disturbing. She believes that adding "in space!" to anything makes it at least 40 percent cooler, will try to pet pretty much any animal she meets—this includes snakes, excludes bugs—and once lied to her friend that she had climbed all the way up to Tintagel Castle in Cornwall, when actually she'd only gotten to the beach, realized it was really high, and chickened out.

She aspires to be a cynical misanthrope, but is unfortunately held back by a sunny disposition and an inability to be mean to strangers. If TA Moore is mean to you, that means you're friends now.

Website: www.nevertobetold.co.uk

Facebook: www.facebook.com/TA.Moores

Twitter: @tammy_moore

BONE
TO PICK

TA MOORE

Cloister Witte is a man with a dark past and a cute dog. He's happy to talk about the dog all day, but after growing up in the shadow of a missing brother, a deadbeat dad, and a criminal stepfather, he'd rather leave the past back in Montana. These days he's a K-9 officer in the San Diego County Sheriff's Department and pays a tithe to his ghosts by doing what no one was able to do for his brother—find the missing and bring them home.

He's good at solving difficult mysteries. The dog is even better.

This time the missing person is a ten-year-old boy who walked into the woods in the middle of the night and didn't come back. With the antagonistic help of distractingly handsome FBI agent Javi Merlo, it quickly becomes clear that Drew Hartley didn't run away. He was taken, and the evidence implies he's not the kidnapper's first victim. As the search intensifies, old grudges and tragedies are pulled into the light of day. But with each clue they uncover, it looks less and less likely that Drew will be found alive.

www.dreamspinnerpress.com

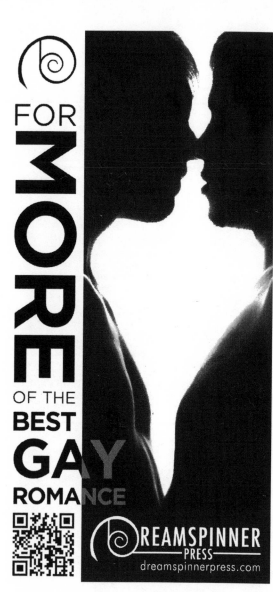